MAKE MY WISH COME TRUE

MAKE MY WISH COME TRUE

Rachael Lippincott and Alyson Derrick

SIMON & SCHUSTER

First published in Great Britain in 2024 by Simon & Schuster UK Ltd

First published in the USA in 2024 by Simon & Schuster Books for Young Readers,
an imprint of Simon & Schuster Children's Publishing Division,
1230 Avenue of the Americas, New York, New York 10020

1 3 5 7 9 10 8 6 4 2

Simon & Schuster UK Ltd
1ˢᵗ Floor, 222 Gray's Inn Road
London WC1X 8HB

Simon & Schuster: celebrating 100 years of Publishing in 2024

www.simonandschuster.co.uk
www.simonandschuster.com.au
www.simonandschuster.co.in

Simon & Schuster Australia, Sydney
Simon & Schuster India, New Delhi

A CIP catalogue record for this book is available from the British Library.

PB ISBN 978-1-3985-2924-3
eBook ISBN 978-1-3985-2926-7
eAudio ISBN 978-1-3985-2925-0

Printed and Bound in the UK using 100% Renewable
Electricity at CPI Group (UK) Ltd

MIX
Paper | Supporting
responsible forestry
FSC® C171272

For Poppy

CHAPTER 1

CAROLINE

"Caroline!"

I snort awake, nearly tumbling out of bed as my younger sister Riley's voice shoots me into consciousness better than the twelve alarms I snoozed this morning.

That's what I get for staying up until three a.m. to tinker with my portfolio for my Columbia application, adding in an article I just finished on the local bakery's heavily guarded, five-generations-old Christmas cookie recipe. Apparently a great-aunt had even killed a man to protect it, which made *this* piece a bit more high-stakes than the rest of my reporting about our Christmas-obsessed small town. . . .

If *looks* could kill, though, Riley's might just do the trick. She leans away from my now defunct left eardrum, arms crossed over her worn forest-green Barnwich Soccer hoodie. "Can we *please* not be late for once?"

I grunt and groan a "no" in reply, rolling over to rebury myself in my cozy comforter.

"It's Pancake Tuesday," she says.

I immediately roll back to face her.

"That's what I thought," she adds, before leaving me to my frantic Tuesday-morning routine. I stumble into a pair of jeans and an oversized cardigan, brush my teeth as I pack up my backpack, then add a sweep or two of mascara and enough rings to let people know I like women.

As I head downstairs to the kitchen and the pancakes that are the only thing that could get me out of bed today, Blue, my black-and-white border collie, trots after me, his toenails clicking on the hardwood floors. I smirk when we turn the corner to see Riley spraying a gravity-defying amount of whipped cream directly into her mouth and my two older brothers, Levi and Miles, wolfing down short stacks like it's their job. They show up to Pancake Tuesdays religiously even though they're both in their early twenties now.

"Don't you two have your own house?" I ask as I pour myself a cup of coffee. I turn around just in time for a flapjack to smack me square in the face. Riley snorts as I peel it off and take a bite.

Dad stops his humming over a sizzling pan of turkey bacon and whirls around, apron flowing in the wind, to point his spatula between the four of us.

"One more thrown pancake and you can all forget Pancake Tuesdays for the next year!"

"You're all talk, old man," Levi scoffs, shaking his head.

"Just try me, kid," my dad replies with a challenging smile, but the standoff is interrupted by my mom breezing into the kitchen. Immediately, Dad casts a sideways glance at the clock in the corner, still worried even after twenty-five years about her being—

"Late. I'm gonna be late," my mom mutters as she steals the coffee cup right out of my hands and takes a sip.

Mom commutes from Barnwich to Pittsburgh every morning to work at the law firm she started with her best friend from college and is almost *always* running a few minutes behind. My dad tried setting our clocks forward by five minutes once, but it didn't make a difference. It was like she knew in her bones it was wrong. Thank goodness trains leave the Barnwich station every seventeen minutes, or she'd never make it to work before the morning meeting *she* schedules.

I guess I get that from her, because when my gaze drifts over to the clock too, I see I have all of a minute and a half to shove the rest of this much-needed pancake into my mouth and get out the door.

"Anyway, we need sustenance," Miles says, continuing the conversation. "Got a busy night to prep for the bar tomorrow. Bought a karaoke machine two weeks ago, and Karaoke Wednesdays have been a real game changer." He scrolls through a color-coordinated events calendar on his phone, pinks and yellows and greens flying past.

He and Levi saved up practically every penny since they were both in middle school to open up Beckett Brothers, a bar tucked into the corner of Main Street and Pine, the result of my dad's obsession with *Bar Rescue* and their desire to find their own niche in our holiday-centric Pennsylvania town. They carefully renovated the space together after leasing it two Christmases ago at a heavily discounted price from the owner and also our neighbor, Mr. Burton. Then Riley and I were enlisted to help paint and haul Facebook Marketplace finds, paying us in ice cream in the summer and hot chocolate in the winter. This is the first full year they've been open for business, and they've been giving it all they've got to stay afloat and turn a profit. Trivia, speed dating, live music, and now karaoke, apparently. They'll do anything to keep those doors open. But it's been hard to watch them struggle like so many businesses in our town have these last couple of years.

"I don't know about game changer. My ears are still bleeding from last week," Levi grumbles through a mouthful of food.

So are mine, honestly. He sent me a video of a girl who was attempting to belt out some Celine Dion but sounded like a rooster with a sore throat.

"You'll still be coming to the Hanukkah party, right?" Mom asks, fingertips tapping against what was once *my* coffee mug, worried as always about being late but doing nothing to actually move faster. "I told Grandma you'd both be there."

"Obviously," Miles snorts, selecting a highlighted day on his carefully curated calendar to prove it. "Missing out on her brisket would be a crime."

With Mom being Jewish and Dad being Catholic, this time of year is a flurry of Christmas music, latkes, new socks, and . . . the all-too-familiar disconnect: existing in that liminal space between the two religions.

Not going to church or synagogue but opening Easter baskets and being shipped off to the Jewish sleepaway camp in upstate New York that my mom's whole family went to. Getting a Christmas tree and exchanging ugly sweaters, but keeping the gifts from Santa to a minimum.

Most of all though: not feeling Christian or Jewish enough, especially in a town with Christmas as its bedrock.

4

Levi and Miles never seemed to wrestle with that feeling. They've managed to find their place here in Barnwich quickly. Even with the articles I write, though, I guess I just haven't yet.

"You ready to go?" Riley asks me, stuffing one more slice of turkey bacon into her mouth before scrambling to grab her backpack.

I nod as I toss my last bite to Blue, then steal my coffee cup back from my mom for one more sip before heading off down the hallway to bundle up.

"See you guys later!" I call before squishing a beanie onto Riley's head. I throw open the front door, and the two of us giggle as we slip and slide down the steps and through the snow to Bertha, the ancient silver Toyota Camry Miles was brought home from the hospital in before it was passed faithfully down the Beckett line to me. Riley gets in and starts it up from the passenger seat while I scrape the ice off the windshield *just* enough.

"Wow, really, Caroline? I still can't see anything through that," Riley says as I get behind the wheel.

"I thought you didn't want to be late," I reply, throwing my scraper over my head onto the backseat.

"Well, yeah, but I'd also like to get there *alive*," she says, pulling her seat belt around her. "We should've had a snow day." She rubs her mittened hands together.

"A snow day? In Barnwich? *Please.*" Our near-constant flurry of lake-effect snow is a key factor in what makes Barnwich feel like you're in a Hallmark Christmas snow globe.

I turn the key in the ignition, and Bertha fumfers to life. Her tires fight desperately for traction until we're heading off slowly down the street.

"You got any exams this week?" I ask.

Riley hums an affirmation, mitten hanging out of her mouth as she risks frostbite to text her middle school posse.

"Need help studying?"

She hums another affirmation, still tapping away.

Even though we're running late, I rubberneck my way down Main Street while the car windows defrost a little more. I gaze at all the brightly colored storefronts, the string lights zigzagging directly above us, the red bows and green wreaths on glowing lampposts. The warm and cozy and *exciting* holiday spirit is as impossible to avoid as ever. It's no wonder this place has been a holiday tourist destination for decades, with people trekking to our small town every December for hot chocolate and sleigh rides, homemade gifts and a picture with Mr. Green, the plumber-turned-Santa. Not to mention our Christmas tree lighting remains the fourth biggest in the country.

But the crowds have dwindled since I was a kid. A lot. And even though Barnwich is still magical this time of year, there's no denying everyone's had to work harder to lure people back and keep the mom-and-pop shops along Main Street afloat. It seems like everyone's doubling down on all our traditions, adding pyrotechnics to the tree lighting, upping the cash prizes in our hot chocolate and gingerbread house contests, and giving elf costumes to the drivers of the reindeer-led sleds that coast along Main Street. It's . . . so much and yet something still feels like it's missing.

The thought brings back the swell of melancholy I can't help but feel alongside the excitement this time of year.

"Arden was photographed leaving a club *super* fucked up last night," Riley says, still looking at her phone. My grip tightens on

6

the steering wheel, and what holiday spirit I did have evaporates at the mention of my ex–best friend, leaving just the melancholy.

"Language," I murmur, unsure whether I'm talking about my twelve-year-old sister dropping the f-bomb or the name of the person more synonymous with Barnwich to me than Christmas.

It's been four years since she left Barnwich, and me, in the dust to make it big in Hollywood, but in some ways it's like she hasn't left at all. Her presence, or the now unrecognizable ghost of it, still looms around every corner. From tabloids at supermarket checkouts to viral tweets to TikTok edits carefully spliced together by her adoring fans.

Arden James, Arden James, *Arden James*.

And Riley isn't any help. She insists on keeping me fully up-to-date on any of Arden's happenings I do manage to miss, in extensive detail, even though I want absolutely, positively *nothing* to do with her.

Still, when we pull into the middle school parking lot, I can't help but glance quickly over at the picture Riley's shoving in my face. Arden's long, dark hair and brown eyes are still familiar, yet so *different*. And not just because of the glassy, disoriented haze of whatever she's on clouding her vision.

"You gotta take the bus home today," I say as the screen goes dark and Arden's face disappears. I park the car, and Riley unbuckles her seat belt. "I picked up a shift at Edie's."

Edie's Eatery. The beloved local diner that's another reason I can't forget Arden no matter how much I try. It's owned by Arden's grandma and known for a mean stack of pancakes, which are admittedly better than my dad's, and coffee that could peel your eyebrows clean off.

There's no denying I could use the extra money, but the real reason I work there is Edie. With Arden gone and her parents traipsing the globe, I like to keep an eye on Edie, especially now that she's started to slow down a bit. She's tough as nails, but sometimes even nails need tending to. Like she tended to *us* for years. Milkshakes and loaded omelets and letting us play around in the diner kitchen.

It's just another reason to resent Arden. For leaving Edie behind too.

"Fine, but only if you bring me home a black-and-white cookie."

"Deal."

Riley calls a goodbye before running up the steps to meet her soccer friends, and I zip over to the high school, only a little farther down the road. I groan as I pull into one of the few open spots and see that while Riley's just made it, I'm about to be late, as always.

I grab my backpack and slip and slide my way over the icy pavement up to Barnwich High, then skid straight down the green locker-covered hall to my homeroom class. The bell rings overhead the exact second my butt hits my seat in the back corner.

"Good morning," Austin Becker practically sings, setting down a much-needed caramel macchiato on my desk, a perk of having a friend who works the opening shift at Barnwich Brews.

"Morning," I say, gratefully grabbing it from his golden-brown hands, the long fingers covered in silver rings, as Mr. Fisher stands to take attendance before morning announcements.

When I started high school the fall after Arden left, walking through the double doors on the first day without my best friend was pretty intimidating. But luckily, Becker came just before Beckett, and Austin was new to Barnwich, a clean slate who liked books and Phoebe Bridgers as much as I did. This curly-black-haired, guitar-playing, too-cool-for-school-but-still-won-Home-coming-King-over-his-football-captain-boyfriend guy has been my coffee-delivering saving grace ever since that first day.

I open the lid before taking a sip, and sure enough, there's a new piece of latte art on top. A dog that looks almost like Blue. I let out a low whistle, and he beams while I snap a few pictures.

As I return the lid, Maya, the final puzzle piece in our trio, turns around in her seat, elbows sliding onto my desk. "How's the application coming? You finally send it in?" she asks.

I groan, and her blue eyes slide over to meet Austin's hazel ones. The two exchange a look.

"That well?"

"I just feel like . . ." I shake my head. "Like I don't have anything on it that really stands out, you know?"

Austin laughs, shaking his head too. "You've been editor in chief of the school newspaper since we were sophomores, your grades are ridiculous, *and* you won that statewide writing contest for your piece on Barnwich Brews being rebuilt after the fire."

"Yeah, and I bet like . . . all the other kids applying for the journalism program at Columbia have the same stuff on their applications. If not better. What if all the stuff I've done is too . . . I don't know. *Small town*. Not big enough." Even the bakery article I just added doesn't seem stakes-y enough.

Even with the murder.

I raise my hand as Mr. Fisher calls my name and change the subject. "So, how's Finn?"

Like he heard himself mentioned, Austin's boyfriend, Finn, ducks his golden-blond head into the classroom to wave hello to Austin before Mr. Fisher shoos him out to his own homeroom. Finn's cheeks turn red as I hear his football bros in the hallway give him shit, and Austin rolls his eyes, suppressing a smile.

"The same as ever." He shakes his head. "We're going sledding next week on the first day of break, if you two want to come. Finn says Taylor Hill from the cheer team asked if you'd be there. Seems like she's got a bit of a crush."

Taylor Hill? Crushing on me?

"Sounds fun," I say with a noncommittal shrug, picking at the cardboard coffee sleeve.

"The sledding?" Maya asks, leaning forward, eyebrows wiggling. "Or Taylor Hill?"

I snort and shake my head, *my* cheeks turning red this time. "I just . . . haven't ever really thought about her like that."

I mean, I've noticed she's pretty, objectively. Co-captain of the cheerleading team. Blond hair. Picture-perfect smile. It's just, I haven't really thought of anyone like that. For a while, anyway. I'm open to it. I just haven't felt . . .

I think of Finn and Austin. How you can almost see the sparks between them.

That.

"Still hung up on Julie Shapiro from sleepaway camp?" Austin takes a sip from his coffee cup, giving me a knowing look. "Unless . . . ?"

No.

I glare at him and slap at his flannel-covered shoulder before he can say her name, but a pair of familiar, glassy brown eyes illuminated on my sister's phone screen pops into my head anyway. Just as unwelcome as they always are.

Even though Austin never met Arden, he and Maya both know she was more than just a best friend to me. That I'm always searching for that feeling but I never find it.

I wonder if I could put on my Columbia application that I haven't had *any* romantic life over the past four years. Maybe they'd accept me out of pity.

My teeth dig into my bottom lip, but thankfully the morning announcements end the conversation there. I let my eyes glaze over as I turn my head back to the front of the room and force myself to focus on what matters most.

Columbia.

More than sparks or Taylor Hill or *Arden James*.

This time *I'm* going to get out of Barnwich to chase *my* dreams.

I want this so badly I can taste it. But when I look out the window, at the white flakes drifting slowly down outside, I know that however much I sometimes feel trapped in this Hallmark Christmas snow globe, I could never fully say goodbye. It's not as easy for me to leave people behind.

Or forget them.

After school I head across town to Edie's. The bells jingle as I push inside and am greeted by the familiar checkered floors, worn mint-green leather booths, and row of swivel chairs. The smell of Edie's cooking drifting out from the kitchen makes my stomach grumble, even though lunch wasn't that long ago, and I feel my shoulders relax for the first time all day. My head always feels clearer here, and while all the stress from my looming Columbia application doesn't fade away completely, it feels almost manageable.

"Hey, Edie," I call out, rushing to the back to take my million and one layers off. As I whip around the corner, I almost run smack into Harley, the edgy college student who's worked here for the last two years, juggling two armfuls of plates.

"Whoa there," she says, dodging out of my way without dropping so much as a single curly fry.

Edie's salt-and-pepper hair pokes through the serving window. She waves a spatula in greeting, looking decidedly less chipper than usual. For a barely five-foot-tall Korean grandmother, her presence usually fills up the whole diner. As I tie my apron and pull my strawberry-blond hair into a ponytail, all she says in her thick Southern accent, courtesy of her Georgia upbringing, is, "Well, she really showed her whole ass this time, didn't she?"

I hesitate, some old instinct to defend her bubbling up in my throat.

But instead, I nod. Because she's right, and I don't owe Arden anything. Not anymore.

We don't talk about it again for the rest of the day, but I know what's going on in her head. Edie's always blamed herself on some level. When they lived in town, at least Edie could be there for Arden while her parents fought day in and day out. Or I could, letting Arden in from my doorstep, backpack in tow, to squeeze into my bed for another sleepover.

But Hollywood is too far out of either of our reach. Especially when the person who's there isn't reaching back.

She found fame instead. She doesn't need us anymore.

As I scoop up a double cheeseburger and fries for table three from the serving window, I give Edie a small, reassuring smile, trying to erase some of her guilt. After all, she always said Arden's parents could never stay in one place long. Arden leaving us in the dust was bound to happen when it was all she ever knew.

CHAPTER 2

ARDEN

"Good morning! Good morning! Get your ass out of bed!"

A tsunami of ice-cold water splashes onto my face. I sit bolt upright, coughing, and wipe my vision clear until I see blue eyes and a mess of curly brown hair. My agent, chewing on a wad of green spearmint gum, peers down at me.

"Really?" I grumble, pushing wet strands of hair out of my face.

"Really. You're late . . . *again*," Lillian adds as she moves to the windows to rip open the bamboo blinds.

"L."

Blind.

"A."

Another one.

"T."

A third.

"E."

She draws the last blind, revealing a full panoramic view of Malibu beach, whitecaps splashing over huge dark rocks just off the shoreline. I paid millions of dollars for this view, thinking I'd at least be able to chill on the beach every once in a while, but I haven't touched the sand in two years.

"Yeah, I know how to spell."

A beam of sunlight breaks through the morning cloud cover, and I slap a hand over my eyes, trying to manage my pounding headache.

"You could've fooled me, because you sure as hell can't read your schedule, or any of the five reminders I sent you yester— Oh, hello there," she says, her tone of voice softening just slightly. I peek through my fingers to see a shape moving underneath the sheets next to me. A girl with bleached-blond hair sticking up in just about every direction pops her head out. Even though she's wearing last night's makeup and sporting a hangover to match mine, I gotta say she's one of the hottest girls I've ever seen. That's one thing LA is never running low on.

"Arden? Do you have to go?" she asks, pushing up on her elbow and pulling the sheet up to cover herself. "I thought we could have breakfast. . . ."

Oh God.

"Sorry . . . uh . . ."

Miranda? Jackie? Shit. Did her name start with an L? Or . . . wait. I think it was an A?

Lillian pipes up from the foot of the bed right on cue. "This one's got a commercial shoot she's half an hour late for already, so if you wouldn't mind skedaddling, hon, that would be *excellent*. You can help yourself to a cold-pressed juice in the fridge on your way out."

Lillian pulls me out of bed, and I grab the comforter to cover my jimmies before flashing the blond an apologetic smile as I'm led out of the room.

"Are you trying to kill me?" Lillian mutters, shaking her head while we clomp down the hall toward the bathroom.

"Not intentionally." I sigh.

"It sure seems intentional, Arden. This whole bad-girl thing was just supposed to be a persona for the press, something to get you some attention. It wasn't supposed to bleed into your real life. You remember that, right?"

"I know. I know," I reply, squeezing the bridge of my nose. She says it like it's so easy. Like it's possible to spend years pretending to be something you don't want to be and then somehow not become it. Like she doesn't know how deeply this place gets its claws in you.

"And it worked. Everyone knows you. Everyone wants you. *You're* the one who told me you wanted to pivot, to change your image. If you want people to see you as a serious adult actor now, then you need to pull on your big-girl pants. My God, Arden, at the very least you have to be *on time*."

"I *know*, Lil. I—"

"If you know, then why did I wake up this morning to photos of you high out of your mind, hooking up with multiple people at some party the night before a shoot?"

Because the idea of staying in this big, empty house all alone for an entire night was fucking unbearable.

"I'm sorry. I didn't—" I wipe my hands down my face. "I didn't know there were cameras there. It was supposed to be a private party."

"You're Arden James. You were the second most searched

name in the US last year after Taylor Swift. There are *always* cameras. There will *always be* cameras. This shoot? It's for the Super Bowl. I could have paid for all three of my divorces with what you're going to rake in just to smile and hold a bottle in front of the camera for a flipping hour. I spent a month on the phone with the execs convincing them you were right for this. Pull it together," she says, pushing me into the bathroom. "Take a shower. I already ordered you breakfast from down the street. You can eat it in the car on the way to the studio."

I peek through the opening in the door, giving her an apologetic look. "Thanks, Lillian. I owe you one."

"You're damn right," Lillian says as she taps away on her phone with one hand and hands me a coffee and an Advil with the other. Then she glances up at me, smirking. "Make it two. I also saved you the trouble of pretending you knew her name."

An hour later, Lillian reads off my schedule for the rest of the week as I sit in the hair and makeup trailer, finishing the last of my second coffee of the morning.

"Today you're free after this shoot, but don't go crazy again," she says, eyeing me as my long, dark brown hair is tugged and pulled into place and about half a pound of concealer is applied to cover my dark circles. "You have *the* audition tomorrow with Bianchi."

Bianchi.

"I won't forget," I promise Lillian, thinking about the hundreds of annotations I've added to the script in my bag, the pages worn and ragged from all the prep I've done.

Still, my leg starts to shake at the thought.

I can't remember the last time I actually *wanted* a role, but thoughts of this audition have kept me awake at night for the past month. I went out partying last night because I couldn't stand to be in my own head a second longer.

My career has gone from Disney Originals to being pigeon-holed into straight rom-coms, especially after my record-breaking Netflix debut launched me into the spotlight two years ago.

But *this*. This is a drama about a sapphic Asian American small-town girl who claws her way out of her broken life and into a better one. It feels like it was written for me and me alone.

Like Meryl Streep as Miranda Priestly or Tom Hanks as Forrest Gump.

This role is *mine*.

Plus, I'd be working with the best. Anything Bianchi directs turns to gold. Picked up by A24. Ten-minute standing ovations at Cannes. Oscar noms in more categories than not.

It feels like what I've been waiting for, my opportunity to take my career in a different direction. But I have to show Bianchi that there's more to me than what he's seen so far. That I can do more than deliver funny lines while looking like a smoke show and make some guy fall in love with me in a way that *Variety* loves to call "likable but easily forgettable."

This is the whole reason I want to shift my image too.

Leaning into the young Hollywood train wreck helped get eyes on me like Lillian promised, but it was supposed to be a means to an end, not what I want to be known as for the rest of my life. I'm ready to be taken seriously. I *want* to be taken seriously. I want an Oscar instead of another Teen Choice Award.

I just need one shot. And to get that shot I have to give Bianchi a performance that he'll remember more than my reputation or IMDB page. So I don't know why the closer it gets the harder it is to keep myself under control.

"I know how badly you want it. Don't let yourself down," Lillian says.

Before I can respond, the commercial director busts into the room with none other than Marc Nicholson himself, the heir to the Nicholson bottled water fortune.

I try not to wince at the sound of the door bouncing off the wall.

"I'm so sorry I was late," I say sweetly as I stand up to greet him. The director glowers, but Marc Nicholson waves my apology off with a thick tan hand before he takes mine.

"No trouble at all," he says in a heavy Southern drawl, blue eyes crinkling at the corners as he holds my hand too long. "Wow, it's true what they say. The camera really does add ten pounds." He laughs, his eyes running from my head to my toes and back again. I don't know whether I should laugh or say thanks or smack him, but before I can decide, he nudges the spindly man next to him. "Give her a rundown, Richie."

"Richie," the director, pushes up his chunky glasses, hand sweeping dramatically through the air. "Five different scenes. Scattered throughout time, to show the *legendary* Nicholson water in the past, present, and future. You, present day, getting into a car after an awards show, taking a refreshing sip. You, one hundred forty-six years ago when the company was founded, cracking open a bottle after a long day of washing clothes. You, one hundred forty-six years in the future, Nicholson water bottle in hand as your pod car drives you all on its own. You . . ."

As he continues, my eyes scan the rack of clothes in the corner, going from Victorian chic to George Lucas's wet dream, then to Lillian, whose look tells me to suppress my eye roll.

"I can't believe *the* Arden James is here on *my* set." Marc Nicholson, thirty years my senior, skirts around me, his hand dragging along my back before he leans in so close that I can feel his lips on my ear. "I've got a reservation at your favorite club tonight if you'd like to celebrate." He says it in a whisper so no one else can hear, but even so, Lillian sits upright in her chair, ready to step in.

I shake my head subtly at her and step just out of Nicholson's reach, forcing myself not to wipe the moisture off my ear.

Instead, I throw him a very rehearsed coy look that I've used too many times with too many men. "I wish I could, but I've got an important audition to prep for," I reply before turning back to Richie, who goes off on another tangent about the blocking for the scenes, the vision for the shoot.

I've stopped listening, though, because as it turns out, none of it really matters. I'm just here so that this old rich fuck can ask me to dinner. To try to impress me with a reservation that I could land in my sleep. They could've just about hired a blow-up doll to do this job.

"Got it?" Richie finally asks, and I nod with the utmost confidence.

Get your paycheck and get out.

"Got it."

With my hair and makeup done and my jeans and oversized hoodie swapped for a sparkling dress, they shuffle me off to set.

And lights, camera, action, I do what I have to do.

Overdramatic sips and coy smiles, outfit changes and corny lines of dialogue read off a teleprompter.

After Victorian chic and seventies are done, I head back to my trailer for a lunch break, Lillian following on my heels, tapping away on her phone.

"How're you doing?" she asks as I plunk down into the black swivel chair in front of the brightly lit mirror.

"Well, I started my day off by getting water thrown in my face. So . . ."

"You could've set an alarm," Lillian suggests without looking up from her phone.

"You could've been a little more gentle."

"Well, Arden, after the fifteenth time, it gets a little old. It's not my job to be gentle, sweetie. I'm your agent, not your m—" She stops, looks up from her phone.

My skin prickles.

Mom. Who I haven't seen in two years, along with Dad. Whose issues I thought I could fix with my success.

And in some ways, maybe I did. They stopped fighting over money, but their attention never pulled back to me, and they still didn't seem content. It's what made me finally see that *I* was the reason for their problems, not the solution. The wet blanket on their dreams of a nomadic life.

I remember the first time they left. My mom woke me up with breakfast in bed, fresh orange juice, pancakes shaped like hearts, and a fancy omelet.

"Hey, baby, your dad and I are taking a little trip, but we'll be back Monday morning to take you to set," she said, her voice almost as soft as her hand grazing my cheek, two things I wasn't used to. I didn't realize until I found the container in the trash later that my perfect breakfast was all ordered from down the street. Just like I didn't realize how much things were about to change.

First it was just a few days in Florida or a weekend in Vegas to "reconnect." Then they needed a private jet to Fiji. A month on a yacht in Santorini. Pretty soon I realized I was spending more weeks with the lady hired to clean the house than my own parents.

Then, on my sixteenth birthday, I got a call from my mom when they were supposed to be coming home from Italy to celebrate with me.

"Hey, Mom, what's up?" I asked, hoping their flight wasn't delayed.

"Hey, baby. Listen, we're going to have to extend our trip a few more weeks," she said, as if they were there on business and not frolicking around with *my* money.

"Is there anything else you wanted to tell me?" I asked as my eyes burned with tears.

"Oh, yeah. Lillian got another script for a Netflix something or other. Films in LA. March to June. *Big* money, baby. I gave her the green light!"

I couldn't say anything. I couldn't do anything but hold my breath on my end as tears streamed down my cheeks.

"Ciao, bab—" She hung up before she even finished saying goodbye, let alone happy birthday.

That was the final straw. I couldn't keep letting them use me.

So . . . I got emancipated. I cut them off financially to see how they felt about *me*.

They never came back.

"Sorry," Lillian adds, sincere this time. "I'm gonna grab some coffee. You want anything from crafty?"

I shake my head. "I'm good."

She pats my arm before leaving, and when the door clicks shut, I let out a long sigh. I tilt my head back, the ceiling tiles spinning above me as I swivel around in the chair. Once. Twice.

I look back at the mirror in front of me to see overdramatic blue eye shadow and my dark brown hair curled into massive waves. I tilt my head to study my face before they change it again. I spend so much time pretending to be someone else that sometimes it's hard to recognize the person looking back at me.

Not that that's a *bad* thing. I mean, I love it.

Otherwise, I'd be *just* Arden.

I've been her before, and I much prefer Arden James.

Everybody does.

I pull out my phone and swipe onto Twitter. I'm barely two scrolls in before I see a caption with a picture of me looking like I got run over by a tow truck, snapped as I was leaving the club last night.

Arden James: Too Far Gone?

Okay, well, I don't love *that* Arden James, but that's not *really* me. The paparazzi just always know how to catch you in your worst moments, because that's what sells. Still, I can't deny that there have been more of those than necessary to just keep up appearances lately.

But I can't give it up before I have something else to fill the hole it will inevitably leave behind.

And the perfect thing to fill that hole is this movie role.

I shake my head and swipe to Instagram, liking a picture of an older actor from my first role in *September Blues* and then one of a musician I hooked up with once at a *Vanity Fair* after-party. I only pause in my double-tapping when a familiar diner rolls into view. *Edie's Eatery.* Worn mint-green leather booths, glass bottles of Coke in a merchandise fridge, a counter display case filled with desserts.

But that's not what stops me in my tracks.

Front and center, holding an overflowing plate of my grandma's signature pancakes . . .

Caroline.

I zoom in on her face. The same but . . . different. More mature. Her smile seems more reserved, softer, not like the goofy filled-with-braces grin I remember. But her warm brown eyes are the same. And her strawberry-blond hair that's pulled into a ponytail, a few strands tumbling out.

Natural, which is something I haven't seen a lot of in LA. Girls in this industry start Botox before they're even old enough to rent a car. Not me, though. Not yet. At least my mom gave me something.

I stopped asking Grams about Caroline sometime last year. I don't want to hear secondhand about her college aspirations and her group of friends and a high school experience that I never got. And never will.

That's all behind me. *She* is behind me. And I'd like to keep her there.

But the diner's post does make me realize I haven't talked to Grams in . . . jeez, four months? She used to call me a lot, but

I think I sent her through to voicemail so many times that she gave up. Whenever I pick up the phone to call her, I can't help but think about all the photos of me plastered across the internet, and then I never have the balls to go through with it. And the longer I go without talking to her, the easier it gets to keep putting it off.

"Who's the girl?"

I jump, nearly throwing my phone across the room, as I register Lillian peeking over my shoulder, stirring her coffee.

"Uh." I shift in my seat, clearing my throat. "Just my childhood best friend. Caroline."

"Mmm." She takes a sip of her coffee. "That's it? You were grinning like a fool a minute ago, so I thought she must be someone special. You're not going soft on me now, are you?"

"Never." I tap the side button until my phone goes dark, Caroline's face fading from view. "I thought lunch was only supposed to be twenty minutes," I reply, knowing exactly how to get her off my back.

Lillian checks her watch and then flies out the door. She returns a minute later with the two makeup artists, still chewing their last bites of food.

As I'm poked and prodded by these strangers in this swivel chair, I can't help but think about how if things were different, right now I would be sitting in one of those mint-green booths instead. How I would be wolfing down a plate of my grandma's pancakes with too much butter and *real* maple syrup. I'd be halfway through my senior year. Getting ready for Barnwich's famous Christmas tree lighting.

Would I still be doing it all with Caroline Beckett?

"Ms. James? Is that comfortable?" the hair stylist asks as she adjusts a pin-straight silver wig on my head.

"Huh?" I shake myself back to reality, my futuristic reflection in the mirror startling me for a moment. "Oh, yeah. Sure."

I don't know why I'm daydreaming about Barnwich, when I'm here in LA living the exact life that I always wanted.

CHAPTER 3

CAROLINE

"Almost halftime," Austin groans from next to me as he hands a Gatorade bottle to Nicole Plesac, the best player on the Barnwich High girls' basketball team.

I glance up at the clock to see there are still ten whole minutes left in the quarter.

"Almost?" I snort as Nicole chucks the bottle in our direction and jogs back onto the court. The two of us flail in an attempt to grab it before it hits the ground.

This stellar athletic prowess is exactly why we've been forced to manage the team since freshman year. Barnwich High is small enough to have a "play or manage" sports requirement, and managing girls' basketball not only got us out of gym class but felt like the safest option. Indoors. Great concessions. Short games.

Sometimes not short enough.

"Psst! Beckett!"

I turn around to see Maya laughing and enjoying herself with Finn and his two football buddies, L.J. and Antonio, up in the bleachers. She's actually *good* at soccer, so she doesn't have to worry about filling water bottles and washing pinnies that smell like fermented armpit.

When our eyes meet, she super-not-casually jerks her head in the direction of the cheerleaders and mouths, "Taylor. Keeps. Looking. At. You."

Finn gives me a big grin and a thumbs-up, while L.J. wiggles his eyebrows suggestively beside him, but I roll my eyes and turn back to face the court. Despite myself, though, I casually push a strand of hair behind my ear, then peek over to where the cheerleaders are standing in Barnwich green and white.

And, sure enough, Taylor Hill *is* looking at me.

She flashes me a smile, white teeth glinting in the fluorescent gym lighting.

I do an awkward wave and try for my own sparkling smile, but it's like my facial muscles have forgotten how. Before I can embarrass myself any further, I lean forward, using Austin as a human shield.

"Smooth," he says, and I glare up at him, wanting the waxed hardwood floor to suck me in, never to be seen or heard from again.

I manage to make it to halftime before glancing back over at Taylor. While Austin and I hand out water and towels to the team, Taylor and the rest of the cheerleaders jog onto the court, performing cartwheels and flips that would for sure break my neck. I watch her move just past Coach Gleason's shoulder, and, well . . .

Yeah.

There's no denying she's nice to look at.

Nice face, nice hair, nice . . .

My cheeks turn red and I look away, busying myself with putting the bottles back in the carrier.

I mean, maybe I *am* expecting too much too soon. Maybe this *could* be the start of something?

Austin looks up from his phone as I sit down next to him and shake myself out of my Taylor-Hill-filled thoughts. "Finn just told me everyone's going to Barnwich Brews after the game for hot chocolate. Which is *great*, because I think I've finally nailed the perfect base for the competition. Rich and sweet, but not *too* sweet, you know what I mean?" he says, thumbs already tapping out a reply. The hot chocolate competition is a big deal around here. The winner gets a cash prize, Barnwich notoriety, *and* the honor of pulling the switch at the Christmas tree lighting. It's a sixty-year-old tradition, but the honor of pulling the switch was added the winter before last in an attempt to lure in out-of-towners to compete. Which hasn't really happened.

One thing I know for sure, though, is that this is Austin's year to win it. He's been working tirelessly to perfect his recipe, and he's already breezed through three rounds of heated competition to make the finals.

He nudges me, his eyebrows rising questioningly. "You in?"

I open my mouth. "Ugh. I want to, but I have to put out a small fire with the paper. Kendall messed up the formatting on—"

"Hi!"

I'm cut off mid-sentence as an out-of-breath Taylor Hill plunks down onto the bench in between us, her arm brushing against mine.

"Hi," I say as her blue eyes study my face beneath her sparkling silver eye shadow.

She smells nice. Fresh. Like clean laundry.

"Are you going to Barnwich Brews after the game?"

"We were *just* talking about that!" Austin says, giving me a mischievous grin over Taylor's head. "She was about to make up some excuse about something to do with the school paper."

"You should come," Taylor says, and nudges me. "I'd love to hang out with you more."

"Well, I . . . umm." I stumble, something about her confidence and the way she's looking at me knocking me off my guard the tiniest bit. Something about it is familiar. Almost . . . *challenging.*

For a minute I see Arden across the booth from me at Edie's, leaning forward, the dare in her eyes before it's even on her lips.

I push the image away, but the challenge remains. I mean, I *could* ask Caleb Harvey to put out the fire. He's a shoo-in for editor in chief next year and always eager to help. Sometimes a little *too* eager. But it would be nice not to worry about my application or school or the paper for just one night. To worry about something or someone else for a change. I think again of those glassy eyes, how different that person is now. Maybe I could be different too if I just said yes for once. "Yeah, I, uh . . . I . . . Caleb Harvey? He could maybe . . ."

"Caleb Harvey can what?" Taylor asks, an amused smile on her face.

"The newspaper . . . he can . . ." I shake my head, trying to get my shit together. "Yeah, I guess I can hang out for a bit."

Wow. Way to play it cool, Beckett.

"Taylor!" Coach Stevens, the cheerleading coach, calls, hands on her hips. She jerks her head in the direction of the rest of the squad, dark ponytail swinging.

"Gotta go," Taylor says, casually reaching up to pluck a piece of lint off my shoulder. "See you after the game."

"See you," I call after her a beat too late, and Austin lets out a low whistle.

"Phew. That was painful." He scooches closer, closing the gap Taylor made. "Guess Julie Shapiro didn't show you any moves up at camp."

I snort and shake my head. "Oh, shut up."

After our team wins the game, we head out with Maya to meet everyone at Finn's pickup truck, parked underneath the orange glow of a lamppost.

"So, Beckett," Antonio says when we approach, exchanging a look with L.J., both of them grinning. "Taylor Hill?"

"Shut up, Antonio," Maya and Finn say at the same time. Finn reaches out to pull Antonio's black beanie down over his face for good measure.

Austin slips his hand into Finn's and Finn quickly looks up, blue eyes wide. "Babe, your hand is freezing. Where are the gloves I got you?"

I smile and tilt my head back to watch the falling snow, white specks against the grayish-orange sky, while Austin makes up some excuse to avoid telling Finn he would rather be caught dead than wear red leather gloves.

"It's freezing out here," I mutter as I shuffle from foot to foot, wishing I hadn't worn a skirt to school today and pretended that my sheer black stockings actually had the ability to keep my legs warm.

"I know, right?" a voice says behind me. Before I can turn, a warm letterman jacket slips onto my shoulders. Taylor appears at my side with Lindsay, L.J.'s girlfriend and her co-captain on the cheer squad.

L.J. lets out a low whistle as he puts an arm around Lindsay. "Hill, I'll give it to you. That was smooth."

"Yeah," Lindsay says. She looks up at him, patting his chest. "Maybe you can learn something."

He opens and closes his mouth as everyone laughs. I cast a sideways glance at Taylor, who's rubbing her arms with a small smile on her face, still radiating confidence while I blush from head to toe.

Finn nods to his truck. "Ready to go?"

"Finn. We are not all fitting in there," Maya says even as Antonio throws open the back door and dives in.

"Sure we can! It's like . . . a half mile away."

Everyone piles inside, giggling as we struggle for seat space. Being the shortest, I somehow end up on top of the pile, with my face pressed up against the cold window while we all shift into position: L.J. with Lindsay on his lap, Antonio with half a cheek on the seat, Maya practically underneath him, Taylor . . .

Taylor practically underneath me.

"Everybody hold on," Finn calls from the front, and my eyes meet Austin's in the rearview mirror as Taylor wraps her arms around my waist, taking Finn's suggestion to heart.

"Is this okay?" she whispers into my shoulder, and I nod, but my cheeks turn red again as the truck lurches forward and my hand reflexively grabs ahold of her arm to steady myself.

"Sorry!" Finn calls before pulling out of the parking lot and down the road into town much more slowly. I quickly slide my hand off her arm, but her grip on me doesn't waver.

The ride isn't far, but the whole time I'm too distracted to pay much attention to the conversations around me. *Is my hair in her face? Did I remember to put on deodorant? Is my butt crushing her thigh? Why did I leave the paper in Caleb Harvey's delicate little hands? Did I leave the oven on?*

I finally remember to breathe when we pull into a space right outside Barnwich Brews' cool black exterior, a Christmas-light-wrapped sign swaying lightly in the breeze.

I push the truck door open immediately, but Taylor's arms wait a beat before releasing me. Once they do, I tumble less than gracefully onto the sidewalk. I nod hello to a group of elves jingling past after wrapping presents at the toy store as I right myself and smooth out my skirt.

Maya links her arm with mine as we head inside, leaning in to whisper, "*Relax*, Caroline."

Me? *Relax?* That would be a first in eighteen years of life. I try anyway, taking a long, deep breath, the warm smell of coffee filling my nose.

"You don't *have* to date her. You don't have to like her! Just, you know, see if maybe you could."

Yeah. Okay. I think I can do that.

I nod and she gives my arm a squeeze.

Austin gets to work on our hot chocolates, mixing and measuring a powder he pulls from a plastic bag that just happens to be tucked into a pocket of his backpack. His brow furrows in concentration as he works, his movements careful. Precise.

Finn lets out a wolf whistle as we watch from the other side of the counter, and Austin can't help but crack a smile. Then he looks up from his concoction with a halfhearted glare.

"Finn. I swear I won't make you one if you make me mess up the temperature."

Finn's eyes widen, and he mimes locking up his lips and throwing away the key.

We watch Austin pour and sift, then finally add the perfect amount of whipped cream to each mug before we grab them and pile into a booth in the back. Taylor slides in beside me, and I see her take a sip, then reach her hand up quickly to wipe off the milk-foam mustache left behind.

I remember thinking how cool she was when she came out. One of the most popular girls in school, on the cheerleading squad, homecoming queen material, a *lesbian*. And now she's so casually and sweetly putting her *very* cozy letterman jacket over *my* shoulders. For a moment I can start to see it. The classic high school experience with a sapphic little twist. Kissing in between classes in the back stairwell or at halftime after her routines, study dates at Barnwich Brews with Taylor reading my articles in the corner booth, pancakes at Edie's with our friends, holding hands at the Christmas tree lighting, the glow of the lights feeling maybe a little less melancholy.

So, when her leg brushes up against mine, I . . .

I don't move mine away.

I try to keep thinking of what could be, but somehow the contact makes me think instead of what was. A dark-haired girl's knee knocking into mine, her brown eyes gleaming mischievously on a snowy winter day, sleds clutched in our hands as we skipped school, all red noses and icy fingers. Back when I had not just a best friend, but a crush so big it felt like it couldn't possibly be contained inside me. Like one day my heart would just stop from the weight of feeling so much for her.

Part of me is glad she left when she did, because there's no way I could have kept that secret if I had to be close to her for one more winter. And if I had told her, having her say she didn't feel the same might have been the only thing that could have hurt more than watching her car drive away.

CHAPTER 4

ARDEN

"On time," Lillian says, impressed, when she pulls open the door to see me already sitting in a black plastic chair, waiting to be called into the audition room.

"Early," I say with a grin, taking a quick sip of my latte as I go over my well-worn script one last time.

She plunks down next to me, and the chair squeaks noisily as she shifts right and left, trying to get comfortable. "Jesus Christ," she mutters. "This is *Bianchi* we're talking about. You'd think these chairs wouldn't be stolen from a middle school guidance counselor's office."

I snort and glance up at the clock to see I still have five minutes before, you know, quite possibly the most life-changing audition of my career. I take a deep breath, feeling my heart beating too fast to be able to put on the performance I know I have to today.

"I'm gonna run to the bathroom," I say, nodding to a door halfway down the white-tiled hall.

"Script!" She holds out her hand, eyes just barely flicking up from her phone. I look down to see I'm white-knuckling it.

"Don't want you to dunk it in the toilet. Might as well leave your purse too."

"I need a tampon," I lie, but as I walk past her, she reaches out and grabs the strap of my bag.

"Your period's not for another week."

"Okay. You know *way* too much about my life." I yank on the purse, but she doesn't loosen her grip. "Oh my God. Lil, it's a beta-blocker, not cocaine." But still, she doesn't let up, and finally I release it with a sigh and head for the bathroom empty-handed.

I close the wooden door and lock it behind me, letting out a long exhale as I rest my head against it and squeeze my eyes shut.

"*Relax*, Arden. You got this," I mutter.

I've done *hundreds* of auditions. And yet, in so many ways, this feels a lot like my first. Like I'm thirteen again, standing in a line of girls at an open call in Pittsburgh. The role was for the little sister in a movie where two kids lose their parents in a wildfire. I wanted that part so badly, it felt like *I* would die if I didn't get it. I got more and more nervous as the line grew shorter, and the only thing that calmed me down was my Grams standing there all day with us.

Us.

Me and Caroline.

She didn't have any interest in acting. My parents didn't either, not until after I started making money doing it, but unlike them, she went with me anyway, because, well . . . we never really did anything without each other.

I didn't get the part that day and I didn't die, but I cried all night long. Caroline stayed up with me, though, and she didn't seem to mind when my tears soaked through her pillow. I just knew even then that I wanted to be a part of one of those movies that you feel in your bones. The kind with scenes that have you looking just above the screen so the tears don't spill over and dialogue that makes you forget that some writer made it all up.

A movie like this one.

When my heartbeat finally slows, I head to the bathroom sink to scrub my hands with cold water and then stare at my reflection in the fluorescent bathroom light. I opted for minimal makeup today, just a few strokes of mascara, a tinted moisturizer, and a whisper of blush. Bianchi is known to take a liking to things that come across more . . . authentic. Natural.

Not exactly the words I'd use to describe my public image, but that's what acting is for. When he sees the performance I'm about to put on in there, when he sees me transform into his character, he'll be begging me to take the role.

He'll see that this isn't his movie. It's *ours*.

I shut the water off and grab a few paper towels out of the dispenser, before heading back out to Lillian, who hands me my script but keeps my purse.

"You good?" she asks.

I nod and close my eyes, going into my usual routine of replaying the audition scene in my head, practicing my inflections, my pauses.

"Arden?" The black door in front of us bursts open. Out pops the head of a production assistant wearing a baseball cap, curly black hair sticking out from all sides.

We both stand, and Lillian pushes me forward to follow him into the room.

"Give me that," Lillian hisses, grabbing the script and shoving it into my purse. "Don't want to seem like too much of a try-hard."

"What if I forget my lines?"

"Arden, you highlighted the living shit out of this. You'll be fine."

I plaster a smile on my face as we cross the threshold, and *there*, sitting at a table with a casting director, is Bianchi. Unruly brown hair with traces of silver, wire glasses, and a tweed jacket. His arms are crossed in front of his chest.

"Arden James," he says, with a small chuckle, holding out his hand, a ring on his pinky finger. "Can't say I expected to see you at an audition like this."

I shake it. "Well, I'm a huge fan of your work. I really loved *Unfinished*."

"*Unfinished*?" he asks, eyebrows rising in surprise, as I shake the casting director's hand too. "Not a lot of people know about that one. No one really bothers to watch anything prior to *Blue Skies*."

"Then they miss some of your best," I say, and he nods, impressed, before he scans the script in front of him.

"We're going to have you read the scene where Anna has the confrontation with her sister after she returns back home for her mother's funeral." He glances over at the PA, who is clutching a sheet of paper, and then back at me. "Do you need my script, or . . . ?"

"I have it memorized," I say, turning my attention to the PA and nodding. "I'm ready whenever you are."

"Anna? What are you doing here?" he says, reading off the paper, his voice a monotone.

"I—I heard about Mom."

"You're too late. She's dead."

"I didn't come back for Mom. I came back for *you*."

I'm swept up in the scene as the two of us go back and forth. Despite his monotone, in my head the PA *becomes* my sister, who I haven't seen in years, who I left with my deadbeat parents so I could move to a place where my girlfriend and I could finally be together.

Still, I know I need more. I try to unlock a memory to build enough emotion to carry me through the end of the scene.

The dog's death in Marley & Me.

The little boy chasing after his grandmother in Minari.

The first five minutes of Up.

I try it all, but nothing is doing it for me today.

My palms start to sweat. If I'm going to land this part, I have to make Bianchi *feel* my performance.

Just when I think it's not going to happen . . .

An image suddenly pops into my head.

A fourteen-year-old girl in a puffy pink coat and a pair of blue jeans with a hole in the left knee from when I made her climb a tree with me that summer, standing on the sidewalk outside my old house. I can see myself waving to her out of my parents' back windshield as they drove me toward the airport to start a new life in LA.

Tears fill my eyes, the room blurs in front of me, and finally I feel the character settle into my bones, because I *know* her. I *am* her. I left my small town too. I left my home. I left my best friend and my grandma and everything to come here, because I had a wild, crazy dream . . . and more to lose than I imagined.

"I never *wanted* to leave," I say. For the sake of this scene, I let myself believe that it's true. I pause, letting the moment breathe, allowing there to be silence, ear-ringing anticipation.

My chest heaves. I remember my hand pressed up against the glass as my best friend cried on the other side. I remember saying, *See you at Christmas*, because even though I didn't think it was for good then, I couldn't bring myself to say goodbye.

And then . . . she was gone.

Tears fall down my cheeks, and my breath is ragged as I deliver my final line.

"But no one ever told me I *could* stay."

I remain in character for an extra second before locking that memory back in its box, where it needs to stay. I straighten up and wipe the tears out of my eyes.

I glance quickly around the room, trying to gauge everyone's reactions. The casting director and her assistant are looking at each other, mouths slightly agape, eyes shining. The PA reading lines with me is smiling with a look of disbelief, but I don't know if it's because I'm me, or he actually thinks I did well. The biggest sign is Lillian. She's sitting in her plastic chair by the door, her phone screen lit up, but for once she's not looking at it. When I meet her eyes, she gives me one subtle but firm nod.

Still, there's only one person in this room whose opinion matters.

Finally, my gaze lands on Bianchi, sitting front and center. His arms are still crossed over his chest, his feet are planted firmly on the floor, and his expression is completely unreadable.

I refuse to let it intimidate me, though. I stare right back until he finally speaks.

"You know, Arden, I've been sitting in this room for five hours, watching audition after audition." He nods behind me. "The best of the best have walked through those doors, actors who I've always thought to be, frankly, more talented than you. Actors who I've *always* wanted to work with. And you come in here, Netflix's little darling, and . . ." He looks down, shaking his head.

Shit.

He hated it. That's it. I *knew* I'd overdo it if I let myself—

"You outshined them all," he finishes, looking up at me, the corner of his mouth pulling up into a half smile.

What?

My eyes flick to Lillian, who is absolutely beaming, which confirms that I really did hear him correctly.

Holy shit.

Holy shit.

"But," he says, holding up a hand before I can say anything. "I can't give you the role."

"Wait, *what?*"

Is he joking? He has to be joking. I search his face for some sign that he's just messing with me but don't find one.

"I don't understand. You *just* said—"

"I know what I said." He leans back in his chair, alarmingly casual for someone who just, you know, metaphorically spit in my face. "But I also don't live under a rock. I know what they say about you, Arden James."

He holds up the script that I spent weeks, no, *months* memorizing.

"This script is the best shit that's come across my desk in

42

about a decade. A *decade*. I can't have you ruin it when you can't get out of bed on a Monday morning to be on set."

My stomach drops. This can't be happening. "I've been nothing but professional since the moment I walked through those doors."

He stands up from his chair and pretends like he's arranging some papers on the table.

"I'm sorry, Arden. Maybe in a few years when you've grown up a little."

My reputation is not going to be the thing that stands in the way of this role.

"You've got to be kidding me." I shake my head and take a step forward. "I see what they say about *you*, too. A raging alcoholic who could barely finish his last movie?"

He smirks, because we both know that was just tabloid bullshit last year.

I seize my opening. "You of all people should know you can't believe everything you see on the internet."

He just cocks his head, looking amused. "But photos don't lie. So if it's somehow not true, why would you *want* to be seen and photographed as someone who parties with a different girl every weekend?"

Bingo.

"Because," I say, my mouth curling into a grin, "it's kept me one of the biggest names in Hollywood. I'm not an idiot. I practically grew up in this industry, and I've learned exactly how it works. You want to be bankable for a studio? Keep fans watching your movies? You have to stay trending. You have to make yourself interesting." It's not technically a lie. At least, in the beginning it was all pretend.

"Well," Bianchi says. "That's the other problem. This role, Arden. I'm looking for someone more . . . small-town. More genuine. More homegrown, less Hollywood. Okay? Someone who could better embody the role. Look, there's no denying you have the talent. You know that, but that doesn't mean—"

"Barnwich, Pennsylvania, Michael," Lillian pipes up, getting up out of her chair in the corner. "Ever heard of it?"

He squints at her and shakes his head, though I'm not sure if it's in answer to her question or because she just first-named him.

Either way, she laughs, heels clicking as she slowly walks over to me. "I guess you didn't do your homework. That's where I found this one, working at her grandma's diner in the middle of fucking nowhere. I ended up stuck there on the way to a wedding. The whole town is the size of a goddamn postage stamp." She pats my shoulder, the lie rolling off her lips so smoothly that I almost believe it myself when I know she didn't sign me until *after* I came out to LA. "Creating that kind of image for her was one of the most difficult things I've done in this business, because she's the polar opposite. You couldn't find someone more homegrown. Someone *less* like the person those tabloids make her out to be. Loves her grandma's pancakes and the clean Pennsylvania air and her normie longtime girlfriend back home. Caroline."

My . . .

My *what*?

I try to stop my eyes from bulging out of their freaking sockets as Lillian and I stare at one another.

"Yeah," I manage to say, as I try not to black out. "My . . . girlfriend."

Bianchi lets out a laugh. "Your . . . your *longtime girlfriend*?

Why haven't I seen an article about *that*, then?" he asks.

Yes, Lillian. Enlighten us. Why haven't we seen an article about that, then?

"You haven't seen an article . . . *yet*," she says.

"Yet?" I squeak, and Lillian gives me a look.

"Right! *Yet*. Listen, Michael. If I were in your position, I'd be apprehensive about hiring her too. I mean, come on, the last round of photos were a real hot mess."

Okay. I don't think taking a shit on me is going to help right now, Lil.

"*But!*" she continues, giving me a reassuring glance. "It's because we're about to pivot Arden's image. She's ready for her transformation moment, to mature into the woman she really is. And what better way to do it than with Arden's first and only feature interview, all about her and the girl she's always loved, finally ready to face the world. It'll be posed as a new relationship to the public, but Arden and Caroline? They've been together forever. Like peas and carrots," she says, arms folded confidently over her chest.

I know she's saving my ass. I know it might even work. But an *interview* about a girlfriend who doesn't even exist? Is she losing her mind?

Bianchi's looking at me expectantly, like he's waiting for me to confirm it all. So I do what I do best. I get into character. "Yeah, I'm actually going to be shipping out tomorrow to see her. Heading back home for the holidays. Good old Barnwich practically turns into a Hallmark movie set this time of year. I never miss it."

It's Lillian's turn to burst a blood vessel. I can see her carefully color-coded schedule flashing through her mind, suddenly shot to shit. But she rolls with it.

"There's going to be a write-up in *Cosmo* all about it. I mean, come on, Michael! What is more 'genuine' and 'home-grown' than our Hollywood star here"—she throws an arm over my shoulder—"settling down at last, spending the holidays in her hometown with her childhood sweetheart and then snagging the lead in Bianchi's most anticipated work yet, *Here to Stay Again*?"

I look at Bianchi to see he's chewing his lip thoughtfully, his gaze calculating. My heart hammers in my chest, equal parts hope and fear and anticipation.

"Well," he says finally. "We don't start pre-production until the new year. No need to rush the process. I look forward to reading the article." He raises an eyebrow, then pats the script in front of him. "If there's a Christmas miracle, then maybe we'll talk."

No fucking way.

No fucking way.

It's only a maybe, but it's a hell of a lot better than the no it was.

"We will," I say when Lillian's grip tightens around my shoulder. "Well, I've got a flight to catch!"

After a final round of handshakes, Lillian and I bust out the front doors and into the parking lot.

"I can't believe that worked," I say, and she whacks me with her purse.

"*Gone until after Christmas*, Arden?" she says. "I'm going to be on the phone for the rest of the day fixing this!"

"And calling in every favor you've ever accrued for that article in *Cosmopolitan*," I add.

"Oh my God. What have we done?" she asks, already pulling her phone out.

"We?!" I laugh. "You're the one who made up the girlfriend shit! I was just going along with it."

"Well, I had to." She shakes her head and hands me my purse. "Haven't seen this kind of fire in you in years. Plus the payout will be worth the headache."

I smile at her, swinging my bag up onto my shoulder.

"I'm booking us on a flight into Pittsburgh tomorrow morning. I'll pick you up at—"

"Whoa. Whoa. Whoa." I hold my hands out in front of me, twisting my face up in confusion. "You're not coming with me."

"The *hell* I'm not," she replies, looking up from her phone to me.

"Lil. No offense, but I'm not bringing my agent home for the holidays. How's that going to look to whatever writer they send out to cover the story? It's not exactly going to make me look homegrown." Not to mention I can't imagine Lillian and Grams in the same room, let alone the same house.

"But . . . what if you need something?" she asks, sounding genuinely concerned for me.

"Then I'll ask my grandma." I take a step closer and put my hand on her shoulder. "Hometown girl, remember?"

She takes a deep breath and holds it while she thinks. "Fine," she says. "Fine."

"Thank you."

"Plus, you'll have Caroline," she adds.

"Huh?" I ask.

"If you need something, you can always ask your best friend,

47

Caroline," she says. "You're going to have to ask her to be your girlfriend anyway." I nod, even though something tells me "best friend" isn't necessarily the label Caroline would use to describe me anymore.

I let out a long exhale, thinking of the girl in the Instagram photo. Is she still the same girl I spent all those years running around Barnwich with? Who would invite me to stay over on school nights when my parents were yelling so loud I couldn't even focus on my homework? Whose family always treated me like their own? Who was game for any scheme I'd come up with?

We were Arden and Caroline, glued at the hip, always a package deal. I thought she'd be in my life forever. But even after all the years between then and now, I still feel our connection. When you have a friendship as tight as ours was, it doesn't simply evaporate.

I just wonder if Caroline feels the same way.

CHAPTER 5

CAROLINE

"She's got you doing lights!" Harley calls as she takes out a tray of coffee for a small group of tourists.

"Lights . . . ?"

I lean over the counter, reading the list of stuff Edie left for us to do before she headed home after the breakfast rush.

Next to my name, written in red ink, is *Hang Christmas lights up outside.*

Outside? I grimace and peek out at the steadily falling snow, my hands still just barely warming up from the drive over.

I'd admittedly noticed the lights weren't out yet, but Edie hasn't exactly been in the Christmas spirit the past few years. It's only two weeks out from the big day, and as I gaze around the diner, I can feel the shift from past years inside, too. This place used to be full and merry, abuzz with holiday cheer by early November. Now, at a table by the jukebox, Mrs. Tucker tries not to cry about her stationery store going under.

Now, Barnwich is struggling to hold on to what it once was.

"They're in the supply closet," Tom says, sticking his balding head out the serving window. "Top shelf."

Tom has worked in the kitchen since I was a kid. He's the only other person Edie trusts with a spatula. He nods toward the front door. "Ladder's in the back of my truck. The hooks should still be there from last year, so you just gotta . . ."

He does a looping motion with his spatula that means nothing to me.

"*Lights*, Edie?" I mutter as I grab my jacket and pull it back on, then clomp to the supply closet. I throw open the door and climb over mops and brooms and buckets to get to the shelf where a spool of Christmas lights sits on top of an open box filled with decorations covered in a thick layer of dust.

Arden's favorites. A dinged-up glowing Santa Claus. A blow-up reindeer. A wreath we made in fourth grade.

Edie's full display hasn't seen the light of day since Arden left, I realize.

I head outside with the lights, pull my hat on, and crane my neck back to see the hooks Tom mentioned trailing the entire length of the place. I let out a long exhale that sends my breath swirling around me before grabbing the ladder from out of Tom's beat-up red pickup truck and dragging it to one corner to get started.

"Of *course* I forgot gloves today. . . ."

I climb cautiously up the ladder, nearly slipping off a metal rung. Once I'm sure I won't face-plant, I stretch to hang the first few feet of lights, but the cord slips off the hook about eight times before finally staying put. Teeth chattering, I slowly but surely make my way back down the ladder, move it, and start all over. I repeat this again and again along the row of windows, until finally I reach the last two hooks on the opposite side.

I hear a knock on the window and look down to see Harley holding up a steaming mug of hot chocolate, the top overflowing with whipped cream, a tantalizing reward waiting for me at the end of this string of lights. She gives me a thumbs-up and I try to return it, but my hands are too numb to fully commit.

I peer up at the final two hooks and stretch to loop the strand of lights around the first. But when I try for the second, it's *just* out of reach.

"Shit." I *really* don't want to move this ladder yet again. My mind is already on the hot chocolate I'm about to drink.

I scooch toward the edge of the ladder rung and stand on tippy-toes, my arm outstretched as I strain, trying to hook it, and—

Yes!

Wait.

Fuck.

The ladder starts to sway underneath me, and before I can stop it, the whole thing topples to the right, dumping me into a snowdrift left over from when the parking lot was plowed.

I lie there for a few seconds, letting snowflakes collect in my eyelashes as I stare up at the sky and . . . *Arden James?*

"Hi, Caroline," she says, the right corner of her mouth ticking up into a shockingly familiar lopsided smile.

Jesus. How hard did I fall? I must have smacked my head on the way down.

But then she kneels and holds out her hand for me to take, and when I squint at her face, framed by her dark brown hair, the long eyelashes overtop even darker eyes, I realize it's the same but . . . different. Older. *Prettier,* a voice whispers somewhere deep inside me. I look at her extended hand, note her rings and painted fingernails, but it's the tattoo I've never seen before peeking out underneath the sleeve of her denim jacket that convinces me.

She's . . . here. Actually *here* in Barnwich.

I brush her hand aside as I stand up and fix my hat.

"What . . . *what are you doing here?"*

"Home for Christmas," she says like it's obvious, slipping her hand back into her jacket pocket. "How would you feel about being my girlfriend?"

I push her into the snowdrift.

As Arden flails around in the pile of snow, I dust myself off, then plug the lights in so Edie's bursts forth in a small attempt at holiday cheer. Nodding with satisfaction, I force myself to focus on my hot chocolate reward instead of whatever the hell is going on here.

I return the ladder to Tom's truck and move to head inside, but Arden chases after me.

"Caroline, *listen,*" she says, catching the door as I push through it. "Do you know Michael Bianchi? The director?"

Of course I do, my brain answers immediately, but I ignore her and keep walking into the diner. Heads turn and eyes widen at the sight of Arden. The few tourists stop eating to pull out their phones and snap pictures, which only makes me angrier, but she just continues talking.

"Okay, so there's this movie. This role. My *dream* role, right? And I crushed the audition, but he's looking for someone a little less, uh . . ." Her voice trails off as I push through the doors to the back.

"Of an asshole?" I supply as I rip my hat and jacket off. Arden just snorts.

"I was gonna say less messy and controversial, but yes, sure. That works too. Tom! Hey!" Tom comes over to scoop her up into a hug while I pull my hair into a ponytail and tighten my apron. I use the distraction to push back out of the kitchen and away from her.

I've barely dropped off waters and menus at a table before she reappears, trailing after me. "He's looking for someone who's more 'genuine' and 'homegrown.' So my agent, Lillian, came up with an idea. Technically a, uh, lie, I guess, but to show the truth that I do come from a small town."

I grab a bin and start clearing off a table while she stops to say hi to Mrs. Clemente, our second-grade teacher, and signs one of the paper place mats for her granddaughter.

I push the silverware, plates, and napkins into the bin and try to steady myself, but all I can think is *there she is*. Actually *here*. I cast a sideways glance to see her leaning casually against the booth, all charm and warm smiles, her undivided attention on Mrs. Clemente, making her feel like she's the only person in the entire room. Her hands move as she talks, her nose wrinkling, her head tilting. So much the same that it makes my stomach twist.

As I begin to clean the next table, Arden, still half a foot taller than me, pops up beside me and continues the one-sided conversation like she never left.

"She told Bianchi that I'm from the Christmas capital of Pennsylvania. And that there's going to be an article in *Cosmopolitan*, my first feature, all about the twelve magical, snowy days I'm spending back home with my, uh . . . my longtime girlfriend, Caroline."

I drop a handful of mugs back onto the table, my eyebrows shooting through the damn ceiling as my head swings up to look at her.

Arden nods with the gleam of a scheme in her eyes. It's all too familiar in that painfully nostalgic sort of way.

She wants *me*, Caroline Beckett, to pretend to be her supposed longtime girlfriend? If I wasn't so pissed off, I would be rolling on the floor laughing right now.

Even Mrs. Clemente, who still doesn't know how to turn on a computer, let alone go on Instagram, has probably seen a picture of Arden shit-faced and stumbling out of a bar with her newest flavor of the month. Or week. Or hour. Who's going to believe this?

She must see my expression, processing all this bullshittery, because she begins to clarify. "At least, that's what *Bianchi* thinks the truth is. To the public, it'll be a change brought about by my, uh, finally requited love for my childhood best friend."

Finally requited?

I feel like I'm going to be sick.

She leans closer to me, her face inches from mine, and I hate the fact that after all this time she smells the same. Warm and rich and earthy, not like some expensive perfume she bought on Rodeo Drive.

"Listen," she says, her voice softer now as she looks past me at the room of people. Her eyes land on Mrs. Tucker by the jukebox. "Don't do it for me. Do it for the town! Think about what great publicity it could be. A wintry fluff piece like this will have everyone flocking here for their holiday cheer! Even just driving down Main Street, I can tell there's been a bit of a drop-off. Barnwich isn't what it used to be."

I pick up the bin and head back toward the kitchen, my heart hammering angrily in my chest that she's using *this* as a tactic. My love for a town that she abandoned.

Arden follows. "What do you want? I could pay you some—"

That's the final straw. I slam the bin down on the counter and whirl around to face her. "Let me get this straight. You disappear *four* years ago. You don't call me. You don't text me. You don't come home *once*, not even for Christmas like you promised you *always* would. And now you drop back in, thinking you can bribe me into agreeing to be your *fake girlfriend* and telling the whole world about it?" I laugh and shake my head. "Are you out of your mind?"

She doesn't answer. The two of us stare at each other for a long moment before I turn around and grab a rag to angrily wipe down the already-clean counter.

When I stop scrubbing and look up at her, I'm not sure what's more a ghost of themselves, Barnwich or Arden James. She might have the same face, the same smell, the same voice, but I don't even *recognize* the girl across from me.

"And how dare you pretend you care about this town and the people, Arden! Have you even seen Edie yet?"

She looks down for a fraction of a second, which is answer enough. I shake my head, throwing the rag into the dirty water.

"That's what I thought."

Arden opens her mouth like she's going to say something back, but before any words can come out, she seals her lips into a straight line, turns, and makes a beeline for the parking lot, leaving just as suddenly as she arrived.

CHAPTER 6

ARDEN

"Fuck."

I hit my palm against the steering wheel, and my hand practically splinters from the frostbite I've probably gotten after all of ten minutes in Barnwich.

Fuck the cold. *Fuck* this stupid article. *Fuck* . . . well.

Me.

For thinking Caroline would want to help me with anything at all. For thinking there was a slight possibility of rekindling our friendship after all these years.

Sighing, I turn up the heat to full blast before looking into my rearview mirror. My gaze lands on Caroline on the other side of the diner window, sipping from a white mug while she talks to a girl with hot-pink hair.

Are they . . . dating? I can't see the two of them together. But maybe I'm so focused on the plan that I don't want to. I never considered that that could be a possibility, that she might not even be able to fake date me if she's dating someone else for real.

I watch her for a long moment before throwing the car

into reverse and heading out of the parking lot toward the opposite side of town, where Grams lives. Her house is a small bungalow between the Christmas tree farm and Cemetery Hill, where everyone goes sledding in the winter. Or did four years ago, at least.

I peer out the window as I drive, at the lights strung up on every storefront and the wreaths hung on black lampposts, perfectly spaced along Main Street like a Christmas postcard. People mill about, and a few heads turn as I go by because of *course* Lillian rented me a fire-engine-red Corvette instead of something norm— *Shit!*

I try to hit the brakes at the stoplight, but there's no traction, and I end up sliding halfway into the intersection before the car comes to a stop.

"You're not in LA anymore, Arden," I mutter to myself as I give an embarrassed wave of thanks to the mom in the minivan who dodges me like a true professional.

I look over to see if any more cars are coming, but instead I catch sight of a new sign, swaying gently in the breeze. BECKETT BROTHERS BAR.

No way.

My fingers tap excitedly on the steering wheel. Levi and Miles. They actually did it?

Someone honks from behind me, and I pull my gaze away to see that the light is green. I throw up another hand of apology before hitting the gas gently this time.

It feels so . . .

Strange to be back here. Back *home*.

In so many ways, it's like someone pressed a pause button

while I was gone and everything stayed frozen, suspended in time. But like the Beckett Brothers sign, when I look closer I see that that isn't the truth. Edie's new pink-haired employee. The gray in Tom's sideburns. The blacked-out empty storefronts.

The way Caroline looks at me, like I'm the last person she wants to see instead of the first.

And now, my Grams's house. Dark except for the kitchen light peeking out through the blinds. Not a single string of lights. Not a garland or wreath. Not her gigantic inflatable snowman or Santa Claus bouncing around in the front yard. And worst of all, not even a tree, decorated with fifty years' worth of ornaments, glowing in the living room window.

I swallow hard as I get out of the car and take it all in from the driveway, dropping my bags at my feet and feeling my chest get heavy with guilt. Of course she hasn't done any of that. How would she manage it by herself? I left her here all alone. Me and my parents, gone all at once. And none of us came back. We didn't even let her visit me in LA either, because they didn't want her to see they were never there, and when things got messy, I couldn't stand the thought of her seeing that part of my life, which now is just . . . my whole life.

Will she even want me here after I've stayed away for so long? I shouldn't have just assumed she'd let me stay here, like I assumed Caroline would want to see me.

But there's only one way to find out now. I stoop to pick my stuff up and slowly walk to the front door. I knock, and my heart hammers at the sound of her shuffling around inside.

"Just a minute," she calls out, and hearing her thick Southern drawl in person sends tears I didn't expect springing into my eyes.

I don't even have time to blink them back before the door swings open and there she is.

Grams.

Salt-and-pepper hair. More salt than pepper now. Crow's feet around dark brown eyes. A thick cardigan because she never did get fully used to the Barnwich cold.

We stare at each other, for the first time in four whole years, for what feels like an eternity.

I look down at my feet, eyebrows furrowing as I struggle to find words, but she finds them first.

"Oh, Arden."

And then she's there, wrapping me in a hug without me having to say anything at all.

I squeeze my eyes shut and feel her breath hitch just once underneath my palms. My Grams who never cries, fighting to keep it that way.

Finally, she pulls back and pats me on the face. "Come on, I'll make you that meat loaf you like." She peeks past me at the Corvette in the driveway, smirking as we head inside. "Well, if you'll still eat it. Look at you, Miss Fancy Pants."

I laugh and drop my bags in the entryway, then hold up the keys. "I was going to see if you wanted to drive it for the next two weeks, but if you don't—"

She swipes the keys out of my hands so fast my hair blows in the breeze. "Oh, well now, let's not get ahead of ourselves."

We walk into the kitchen, and I can't help but smile at the familiar white cabinets, the wooden breakfast nook in the corner, the refrigerator covered in Christmas cards and photos and newspaper clippings.

I watch as she dumps, pours, and sprinkles all the ingredients into a metal bowl, measuring everything by eye just like I remember.

"Well, come on," she says, turning around to face me. "This meat loaf isn't going to mix itself."

I breathe a sigh of relief at the ease in her voice and roll up my sleeves to help. I wash my hands and then sink them into the bowl of meat and eggs and milk and whatever else she puts in there that makes it so delicious, to start mixing away.

"How's, uh . . . how's the diner treating you?" I ask as we fall into a familiar rhythm.

She snorts. "Same old, same old. Tom is a pain in my ass. Numbers are down even further this season, but the tourists who do come are showing up with odd demands now, asking for 'oat milk' and kale. Do you know they make a burger without the meat now? If there isn't any meat, what the hell is it?"

"They're actually pretty . . ."

I shut my mouth before the look she gives me turns *me* into a burger.

"Other than that, things are peachy keen. Always something that needs fixing, always a bill to be paid, but that diner has been open for thirty-five years, and it'll be open for another thirty-five to come." She slides the meat loaf into the oven and moves on to peeling potatoes.

"You know I can—"

She holds up her hand, stopping me. I've sent her a check every month since I left, and not one of them has been cashed.

"Why?" I ask. When she doesn't answer, I try again. "Why won't you take my help?"

She lets out a sigh, shaking her head.

"That's why," she says without looking at me. Her famous line from my childhood. The conversation ender. I wish she would take the money, but no one, and I mean *no one*, is prouder than Grams. She has to do everything herself.

We're both quiet while she puts the potatoes on to boil.

When she speaks again, she changes the subject. "I saw that new movie you were in. The one with the time loop," she says.

My mouth drops open in surprise. "You saw *Operation Sparrow*?"

"I watch everything you're in, Arden," she says, stabbing a potato with a fork.

"What . . . uh . . . what did you think?"

She shrugs. "Eh."

"I agree," I say, leaning forward conspiratorially, and the two of us grin at one another. "I mean, the ending?"

"Oh Lord. When you fell in love with that asshole? Just ridiculous." She taps me on the side. "Get me the milk for the mashed potatoes."

I head over to the refrigerator to grab the 2 percent, but my hand freezes on the handle as I look at not just Christmas cards from loyal regulars, but articles about me, even reviews of some of my movies and TV shows. Thankfully, none of my tabloid photos have made the cut. But then I reach out to touch the corner of a different photo. Of me and Caroline, sitting on the barstools at the diner, black-and-white cookies in hand, barely a single front tooth between the two of us, her cheeks rosy from the cold. I lift it up to reveal the newspaper article behind it, but this one isn't about me. It's a piece about Edie's Eatery, and below the title it reads *by Caroline Beckett*.

"You seen her yet?" Grams calls out to me, shooting me a side-eye as she strains the potatoes.

"Yeah, I . . . well . . ."

I huff and let go of the corner of the picture so I can bring the milk over to her. I hop up on the counter to tell her everything that happened at my audition with Bianchi and Lillian while she mashes.

"So I asked Caroline, and she—"

"Read you the riot act?"

"Well, yeah. Pretty much. Told me I had some nerve showing up here after four years and asking that of her." I swing my legs, calves hitting lightly against the cabinets.

The timer dings, and I slide off the counter to get the meat loaf out of the oven and bring it over to the table.

"So, what now?" Grams asks as we sit down, and I take a bite of my favorite meal on the entire planet, the flavors melting in my mouth, sweet and juicy and tangy.

It's even better than I remembered it, when I would lie awake at night in my empty mansion in Malibu, convincing myself that I didn't miss this meat loaf or all these small moments sitting across from Grams in her cozy kitchen.

"I don't know," I say with a shrug. "She didn't say yes."

"Did you really expect her to?"

"I mean . . . yeah?"

"Arden." She lowers her brow and looks straight into my soul.

"I don't know, Grams," I reply, setting my fork down.

"Well, I can't speak for Caroline, but I can speak for myself." She looks down, like she can't bring herself to look at me, which makes me feel sick. "You've been gone for four years, and finally,

finally, you come back to visit us . . . and it's all just a show for some magazine? How do you think that makes Caroline feel? How do you think it makes *me* feel?" She looks up at me at last, her eyes shiny.

"I—I don't know," I reply, my throat aching too much to say anything else. Shame I've tried so hard not to feel washes over me.

"Well." Just when I think she might ask me to leave, she reaches across the table to place her hand over the back of mine. "Maybe you should spend some time thinking about it."

I place my other hand on top of hers so they're sandwiched together, and as hard as it is for me right now, I look her straight in the eyes.

"I'm sorry, Grams," I tell her, even though I know it's not enough. Even though I should have said it the second I walked in.

"I know you are." She slips her hand out of mine and puts another slab of meat loaf onto my plate. "Let's eat before it gets cold."

I pick up my fork, and she eases the tension by telling me about the new menu options at the diner, but I can't stop thinking about Caroline and what it must have looked like from her point of view today. Me busting in like she'd just go along with my schemes again, as if she owes me anything.

That's when I realize there's one thing I owe *her*. One thing I've owed her for a very long time now.

An apology.

CHAPTER 7

CAROLINE

I pull open my kitchen cupboard, eyes glazing over as I stare at the pile of plates in front of me.

Arden.

I can't believe she's here in Barnwich. Part of me still thinks I must have wrecked it too hard off the ladder, because it's just so completely unbelievable that she was actually at Edie's diner, asking me to—

"Earth to Caroline," Riley says through an empty paper towel roll, pressing one side flat against my ear.

I swat her away and grab the plates. I place one down in front of every chair at the table, as Miles trails behind me, adding a cup next to each.

"You good?" Levi asks, juggling an armful of utensils.

"Yeah. Just . . ."

Annoyed? Shocked? Wondering if the universe is playing some giant trick on me?

"Tired," I settle on, as my phone buzzes in my back pocket. I expect to see Taylor's name, since we've been casually texting since the basketball game. Or, she's been casually texting, and I've been stressing over every word I send back. We like the same canceled sapphic TV shows, the same kind of pizza from Taste of Italy (*with* pineapple) the same kind of music. And, well, slowly but surely it's starting to feel *good*. Maybe not romantic just yet, but good.

Instead of a text from Taylor, though, it's a message from an unknown number that appears over Blue's fuzzy black ears.

are you busy?

who is this? I reply, though I'm pretty sure I know the answer.

My phone buzzes again and a selfie of Arden pops onto my screen, confirming my suspicion with a thumbs-up and a cheeky smile.

got your number from grams :)

I feel a flash of annoyance, because my number has never changed in all these years. Only hers did. I let out a long sigh and start to type out that I'm about to eat dinner when there's a knock on the front door.

I look slowly up from my phone, eyebrows furrowing. Mom and Dad exchange a quizzical look too overtop the enormous serving plate they're dumping the pasta into.

No. It can't be. I glance down at the selfie Arden just sent, recognizing the white columns of our porch, a blurry Bertha parked just past her head.

"I got it," I squeak out, walking briskly down the hall.

When I throw open the door, sure enough, there she is, standing underneath the glow of the porch light, snow in her long brown hair. She stops blowing on her hands to grin at me, and I roll my eyes.

"You have got to be kidding m—"

The words aren't even out of my mouth before Blue zips past me, launching himself at Arden, his body a blur from all the wiggling.

"Traitor," I mutter, shaking my head as she stoops down to scratch his ears and Blue coats her in kisses. Though I guess I shouldn't be surprised: she's the one who gave him to me.

"He's gotten so big," Arden says, and I remember how small he was that day she rescued him off the side of the road, a tiny head popping out the neckhole of Arden's sweatshirt, the two of them soaked through and shivering from the rain.

"Funny how time works," I say instead. She winces and stands, brushing her pants off.

"Listen, Caroline. I wanted to say—" she starts, but then a voice shouts loudly from the kitchen.

"Who's there?"

I frantically try to think of a way to hide her before they can invite her in, but before I can slam the door in her face or grab her arm and shove her into the hall closet, Levi peeks around the corner, followed by Riley and Miles. "Oh shit!" Levi says. "It's Arden!"

I barely have time to get out of the way before everyone comes barreling down the hallway, a chorus of footsteps and voices.

"Oh, Arden! Look at you!"

"Did you get taller?"

"Why are you in *Barnwich*?"

"Is Scarlett Johansson as hot in person as she is on TV?"

My dad whacks Levi for that last one before pulling Arden inside, and soon everyone is hugging and laughing like it's Christmas morning and Santa Claus himself has come busting through our front door.

"You have to stay for dinner!" my mom says, squeezing Arden's face between her hands.

"Oh, I ate at my Grams's," she tries, but my mom is already grinning, an eyebrow ticking up.

"Marc made his chocolate mousse brownies. . . ."

Arden's eyes widen, and she looks at my dad, who nods. "A double batch."

"Well, I mean . . . in that case . . ."

The words are barely out of her mouth before Miles helps her take her Saint Laurent jacket off and chucks it in my direction to hang up in the closet.

"Unbelievable." I shake my head after it smacks me in the face. But everyone is already halfway down the hall, leaving me in the entryway while they whisk her off to dinner.

I hang up the jacket, then squeeze my eyes shut, taking a deep, steadying breath. In . . . and . . .

I pop an eye open and glare at the jacket in front of me, my attempt at a peaceful moment ruined by Arden's sandalwood smell radiating off the expensive fabric.

Groaning, I close the closet door and clomp down the hall to find her squeezed in next to Riley, who is already talking her ear off, directly across from my empty chair.

"My soccer team? We're the best. Coach thinks we have a *really* good chance at making states next year, since we have so many returning players."

"States?" Arden says, her eyes remaining focused on Riley as I slide into my seat. She's always had that ability to give her

67

undivided attention to whoever she's talking to, like earlier at the diner, but it's been made all the more magnetic by her time in Hollywood. "That's super impressive. You guys must be really good."

She's a talented actress, I'll give her that much.

"Do you think if we made it to states, you'd come watch?" Riley asks.

"Uh, yeah. Maybe!" Arden says, and I can't help but chuckle into my water glass.

"Don't get your hopes up."

Levi kicks me as he hands me a plate of pasta, and I glare at him. Of course they're acting like nothing happened. Like she didn't ditch me, and all of us, for that matter, only returning when it benefits her.

Since clearly no one else is going to say anything, I do my best to focus on the noodles in front of me instead of the girl across from me, but it proves to be . . . incredibly difficult. She talks to Miles and Levi about the bar, insisting she has to come check it out. She talks to my mom about the firm and finds out they apparently both know the same pain-in-the-ass lawyer in the entertainment industry. She talks to my dad about the new pasta recipe he tried tonight, telling him how the celeb-frequented Italian spot down the street from her house couldn't hold a candle to it.

And all I can do is sit here and watch them fall for her act, while counting down the seconds until this dinner is over. Until she is out of this house, with her familiar laugh and familiar movements and familiar smell but completely unfamiliar life.

No, better yet, until she's out of Barnwich altogether, and I can just keep remembering her as the Arden who once was instead of the Arden who is, the reality of her homecoming souring the one I used to dream about even further.

"So," my mom says as she puts down her fork and laces her fingers together. "What is a big famous Hollywood star doing back here in Barnwich?"

"Well." I look up as Arden's head turns toward me. She avoids my gaze, clearing her throat. "I'm, uh . . . here for an article. In *Cosmopolitan*."

I laugh, and everyone's attention shifts to me.

"Way to conveniently leave out the bit about how you lied to a director and now you need me to 'pretend to be your girlfriend' to save your reputation for a part."

Arden gives the table a sheepish grin, and Levi and Miles try not to chuckle, hiding their faces in their napkins.

Riley, meanwhile, has far less subtlety. "Who would believe *you're* dating Arden?"

My cheeks burn, and I grab ahold of my water glass and take a long sip.

"Hey," my dad says, giving me an enthusiastic smile. "Maybe you can find a way to add it into your extracurriculars for your college application!"

Sure. *Dating Arden James.* An extracurricular. I'll put that down right next to *editor in chief.* I mean, I want to *write* articles, not *be in them.*

I cross my arms over my chest, tilting my head back to look up at the ceiling as my mom squeezes Arden's arm.

"Well, whatever the reason, let's toast to Arden! *Home for Christmas.*"

I . . . am so done.

"Yeah," I snort, pushing my chair back and getting up from the table. "About four Christmases too late." My plate and utensils clatter noisily as I drop them into the kitchen sink and then head for my room.

CHAPTER 8

ARDEN

Without a second thought, I push back from the table and dart out of the kitchen, trailing Caroline's strawberry-blond ponytail up the wooden stairs.

"Don't follow me," she says without looking back.

I do anyway, down the familiar hall to the doorway of her bedroom, where she whirls around to look up at me, brown eyes aflame.

"Arden. Get this through your head. We're not friends." Caroline points to herself and then to me, finger tapping lightly against my chest. "We *were* friends, but we aren't now, okay? You made that clear when you left." She slams her bedroom door shut between us, and the wood practically grazes the tip of my nose.

I take a deep breath and lean my forehead against it, thinking about the reasons I never came home, the reasons I didn't call. Reasons that Caroline couldn't possibly understand.

Part of me wants to leave again now, abandon my plan and head for the Hollywood Hills. But I think of what Grams said and force myself to reach out and turn the knob. I ready myself to dodge anything she might throw at me as I push inside, but instead I find her typing away loudly at her desk in the corner.

"Caroline, listen. I didn't come here to intrude on your family dinner. I came to say I'm sorry. And I know those words aren't enough, but I am. For what it's worth, I bet your dad's right. This could be a big opportunity for both of us, and I'd hate for you to miss out on it because you're mad at . . ." I trail off, waiting for her to say something, to acknowledge me in any way at all, but she just keeps her back to me, working away.

"Did you hear me?" I follow up. Still nothing. "Caroline. Can you look at me? Talk to me? I'm trying to—"

"Give me a half-assed apology?" she mutters under her breath.

"Oh my God." I throw my hands up, exasperated. "I'm just trying to have a conversation. *What* are you even working on over there?" I ask, walking up behind her.

"My portfolio for my Columbia application."

Portfolio?

I look above her desk and find a bunch of framed articles hanging on her wall, a first-place plaque for a Pennsylvania state-wide journalism contest next to them. And then I remember the newspaper article hanging on Grams's refrigerator.

"All these prizes for your articles . . . You must be a shoo-in."

"Yeah, well, those awards might not be impressive enough. They have a four percent acceptance rate. I'm not a 'shoo-in' for anything," she bites back.

I take a second to chew on it.

I can't make her accept my apology, but maybe she doesn't have to in order to do this with me. Maybe it just needs to benefit us both.

I take another step forward, as I come up with something I *know* will get her to sign on. Something she'd be out of her mind to turn down.

But Lillian is going to kill me.

"You can write it," I blurt out.

Her fingers finally stop clacking against the keys.

"What?" she asks, cocking her head slightly to the side, even though she's still staring at her computer.

Got her.

"You can write the article for *Cosmopolitan*," I tell her.

She does a one-eighty in her swivel chair to face me. "You're bluffing. They would never let me write it."

I continue quickly, wedging my foot into this gap before she changes her mind and shuts me out again. "They'll do it for Arden James," I reply, because we both know it's the truth. "How do you think a feature byline in one of the most widely distributed magazines in the world would look in your portfolio? Columbia would probably be begging for you to come study journalism with them."

I look at her expectantly as she sits there, looking shell-shocked by my proposal.

"That *is* what you want, right?" I ask, and she nods. "See, you and me? Like it or not, we're the only ones who can help each other right now."

She spins back around in her chair and sinks her head into her hands. Her elbows rest on the desk, and her fingers rake through her hair like it's the hardest decision she's ever made.

Come on, Caroline.

"We don't even have to be friends again," I add, just in case that'll tip the scal—

"Fine," she says immediately, like a punch to the left kidney.

"Fine?" I ask. "To the article or not being friends?"

She faces me again, a few strands of hair now loose from her ponytail, but ignores my question, asking instead, "When is it due?"

"Uh . . ." I think back to my phone call with Lillian from the plane. "Due first thing Christmas morning. It's going live on Christmas Day. I'll be gone and out of your hair the next day, and my agent already came up with the title: 'Twelve Days of Arden James,' since we've got twelve days until then if we start tomorrow. She was going to have the interviewer follow us for twelve wholesome holiday dates." I make sure to put air quotes around "dates." "We both know I've been photographed out with a girl once or twice . . ." Caroline snorts and raises her eyebrows, but I ignore her. "*So*, for the sake of me not looking like a cheater, we'll frame it like we're childhood best friends who are finally together after pining for each other all this time. So you could just sort of . . . I don't know. Write down how great it is to finally be together, to be spending the holidays falling in love with such a *humble*, down-to-earth, small-town gal like—"

"Just stop," she interrupts me again. "I'm not going to write some bullshit fluff piece for you. If I'm going to do this, it's going to be on my terms."

"Okay, okay." I put my hands up in surrender. *Jeez, she really takes this seriously.*

"And obviously there has to be some sort of fake breakup down the road. I don't have any desire to be your fake fiancée. Let alone your fake wife."

"*Obviously,*" I reply. *Caroline Beckett, my wife. HA!* "So, what's the plan then, Rachel Maddow?"

I see her shake her head at that, but for the first time there's a hint of the corner of her mouth pulling up. She doesn't answer once again, though, so while she types God-knows-what on her laptop, I take a spin around her room.

It's very different from how I remember it. The walls have gone from white to a deep green. Polaroids of the two of us have been replaced with pictures of her new group of friends looking down at a camera that must've been on the ground, judging by the angle. The flash blew them out and you really can't even tell one face from another, but you can tell from the poses they're *real* friends. One thing I haven't found a lot of in LA. I walk over and lightly touch the corner of another photo, this one with Caroline all smiles while a black-haired boy with rich brown skin has an arm slung casually over her shoulder. On her other side, a girl with bright blue eyes rests her head on Caroline's other shoulder. I think I might recognize her from art class back in middle school, but I haven't thought of it in so long it's hard to be sure.

"All right. So, I like the title and I like the twelve dates idea," Caroline speaks up finally from where she's been typing away, but my mind is still on the photo.

"Who are they?" I ask, pointing to it.

She lets out a long sigh. "My friends, obviously."

Clearly I'm not going to get more than that, so I move to the bookcase, fingers trailing along the top shelf, where a few more journalism awards and plaques rest against the wall.

"Impressive." I pick one up, a first prize for a Pittsburgh journalism contest, and hold it up to her. "When did you get so interested in journalism?"

"The summer after you left." She clicks her pen a few times.

"There's a *ton* of cute stuff we could do around Barnwich right now. I mean . . . even with the decline, this place is full of holiday activities. So we won't have any shortage there. But how can we . . ." Her voice drifts off as she taps her chin in thought.

I pick up the Columbia coffee mug from her bedside table. "Why Columbia?"

"Arden. *I'm* supposed to be the one interviewing *you*."

Resigned, I put the mug back and plop down on the end of her bed to wait quietly as she thinks. Eventually she smiles to herself and starts typing again, so focused she doesn't even notice a strand of hair falling into her face.

"I'm going to come up with twelve questions, one for each date. Twelve deep, personal questions that give people a look into the real Arden, not just 'Arden James.'"

"*Pfft*, good luck with that. *I* don't even know who the real Arden is," I say, before realizing what I just admitted. "I mean . . . never mind." I shake my head.

Caroline peeks over her shoulder at me and gives me a once-over. Then she closes her laptop and gets up, so I do too. We walk toward each other until we meet in the middle, right by her doorway. "Well, you better figure it out if this article is going to get me into Columbia," she says, and then firmly guides me right out the door and back into the hallway.

"Wait." I reach my hand in and catch the door before she can shut it in my face again. She looks at me, annoyed, but this is important. "People will recognize me when we're out and about, so we're going to have to pretend to date the entire time, not just in how you write the article. We have to make it convincing." I wrap my fingers around the door handle and meet her eyes, my heart pounding with . . . excitement? Yeah. I think I'm actually getting a little excited about this new role I get to play. "Think you can do that?" I ask.

She nods, but I can see her biting the inside of her cheek, a tell that she's nervous.

I pretend I don't notice.

"Good," I say as I step back into the hallway. "I'll see you tomorrow."

I head down the hall, slowing as I approach the steps I've walked down hundreds of times, a rush of memories washing over me. Running down to catch the school bus. Scrambling up to watch a rom-com instead of doing our homework. Tiptoeing back and forth to get a midnight snack, trying not to step on the creaky second-to-last step. Caroline's hand brushing against mine the last time . . .

For just a moment, a strangely familiar feeling swims into the pit of my stomach. A sort of warmth that I can just barely remember, because I haven't felt it in four years.

Because I don't want to feel it anymore, I remind myself. What good would it even do to patch things up? My life will never be here again.

So I start down the stairs and keep moving forward like I always have. Like I always will. Knowing that time and distance will chase these feelings away again when my twelve days are up.

CHAPTER 9

CAROLINE

DAY 1

On Friday, the bell has barely finished ringing when I leave calculus, my last class of the day. I whip my phone out of my back pocket as I head down the hall to my locker, frowning when I see I don't have any new notifications telling me what the hell to expect today.

I knew I should've taken control of planning the dates.

Of course I can't trust—

"Still nothing from your girlfriend?" Austin asks, leaning against his locker while I pull mine open and glare at him.

I gave him and Maya the rundown last night over FaceTime, and, as expected, they were super not chill about it. For different reasons. Maya because she is so Team Taylor I think she's getting shirts made, and Austin because he has some romantic delusion that this will lead to a *real* romance with Arden.

Still, they've promised not to say anything. They're the only two people other than my family who can know this whole little scheme is fake.

Well, *three*, because let's be honest, Austin definitely can't make it through the day without telling Finn.

"First of all, *don't*," I say, grabbing my history textbook and shoving it into my tote bag. "And second, no. Still nothing."

"Wait. *Still?* Your *girlfriend* is ghosting you already?" Maya says, popping up next to me, mouth twisting in disdain as she says the word. "Have you told Taylor yet?"

I lean forward, hitting my head against my locker door in reply. Make that four.

"Told me what?" a voice asks, and I immediately lift my head to see Taylor standing there, already in her cheerleading uniform for the boys' basketball game in an hour, looking absurdly pretty.

She smiles at me like I'm exactly who she wants to see, and that makes this a million times worse. Leave it up to Arden to crash into town and ruin my first real potential romance.

While some part of me is slightly relieved that I don't have to struggle to figure out my feelings, it's still annoying that I probably won't even get a chance now.

"I . . . just . . ." I sling my tote over my shoulder and grab her arm to pull her into a nook by the stairwell, Austin and Maya shooting me supportive grimaces as I go. "Listen, Taylor, I . . . I like you."

It's not a lie. Now that I'm getting to know her, it's hard not to like her. You can see why just about everyone at Barnwich High does. She's the person you *want* to be friends with. She's fun, and she makes me laugh, and she's easy to talk to. Will I ever feel like my heart is going to stop from the weight of feeling so much? Probably not. But maybe that was just preteen melodrama fueled by a Taylor Swift playlist and one too many romance movies, more than love. Things with Taylor could be easy. Fun. Not complicated. Who says that can't turn into love too?

Her blue eyes light up, and I want the ground to suck me in, but I force myself to continue on before she can say anything.

"But I . . . well . . ." I have no idea how to frame any of this in a way that doesn't seem actually insane, so, I just blurt out the truth. "For the next twelve days, I'm going to be fake dating Arden James so I can write an article about it."

"*Arden James?*" She laughs, but stops when she sees I'm serious. "Wait. Seriously?"

I nod, grimacing. "We were best friends growing up, and she breezed back into town yesterday, begging me to do it to help her image. And I *really* don't want to help her, but this could make such a huge difference for my Columbia application, you know? A byline in a magazine as big as *Cosmopolitan*? And I obviously don't expect you to like . . . wait until this blows over, or to—"

"I can," Taylor says with a shrug.

I stop, frowning. "What?"

"I'll wait," she says easily.

"You will?"

"Yeah." She gives me a smile that for the first time I think I could probably fall in love with. "I've liked you for longer than just this year, Caroline, even though it took me a century and a half to actually get the nerve up to talk to you. If I have to wait another few weeks, I can do that."

Hearing that makes me like her more, even though it's hard to believe that this outgoing, confident girl who has no trouble talking to anyone was somehow too shy to talk to me.

Me.

I groan and bury my face in my hands. "That is so sweet. You're making me feel even worse."

Taylor laughs and pulls my hands away, then tugs me back toward the hallway. "Come on. I'll walk you out."

As we head for the exit, she pulls lightly on my jacket sleeve. "So," she says with a smirk. "When's your first date?"

"It was supposed to be today, but I haven't heard anything." I check my phone to see if I've miraculously gotten a message in the last five minutes. Nothing. I let out a frustrated sigh as I push angrily through the doors. "This is so typical Ar—"

I skid to a stop when I see her leaning against Edie's ancient blue Volvo station wagon, a swarm of people surrounding her. She grins when she sees me, and pushes off the hood of the car, raising one hand to say hi.

So many heads turn to look at me that I instantly want to die. "Oh God."

I turn around to head back inside the school, but Taylor stops me.

"Whoa, whoa, whoa. You've got an article to write, Beckett!" she says, blue eyes crinkling at the corners. She leans forward to whisper in my ear, her floral clean laundry scent washing warmly over me. "Just don't fall for Arden James, okay? Because I'm banking on a New Year's kiss from you."

I laugh and she pulls back, her cheek brushing lightly against mine before she pushes me in the direction of the Volvo and the shitshow of the next two weeks.

When I get to the bottom of the steps, Austin grabs ahold of my arm, helping me worm through the crowd of people, a path forming when Arden moves to meet us in the middle.

"Holy . . . ," he mutters as we get closer. "She's even prettier in person."

I hate the fact that he's right.

"What are you doing here?" I say, crossing my arms over my chest as I'm pushed into her.

Arden catches me, feigning shock at my tone. "What do you mean, babe? I'm here to take you on our date," she says, and the crowd of people around us audibly gasps. The corner of her mouth ticks up as she taps her watch. "We've got to get moving."

You have to be kidding me.

Her eyes flick behind me, and I look back to see that Maya and Taylor have joined Austin. She raises her hand in greeting. "Hey. I'm Arden."

"Obviously," Austin says, and the two laugh like they're old pals.

"I remember you from art class," she says to Maya, who is glaring at her. "Mrs. Schultz. You did that cool paper model of a bird."

"Yeah," Maya says, her stony resolve crumbling slightly. "You helped me launch it out of the second-story window."

"Yeaaah," Arden says, nodding. "I actually do think it flew for a couple of seconds before, you know, *the crash.*"

My head swings back and forth between the two of them, and now Maya's actually cracking a smile, even though she quickly tries to cover it. How did I not know this? I mean, we've discussed Arden before, but only what she means— *meant*—to me.

Then I see Arden's gaze land on Taylor, and something silently passes between them, but I can't tell what.

I barely have time to process it because Arden takes a step toward me, grabbing my wrist and pulling me closer so she can slide an arm around my shoulder. Annoyingly, my stomach flutters and I grimace, about to push her off, when she leans closer to me, nose grazing my ear.

"People are watching, okay? I know it pains you, but just play along. Like I said last night, it's only twelve days."

I glance over to see that, sure enough, a few people in the crowd are snapping pictures of us super unsubtly. The flash on Arthur Thompson's phone even goes off before he fumbles to shove it back into his pocket.

I look back at Arden, her face still close. Finally, I nod.

"Well, we better head out," Arden says, looking at Austin and Maya and Taylor, who is shaking her head.

"Have fun!" Austin says, slinging his arm around Maya, who is crossing her arms angrily over her chest.

"Take care of her," Taylor calls with a confident smirk on her face that's scarily like Arden's. It makes me blush, and Arden pauses for just a second before she opens the car door for me. Once I slide into the rusty Volvo, I watch as she makes her way around the front of the car, waving goodbye to the crowd, which reluctantly starts to disperse.

I roll my eyes and reach up to pull my seat belt on. "So, where are we going?" I ask as she hops in.

"Christmas tree farm."

I snort. "We already have a Christmas tree. Or didn't you notice yesterday when you crashed dinner?"

Arden doesn't say anything. She just starts the car and checks the rearview before pulling slowly out of the parking spot. I glance out the window to see that people are somehow *still* taking pictures.

"It's for Grams," she finally says as we turn onto the main road. "Her house is looking a little bare. Thought it might liven the place up a bit."

I look away, hating how . . . *Arden* that is. So all-or-nothing.

When she's here, it's like at dinner last night . . . She takes up so much space. I always wondered how one person could have enough pieces of herself to give the most to everyone. Always remembering birthdays and graduations and big moments, even for people she didn't know that well. She learned how to knit just to make a hat for our fourth-grade teacher's new baby. When we were ten, she convinced me to stay up until two in the morning to bake Jessica Gallagher a crème brûlée, chocolate mousse, and vanilla sponge birthday cake she'd had once in Pittsburgh and spent a week talking about *eight months* before, because Jessica's parents had just divorced.

And then she left and I stopped wondering, because Hollywood showed me the truth. There had always been a part of me that felt like she couldn't possibly ever be *mine* because so much of her belonged to everyone else. But I know now that those pieces of her weren't all genuine. That so much of Arden James was nothing more than a carefully constructed act.

Just like this is right now.

Her head whips around as a red Corvette flies past us down Main Street, and a lopsided grin appears on her face as she watches it fade from view. "Speaking of Grams," she murmurs, shaking her head, "we traded cars."

The idea of Edie ripping around town in a Corvette makes me grin despite myself. I look out the window to try to smother it.

We drive past the outdoor Christmas market in the church

parking lot, and I have to do a double take, because there are so few people walking around that it almost doesn't even look open.

Jeez, this year is even worse than last.

Arden reaches out to flick on the radio. "All I Want for Christmas Is You" starts to play through the muffled speakers, and she taps along on the steering wheel.

"So we don't have to talk," she says with a small smile.

I prickle because *of course* I didn't want to talk, but it's annoying that she knew that. And maybe also a little annoying that she's fine with it.

Mariah croons the whole way as we head to the very edge of town, past Edie's, to the Christmas tree farm. But when we turn into the parking lot, a rope is pulled across the entrance, the sign dangling from it reading BE BACK LATER.

"Now what?" I ask as the car comes to a stop. Arden chews thoughtfully on her lip as she peers out the windshield.

Then, without a word, she just cranks the car into reverse. My hand flies up to grip the oh-shit handle as she speeds a little farther down the road, the Volvo bouncing when she makes a sharp right turn and pulls onto the grass.

"What are we . . . ?"

"Come on," she says, hopping out of the car.

I unbuckle and follow her to the trunk, eyes widening when she pulls a whole *axe* out of the back.

"For emergencies," she says with a shrug and a mischievous smile.

"Emergencies?"

I chase after her as we go running into the woods, along the edge of the Christmas tree farm.

"Arden. What are we doing?" I hiss, grabbing ahold of her arm.

"What does it look like?" she says, raising the axe as she stops to inspect a Douglas fir. "I mean, Jesus, Caroline. Use some context clues."

"We're *stealing* a tree?" I squeak out.

"You and I both know Grams has been giving the Swansons free apple pie for years," she says, rejecting the fir and zeroing in on a balsam two rows over. She crunches through the snow to get to it while I sprint after her. When I catch up, Arden is nodding her approval as she circles it. "This is the one."

"But it's broad daylight!" I try. "Can't we just come back later?"

"Not if we want to get it decorated before Grams gets home. Besides, nobody's out here."

When I don't look convinced, she tries another angle.

"Caroline, we need content for the article. You want it to be good, right?"

I let out a huff, because *of course I do*, it's the only reason I'm doing this. "Fine. But you're coming back later with a donation. And if we get caught, you better be ready to play the celebrity card, because I am *not* gett—"

I'm cut off by the thwack of the axe.

She barely makes a dent in the base of the tree.

"Never cut your own Christmas tree down before, huh?" I say, and she glares at me, putting down the axe to kneel and inspect her handiwork, a small nick about the size of a paper cut.

"Obviously you did not watch my smash Hallmark hit *Random Axe of Kindness*."

I squint at her. "You weren't in a Hallmark movie."

She grins up at me. "You been keeping tabs on my IMDB?"

I roll my eyes, but my face grows warm. Arden just laughs, then stands and dusts herself off before picking the axe back up and returning to work.

I let her suffer through about a minute of feeble thwacks, her hair tumbling into her face, red from exertion, before I finally hold out my hand.

"Give it here."

Her eyebrows tick up in surprise.

"Caroline, I watched you get hit in the head with the ball thirty-four times in *one month* in our fifth-grade gym class. You remember when you tripped during field day and—"

I grab the axe out of her hand before she can make me relive that particular trauma. "You *know* my dad always makes us help cut down the Christmas tree. Says it's a bonding experience."

"*This* is a bonding experience?" Arden asks.

I snort and swing the axe at the tree, slightly higher than Arden was aiming for, and feel the metal dig into the wood with a satisfying *thwack*. Ten hits later, the wood splinters at last, sending the tree slowly toppling over.

Arden gives me a once-over as I lean on the handle. "Impressive."

We stare at each other for a long moment before the sound of a truck bursting to life on the opposite end of the farm cuts through the silence.

"*Shit*," Arden hisses, grabbing the base of the tree. "Move, move, move!"

We go tripping through the snow, dragging the tree all the

way to the car. We attempt to hastily shove it into the trunk, since there's no time to tie it on top, but the tree is too big to fit inside.

"Hold it in the back!" Arden says as the top branches curve around the windshield. "We're gonna have to leave the trunk open."

I freeze and look back to see Mr. Swanson's truck just visible on the horizon. His horn beeps out a "Jingle Bells" sound that makes this moment even more absurd.

"Get in!" Arden pushes me into the trunk, and I grab ahold of the tree, clinging to it for dear life.

As Arden dives into the driver's seat and guns Edie's Volvo out of there, my chest heaves with unexpected laughter. When I look over the branches of the tree at Arden, she's laughing too, that lopsided grin back on her face.

And I hate that my heart begins to race just a little bit faster.

Hate how much I missed her.

The cold air stings at my eyes as memories wash over me, adventures just like this, sledding with trays we stole from the cafeteria, riding our bikes in the dark so we could sneak into Edie's to make hot chocolate and cookies for the diner staff, convincing our elementary school principal to sanction a school-wide snowball fight. I haven't done anything like that, *felt* anything like that, since she left. While Arden's been off being the main character, I've just been watching and asking, safe in telling other people's stories instead of my own.

I clutch the tree harder as she makes a sharp right turn, and try to swallow it all. It's only our first fake holidate and she's already making things complicated, confusing. If there's one thing

I know from journalism, though, it's that there's no use writing a story everyone's read before. There's no way I'm letting Arden in again, just to watch her walk back out on Christmas Eve.

But now I know how much harder that will be.

CHAPTER 10

ARDEN

DAY 1

"Is this even going to fit through the door?" Caroline groans as we stand side by side, yanking on the bottom of the tree, struggling to pull all ten thousand tips through the narrow opening.

"Of *course* it's going to—"

Thwack!

One of the branches manages to squeeze through and smacks me right in the face. A second later, the tree, me, *and* Caroline tumble through my grandmother's entryway.

"*Ow,*" I grumble, rubbing my forehead while Caroline giggles away next to me. "It's not funny! Could've damaged the ol' moneymaker."

She laughs and opens her mouth to say something before snapping it closed and standing, dusting herself off as she looks away.

Ten steps forward, nine steps back. Still, I can work with that.

After we manage to get the tree into the living room, I run down to the basement to get the stand and the ornaments, but Caroline hovers by the door at the top.

"Still scared?" I call up to her, gazing around at all of Grams's very unthreatening, carefully labeled boxes.

She calls back a very unconvincing "What? No!"

Caroline was never a fan of anything spooky. Basements, scary movies, and ghost stories were a big *no thanks*. I remember she held my hand the whole way through a corn maze one Halloween because Levi told her a bunch of kids lived there, and they were looking for someone to sacrifice to their demon god. Which . . . come to think of it, is actually just the plot of *Children of the Corn*, but we didn't know that at the time.

I get back to scanning the boxes, each one sloppily scrawled on in permanent marker.

Photos.

Dishes and Crystal.

Diner Paperwork.

Callie and Theo Clothes.

My heart sinks at that last one. I can't believe she still has my parents' stuff down here. She should've dumped this box ages ago. If there's one thing I know about Theo and Callie, it's that they'll never come back for what they left behind.

Nope, not going there. I swing my head up and onward, and my eyes finally land on the box labeled *Christmas Ornaments* on the top shelf, just out of reach. I look around for a stepladder or something, but there isn't one.

"You find it?" Caroline calls down to me.

"You want the good news or the bad news?" I call back.

"Good?"

"I found it."

"Bad?"

"I need you to come help me get it."

Caroline grimaces before slowly poking a foot out, the wooden step creaking as she cautiously puts her weight on it. She creeps down the rest of the steps at a glacial pace, head on a swivel.

"Don't worry, Pennywise just left."

She slaps my arm as she steps off the last stair. "Shut up."

I rub where she hit as I point to the box on the top shelf, just above us. "I think we can get it if I give you a boost."

"Give me a . . . ?"

I stoop down and pick her up around her legs. Caroline lets out a gasp and grabs ahold of my shoulders to steady herself. To my surprise, I almost gasp too, but it's at how nice it is to be this close to her after so long. It feels strangely normal in a way I didn't know I was missing. But even if I wanted to, I don't have time to think about it further, because the past four years of staying out late and generally taking shitty care of my body tell me that I have about six and a half seconds before I drop her smack onto the concrete floor.

"Get . . . the . . . box," I manage to grunt out, and she complies, cautiously reaching up to grab it off the shelf.

Once she has it in hand, I let her body slide slowly through my grip until we're face-to-face, her feet touching the ground, the cardboard box between us.

"A warning would've been nice," she says. I notice her cheeks are faintly red, making the freckles on her nose stand out even though it's winter.

While I'm sure it's just from anger at being scooped up without notice, a small part of me wonders if being this close to me makes Caroline Beckett nervous too. If she can feel the ghost of the childhood crush I had on her all those years ago.

God, I hope not. *Focus, Arden.*

I take the box from her grip. "Let's get the tree done before Grams gets home."

I head up the steps as Caroline squeaks out a "Wait for me!" and runs to catch up before the basement monster can grab her by the ankles.

For the next hour, we get the tree set up, adding a red-and-white quilted skirt that my *great*-grandma made and a string of ancient incandescent lights. I make a mental note to upgrade her to twinkle LEDs instead of these fire hazards. Then we dive into the box of dusty ornaments, which clearly haven't been touched since I left Barnwich. My heart fills with guilt just like last night when I pulled into her driveway and there wasn't a single decoration up.

"You okay?" Caroline asks, dipping her head toward me.

"Yeah." I force a smile and shake it off.

We begin to hang each ornament that Grams carefully collected throughout her life, from frosted pinecones on a string, to a handprint of my mom's from when she was a baby, and even a small snow globe of Seoul that she brought with her when she emigrated as a little girl.

As we move through the box, we're both pretty quiet until I begin softly humming Christmas music and Caroline can't help but join in.

Eventually I hear Caroline chuckle as she digs into the bottom of the box. When she emerges, she's holding up an ornament with a picture of us from two years before I left, just a few short months before I first started realizing I had a crush on her.

"Cuuuute," I say, plucking it out of her hands. In the photo, we're bundled up in our winter jackets, our noses red from the cold. "Your earmuffs were adorable, but I always loved that beanie you made me."

Beige with a blue stripe. Very cozy.

"It was too big," Caroline says.

"Yeah, because you used your brother's big-ass head for the measurements," I say, leaning past her to hang the ornament on a high branch next to a figurine of Rudolph, my arm brushing lightly against hers.

"If you would've held on to it, it'd probably fit your 'big-ass head' perfectly now." She laughs.

"Who says I didn't keep it?" I ask, my heels landing back on the ground.

"Please. I don't think it would exactly match your Saint Laurent coat."

"Yeah, it probably wouldn't," I reply, but smile to myself as the two of us hang the final few ornaments. When the box is completely empty, I plug in the lights and we plunk down on the ground just in front of the glowing tree, admiring our handiwork.

We stare at it in silence for a moment before I glance over at her, taking in her face illuminated in the yellow lights, the straight line of her nose, the fullness of her lips, her strawberry-blond hair over one shoulder.

And all at once, I feel it. The warm, cozy, almost euphoric sense of nostalgia for a time in my life that I've all but forgotten. The feeling of being close to someone who once meant everything to me in a place that looks and sounds and smells like . . . home.

It stirs up a memory and gives me an idea.

I hop up and head over to the buffet, where Grams keeps her ancient stereo. I flip through all the CDs until I find what I'm looking for. *Rockin' Around the Christmas Tree* by Brenda Lee.

I pop it in and turn to face Caroline. I smile at her, but she looks skeptically at me while we wait for something to play. As the first notes play out, her eyes widen immediately.

"Come on," I say, reaching for her hand.

"Arden, I don't remember the steps," she says, pulling her hand away from mine.

"I don't believe you." I grab her arm this time and pull her onto her feet and into the open space in the living room.

"I don't feel like it." She tries again, but I'm already starting without her.

"Right. Left. Left. Right. Twirl!" I sing above the music, going right into the dance routine we made up and performed at the diner Christmas party every year.

"Arden, stop!" she says in a loud, firm voice, jerking hard out of my grip before taking a few steps away from me. "I don't want to do a fucking dance with you. Okay?"

"Oh. Okay," I reply, taken aback. "Sorry."

"Don't worry, I'll say in the article that we did the whole routine." She sits down on the rug with her back to me. I take a second to catch my breath, reminding myself that we aren't those kids anymore. I've made sure of that.

I head off to the kitchen to give her some space and check my phone, finding a voicemail from Lillian.

"Just checking in. Making sure Caroline is actually *writing* that article and you two aren't just screwing around all day. It's not too often *Cosmo* lets an eighteen-year-old from nowhere write for them. I don't want any more surprises, Arden. Make sure it gets done right."

I pocket my phone and roll my eyes at that before returning to the living room with a circular blue tin of Royal Dansk cookies. I plop down onto the carpet beside Caroline and hand her the tin.

"Thanks," she says, taking it and then prying it open. "Oh, yum." She laughs and holds the tin out for me to see.

"Aw, shit. They got to Grams, too." I take it from her and dig through the cookie tin, finding it filled with thread, needles, and miscellaneous buttons, not cookies. "God, is there a certain age that old ladies just *have* to turn these into sewing kits?"

Caroline shrugs. "I think it just happens naturally as we age."

I chuckle and shake my head, and then we sit there for a few minutes as time slowly melts away the tension in the room.

"You still gotta ask me a question," I say, trying to stay in business mode now, thinking about Lillian's message. The look in Caroline's eyes changes as she pulls out her notepad and flips through the pages. Very serious.

I bite my lip, trying to stifle a laugh as she clears her throat.

"You're a successful actress with a long list of credits in a number of smash hits, and half the young girls in the US look up to you." Her eyes, heavy with irony, flick up to meet mine for just a sec. "Who do you look up to?"

"Ooh. That's a good one."

I lean back on my hands, thinking about all my favorite actors, the ones I try to emulate, the ones who've made me want to be a part of a movie like Bianchi's. "Oh, man. It's gotta be Toni

Collette. For sure. She turns every role into one that you wish was yours. She's *so* tal—"

"Arden," Caroline interrupts, and I look over to find her shaking her head. "Not someone whose career you want. I mean someone you look up to as a person. This article is supposed to be more personal, right? So *personally*, who do you look up to?"

I chew my lip as I think, and my gaze lands on a picture on the fireplace mantel of me and Grams at her diner. I'm sitting up on the counter while she flips pancakes on the griddle. Of course. Why didn't I name her first? "Grams. She grew up in the South in a first-generation Korean American family. Worked so hard for years with very little education to save up and open her own diner. She kept going when the love of her life died the week it opened. And then she practically raised me when her daughter couldn't be bothered." Another pang of guilt stabs me in the chest for every day she's spent here without me, and all the days she *will* spend here without me, after all the days she gave up *for* me.

I let out a long exhale, feeling Caroline's eyes on me.

"That's admirable. That's the kind of person half the US should look up to," I add.

"Then why don't you honor her legacy if you look up to it so much?"

I stare back at the tree as I try to speak, but all that comes out is a stutter of sounds. How could I possibly explain to her everything that has happened in the last four years? That I don't even remember saying yes to my first part in LA. That I just remember everything happening all at once, getting Lillian and a schedule and a plane ticket to the promise of a better life. That the moment I stepped off the plane in LA, I found out that to get what I always wanted, I had to turn into something I didn't really want to be, and my parents didn't even attempt to protect me from it. And that by the time I was old enough to do it myself, it was too late, because now I needed the numbing and the distractions. She'd probably just call bullshit before I even got a word out.

"I wanted . . . I—I *want* to," is all I can tell her, because it's the one thing I know to be true. "That's why I want a role like this, one that matters."

I'm worried she's going to press for more, but when I look over at her, at the reflection of the lights in her warm brown eyes, she just nods and flips her notepad shut, like she understands that it's all I can give her right now. I guess in all this time that I've been gone and with how angry she's been since I got back, I forgot that she can read me perfectly. She knows exactly when to push, when to ask the hard questions, and also when to let up. She always has.

There's a loud crash and the door bursts open, making both of us jump.

Grams stands frozen in the doorway, slowly shaking her head. "Ah, shit. Jim Swanson was bitching about someone stealing a tree earlier tonight. I had my suspicions when he said it looked an awful lot like my Volvo." She puts her hands on her hips. "Barely here two days and you two are already getting into trouble."

Caroline and I share a guilty smile, and I wonder if she's remembering when we replaced a hundred dollars' worth of Tom's cigarette stash at the diner with candy cigarettes when we wanted him to quit. Or when we replaced all of Miles's stocking stuffers with sticks of deodorant. Or when Levi got his license and we somehow convinced him that stop signs with white outlines were optional, and he almost killed us all.

Okay, *that one* was a little too far, but we were like twelve.

I hop up and throw an arm over Grams's shoulder, innocently leading her over to the tree.

"Could be a coincidence," I say, and she snorts, giving me a look before turning her gaze back to the tree.

"You like it?" I ask after she's had some time to take it in. She nods, giving me a small smile.

"I like it." She pats my side. "Thank you." Her gaze flicks past me to Caroline, my tree-stealing accomplice, the gratitude extending to her, too.

"It's almost eight o'clock, Caroline Beckett. You better be getting home for pizza night unless you plan on committing any other felonies."

Right. Fridays are pizza nights in the Beckett household. My stomach growls at the thought of their deep-dish pepperoni, and I make a mental note to stop by Taste of Italy and pick one up for me and Grams.

She shouldn't have to cook again after her shift.

Caroline smiles and stands as Grams slips out from under my arm to give her a hug.

"I'll drive you home," I say when they pull apart, holding out her jacket from the hook by the door.

I expect her to resist, but she takes it and nods. "Okay." She brushes past me, smelling like floral shampoo and stolen pine needles, and my head turns almost automatically to follow the scent. When I swivel back to say goodbye, Grams is giving me a look, her eyebrow raised.

I roll my eyes at her and grab my jacket and keys, but her look lingers in my mind. I hate how I've barely been here two days and Caroline Beckett somehow already has me feeling like despite what I've told myself, a part of me has been waiting all this time to come home.

Not home, I remind myself. This is why I can't get too close, too cozy. I only have twelve more days here . . . and then I go back to LA. That's home now.

CHAPTER 11

CAROLINE

DAY 2

I chew my lip the following afternoon as I glance from my notepad to my laptop, typing out notes on yesterday's criminal events so I can stay ahead on this article. I stare at what Arden said last night about Edie, remembering how she faltered when I pressed her on it, her entire demeanor changing as a million unspoken things lay between us.

And the worst part is that maybe for the first time since she's been back, she finally looked completely like Arden to me.

But maybe that's what she wanted me to see.

It feels so hard to tell which parts of her are an act. The girl in front of the Christmas tree or the girl who never called. The girl sitting at dinner talking to Riley or the one wearing something outrageous on a red carpet. The girl holding out her hand, asking me to dance, or the one at the diner asking me to be her fake girlfriend for the press.

It's easier to pretend it's all an act. But that only makes it harder to figure out what to write.

I lean back in my desk chair and let out a frustrated sigh.

God, this girl can get under my skin.

There's a knock on my door, and I swivel around to see none other than Arden James herself pushing inside.

"Oh, hey," she says, launching herself onto my bed like we're still thirteen-year-old best friends. Blue uncurls himself from underneath my desk to hop up next to her.

"Really?" I groan, quickly reaching up to smooth my hair before I can stop myself.

She ignores me, propping herself up on one arm, her other hand aimlessly scratching Blue's head. "All right. So we've got two options this evening—"

"No, we don't. I have a basketball game."

Arden nearly chokes on the piece of gum she's chewing, legs flailing as she sits up. "*You?* Play basketball?"

I sigh before she can remind me again of my near-death gym class experiences. If only she could remember something useful, like maybe how to dial my phone number.

"Of course not. I *manage* basketball."

"Oh, phew." She lies back down again. "That makes more sense. The lumberjack routine yesterday was surprise enough."

I glance at the clock in the corner of my computer screen to see it's already five thirty and I should probably get moving. Warm-ups start in an hour. "I actually have to—"

There's a knock on the door and Riley pokes her head in, holding a box of Cheez-Its. "I thought I heard Arden's voice."

Arden motions to the bed and Riley plunks down next to her, Blue in between them. I rub my eyes, exhaling loudly.

"Guys, I have to—"

"Heard you stole a tree from Swanson's," Riley says, ignoring me and holding the box out to Arden.

"Me?" Arden feigns shock as she spits out her gum and scoops out a handful. "I would never. That was all Caroline."

Riley laughs so hard her mouthful of Cheez-Its nearly coats my bedspread. "Mr. Swanson'll probably put up a plaque to commemorate it. It'll become a new Barnwich tourist destination."

Arden smirks as she tosses Blue an orange square, then dusts her hands off before ruffling his ears. "I will personally come back to steal that plaque."

Nice to know there's something she'd come back for.

Riley clocks it too. "So you think you'll come back to Barnwich again even after this article is done?" she asks excitedly. Arden glances so quickly in my direction I'm not even entirely sure I saw it, but I am sure I don't want to hear that answer.

"Can you two take this little hangout session somewhere else?" I cut in. "I have to get ready for the game tonight."

"Jeez, okay," Riley says as they both swing their legs over the bed and stand. "Sorry to bother you. Didn't realize you were suddenly so passionate about your managerial position."

She and Arden head for the door, Blue trotting after them, Cheez-Its clearly more valuable than his loyalty to me. But then Arden pauses, turning back to look at me.

"I'll see you at the game. We'll . . . I don't know. Improvise something for day two."

At the game? I open my mouth to object, but Riley interrupts.

"Come on, Arden," she says, pulling her into the hall and closing the door behind them.

I stand and catch sight of myself in the full-length mirror on the back of my door and instantly want to die. Oversized sweatshirt. Messy bun. No makeup. Like I'm still the fourteen-year-old girl she left here, like I haven't grown up too these last four years.

It doesn't matter, I tell myself.

But it takes me way longer than it should to figure out what to change into.

An hour later the stands are steadily filling up as Austin and I lug the water bottle carriers in for the game against Grand Hudek, our rivals. A spot in the playoffs is on the line tonight, which is something I probably should care about. But, blasphemously, I don't. A season-ending loss would mean I wouldn't have to touch another sweaty pinny for the rest of my days, so while I'm not waving my pom-poms for Grand Hudek, I wouldn't exactly *mind* if they won.

"You think we got it?" Austin asks me. I glance over to see our team warming up. The already small group is down three and without any subs since the twins had to leave early for a Christmas cruise with their family, and Simone Hall tore her ACL. I watch Melanie Anderson, one of our benchwarmers, airball a free throw.

"There's your answer," I say as the ref blows the whistle and Barnwich green and Grand Hudek blue jog off the court to circle up.

As Austin and I bring the freshly filled water bottles over to the bench, he turns to look back at the stands, a wry grin pulling at his lips. "Well, well, well," he says, waving like he's in the middle of a Miss America contest. My head snaps around to scan the crowd.

I slap his hand down when I catch sight of who he's waving at.

I knew Arden would be here. But in Barnwich High green-and-white face paint? Sitting next to shirtless Finn, Antonio, and L.J., whose chests are painted to spell out, *GO, BARN*, and *WICH*?

Maya is the only one sans body paint and thus apparently the only one with more than one brain cell to spare.

But just when I think it can't get worse . . . it does.

Arden grins at me and holds up a massive GO CAROLINE sign.

The phones come out immediately, practically all of Barnwich turning their attention to her. I can see the social media posts now. My entire feed filled with—

I stop when a camera flashes in my face, and I realize all at once that it's not just Arden they're photographing. That it's *my* name on the sign.

I won't just be on some freshman's IG story. This is going to spread way past Edie's and the Swanson Christmas tree farm.

And fast.

I turn around and wish I could melt into the bench.

"You good?" Austin asks as the players take their positions and the ref blows the whistle to start the game.

I nod unconvincingly, and Austin studies my face before leaning forward a tiny bit. "So what's been happening with you two?" he asks, keeping his voice low.

"What do you mean?" I ask as our star player, Nicole Plesac, dribbles past.

"I meaaaan, this is the girl you were hopelessly in love with for *years*."

"And? Did you forget the part where this is fake?" I glance

back anxiously at the stands, as if Arden might somehow hear from ten rows back. "Weren't you *just* telling me to date Taylor?"

"Well, yeah, but that was before *Arden* was back in Barnwich. Looking absurdly beautiful, I might add, even in whatever face paint my boyfriend helped her apply. And I would be shocked if her *pretending to be your girlfriend* didn't stir up some old feelings."

"Austin, she's here for like eleven more days, and then she'll be gone again. What do you want me to say here?"

"I don't know, but you certainly didn't deny that she's attractive."

I sigh, exasperated. "Just about everyone with a Netflix account thinks Arden James is attractive. That isn't groundbreaking."

"Well, you didn't deny that it could stir up some old feelings, either."

I clamp my mouth shut and turn my head away, catching sight of Taylor Hill and her perfect blond ponytail, standing with the other cheerleaders. Despite everything, she smiles at me, and I lift my hand to wave back.

"I'm just saying . . . ," Austin starts again.

"Austin," I say, turning my head back around to meet his hazel eyes, losing my patience, "I feel *nothing* for Arden. If I felt anything, it would be a vague sense of betrayal that makes me angry anytime I find myself accidentally not hating her guts for half a second. Us dating? Is fake. Her being here? Is temporary. My feelings? They're in the past, right where she left me. Okay? Can we please just watch the game?"

He nods, closing his mouth, and the two of us don't speak again until near the end of the fourth quarter.

"Shit, I don't even like sports, and this is making my palms sweaty," Austin says as we sink a basket and pull ahead by two. It has been neck and neck since the half, and the room is buzzing with excitement.

Even Melanie Anderson managed to make a free throw.

Coach Gleason calls a time-out, and Austin and I hop up, handing out Gatorade bottles that are quickly snatched out of our hands. No subs, a blood feud against Grand Hudek, and playoff hopes close enough to taste are absolutely *wrecking* the five girls on the court. You can see it on their faces. Brows sweaty, faces red, a general aura of exhaustion. Even Nicole Plesac looks like she got hit by a bus; her signature pre-wrap headband, festively red and green because even sports are an opportunity for holiday cheer here, is hanging on by a thread.

"There's only *three minutes* left in this game, ladies," Coach barks, chewing noisily on a wad of pink gum. He looks up to the 47–45 score, illuminated in orange. "Just get your ever-loving shit together and hold them back for three more minutes!"

Austin and I have barely collected all the Gatorade bottles, though, before Grand Hudek makes another basket, tying the game once again.

Then Nicole misses a three-pointer, and the unthinkable happens. Melanie Anderson goes to get the rebound and twists her ankle.

The crowd falls silent, watching her writhe on the ground in pain, and Coach jogs out with the trainer. Austin grabs ahold of my arm as Nicole helps her sit up, and Melanie covers her face with her hands while they inspect her ankle. People start to murmur behind us.

"She's just drawing the foul."

"Did she break it?"

"We're done for."

Coach stands as Melanie is helped off the court. He runs his fingers through his gray hair before turning around and locking eyes with me.

Oh no.

He starts walking over, and my stomach drops in panic.

"Oh no, no, no."

"Caroline," he says, like we're in the middle of a world war. "We need you."

"Need me to do *what* exactly?" I squeak out, and Nicole tosses me Melanie's sweaty-ass jersey while the trainer helps her onto the bench in her white undershirt.

"Absolutely not."

"As manager, you're technically on the roster," he says, kneeling in front of me.

"Sir, I am in Doc Martens and a dress."

He glances down at my attire and then up at the scoreboard. "Please. It's only *one minute*. That's it. You're our only hope, or we have to forfeit. Against our biggest rivals. With the *playoffs* on the line."

Just as I'm scrambling to find any way to say no to that, a single voice rings out from the stands.

"Let's go, Beckett, let's go!" Followed by a few rhythmic claps. "Let's go, Beckett, let's go!"

I turn around to see Arden standing on the bleachers, cheering shamelessly. After a beat, Taylor hops up, motioning for the cheerleaders to join in. All around us, other voices begin to echo them until—*oh my God*—the whole gymnasium is chanting. The noise is overwhelming, the floor practically shaking underneath us.

Arden grins down at me, hands coming up as she calls through them one more time.

But this time she chants something else. *"Full stack or bust!"*

I freeze. I haven't heard that phrase for four whole years.

It became our *I dare you*, our battle cry, after she said it over and over again one winter morning when we were ten, to convince Tom to give us each a towering stack of five flapjacks instead of two. It took us seven hours to finish and about a gallon of syrup, but we did it. From that moment on, before every scheme, every holiday adventure, every moment that scared us just the tiniest bit, we'd say it.

And I hate that it fucking works. Before I know it I'm pulling on the sweat-soaked jersey and a pair of basketball shoes that magically appear from the bench, and the crowd roars to life, erupting in fresh cheers.

"Just stick close to number eight when they have the ball," Coach says, pointing at a player about a foot taller than me with bright red hair. "And try not to fall on your face."

"Great pep talk," I say as I head onto the court, already regretting this.

"Wrong way, Beckett," Nicole says, spinning me around as the game starts.

My heart hammers in my chest as I try to follow Coach's instructions. The clock mercifully winds down as I jog back and forth, trying to keep up with number 8 and avoid any and all contact with the ball.

They miss one.

We miss one.

The score stays tied.

"This may be my worst nightmare," I murmur as number 8 catches a pass. In two seconds flat she elbows me out of the way and shoots the ball right over my head to score, putting Grand Hudek ahead by two.

Nicole dribbles down the court, and I scramble to stay ahead of her as the crowd begins to count down.

"Ten, nine, eight . . ."

The girl defending her traps her at half-court, arms flailing wildly, and I see Nicole look to the other players on our team, but they're all heavily guarded.

And then I see her grimace as she turns her head in my direction.

Oh no.

She throws it to me and I miraculously manage to catch it, but then I freeze in place, just behind the three-point line. It's a testament to the sheer insanity of the moment that my first instinct is to swing my head up into the stands to find Arden. She's on her feet, pointing to the basket, shouting, "Shoot it! Shoot it!"

So I close my eyes, which is probably not recommended, and launch the ball into the air just as the buzzer sounds.

Everyone falls deathly quiet, and I pop an eye open to see it spinning around and around on the hoop. All the players just stand there, gazing up at it, except Number 8, who tries to swat it away, but can't reach.

For what feels like ten seconds, the entire gymnasium is silent. Watching. Not a single person says anything.

And then . . .

It goes in.

CHAPTER 12

ARDEN

DAY 2

Holy shit.

Holy shit.

Despite having met barely two hours ago, Finn and I scream and throw our arms around each other as the bleachers shake under our feet, the crowd going wild all around us. Even Maya, who I suspect is not my biggest fan, grabs my arm as we push through the sea of people, running down the steps to the court.

I can't help but smile when I get eyes on Caroline, who still seems completely shell-shocked, but then I see the girl who was with her outside the school yesterday. *Taylor.* Her blond ponytail bounces as she wraps her arms around Caroline in a way that makes my feet stick to the gym floor and sends a pang of jealousy through my chest.

No, not jealousy. It must be worry. Worry that someone will see it and think there's something going on between them when she's supposed to be with me.

As I watch Taylor pull away, though, still beaming at Caroline like the sun shines out of her ass, I realize that I came crashing back into Caroline's life without even thinking about what I might be asking her to give up. *I* haven't really stopped to think about the experiences I missed out on the last four years. Going to school, having a group of friends, making the winning shot in the big game, maybe even dating the head cheerleader. But that's Caroline's life. Her real life.

And I'm not part of it. Like always, I'm just an actor who is playing another part, a guest role this time, with an expiration date. So no matter what's at stake for me, I have no right to freak out or feel anything close to *jealous* when we're not even really dating. Not when I've already potentially upended things for her.

I study her face, the corners of her lips pulling up as they talk. And I can't help but feel like I'm about to intrude. I look away, about to turn to leave, when a hand pushes the small of my back. It sends me forward, practically crashing into the two of them.

"Uh." I raise a hand. "Hi."

"Oh, hey, Arden." Taylor pulls away from Caroline, blue eyes crinkling. "Your girlfriend was pretty great out there, huh?" she says, and then sends a wink at Caroline like they're in on something. *Did she . . . ?*

"Yeah, totally," I say, running my fingers through my hair as I cast a quick look over at Caroline, but her face is unreadable. "Congrats on the win. Never seen someone score with their eyes closed."

She cracks a smile. "You told me to shoot it!"

"Yeah, well, not like *that*," I reply, as Austin and Maya and Finn fill in around us.

And even though it makes me feel guilty yet again, I take a

small step toward her and slide my hand into hers. To my surprise, she doesn't pull her hand away. Relief washes over me like it's some kind of confirmation that she isn't fully into Taylor.

Our eyes lock as our fingers interlace, and I'm thankful that no one can see my face turning red underneath the face paint.

But then I hate myself for imagining I even have a right to feel relieved.

She's the first to break eye contact, and I turn my head to see what she's looking at.

Oh.

My mouth quickly falls into a straight line.

"Hey, guys. Uhh . . ." I trail off as everyone follows our sight line to where a whole gaggle of underclassmen are coming our way, phones drawn. And something tells me they aren't coming to get a selfie with Barnwich's MVP.

"Oh, shit. Follow me," Austin says, hurrying us toward the nearest gym exit back into the school. "A little faster!" I hear him shout, and I swing my head to see a wall of kids pushing through the crowd like zombies in a TV show.

We smash through the double doors and down the hallway, probably looking like a knockoff version of the Breakfast Club.

Maya with her all-black outfit and edgy eyeliner.

Taylor in her cheer uniform.

Austin with his band T-shirt and rings.

A shirtless Finn, painted in school colors.

Caroline, wearing a basketball jersey over a dress with slightly oversized Jordans.

And . . . me, the Hollywood star who has no business being here.

"In here! In here!" Finn shouts, finding an open classroom ahead.

All of us pile in after him. The second he locks the door, we plaster ourselves to the front wall, where we can't be seen, as the sound of clompy footsteps comes barreling down the hall.

"I know you're in there. I saw you!" a girl shouts, blocking the light as she presses her face against the skinny window in the door. We're all dead quiet, and I don't dare turn my head to the left or right. I know if I make eye contact with *anyone* right now, it's all over. After a minute, another face squishes against the window.

"Whatever. You're hotter on-screen anyway!" a boy shouts, the register of his voice announcing that he has yet to hit puberty. Caroline drops her jaw open in disbelief, and her outrage at this prepubescent boy is so funny I let out half a laugh despite myself. She reaches over to clamp her hand over my mouth until the footsteps can fade down the hall, but it's too late. The dam has been broken. The second she releases her hand, I burst out laughing, and so do the rest of us.

"Oh my God. Just when I thought freshmen couldn't get any worse," Taylor says, hands on her knees as she catches her breath. "Arden, your life is *so* weird."

"Right?" Caroline says, clutching at her stomach.

"Does that kind of thing happen to you a lot?" Austin asks.

"I mean . . . kinda. Yeah." I gather my hair into a bun to get it off my sweaty neck. "I gotta admit, though, I've never had so much fun running from them. Usually it's just me hiding alone in a broom closet somewhere," I add.

"Yo, all that running made me *hungry*. I'm gonna grab the rest of the hot dogs from Mrs. M. at the concession stand for us before they get tossed," Finn announces, his hand already on the doorknob. "You guys want any? I could *maybe* try to bring a couple back."

"Wait. She's just going to *give* them to you?" I ask, one of my eyebrows ticking up.

Finn gives me an overly dramatic coy smile. "You're not the only one around here who knows how to put their good looks to use."

"Touché." I laugh.

"I'm coming with," Austin says, grabbing ahold of Finn's hand. "And if any of you *actually* wants a hot dog, I suggest you do the same, as there is zero chance they make it back here."

I scoot up to sit on a desk as Maya and Taylor move to follow them.

"You want to come?" Taylor asks, her hand lightly grazing Caroline's hip in a way that makes *my* skin prickle.

"I think I'll stay. Save me one with ketchup, though!" Caroline replies with a genuine smile.

"I'll protect it from Finn with my life," Taylor adds, putting a hand dramatically over her heart.

I watch her go, hating that I can see what Caroline sees in her. Sweet. Funny. Even in LA probably close to a ten. And most of all, she's *here*.

"A million hot dogs *with ketchup* for our star player," I hear her shout to Finn as the door shuts behind all of them, leaving me and Caroline alone together in the silence.

"So . . . Taylor," I say, swinging my legs.

Caroline glances over at me. "What about her?"

I chuckle at the obvious. "She's cute. And obviously into you."

"Arden."

"Do you like—"

"What if I do? What would it matter to you?" she interrupts me.

"Maybe I feel bad about it," I reply, and my legs stop their rhythmic swinging. "That I came and crashed your love life."

"Well, you didn't. She knows everything. And when this is all over and we eventually break up, Taylor and I are going to pick up where we left off," she replies.

I want to ask her where exactly they did leave off, but I don't.

"She knows everything? Caroline. How many people did you tell?" I ask her.

She shrugs casually. "Taylor, Maya, Austin, F—"

"So *everyone* then," I cut her off, putting my head in my hands.

"Arden, they're my best friends. I'm not going to lie to them."

I take in a deep breath and blow it out, trying to ignore the subtle burn. Okay, it's not like four random people knowing the truth really matters. And if Caroline trusts them to keep our secret, then I guess I do too.

"Fine," I tell her. "And for the record . . . I like Taylor," I add, in case my opinion means anything at all to her, but before she can respond, the crew comes back with enough hot dogs to feed a family of ten.

We sit around on the desks, eating whatever Finn doesn't scarf down, and we talk about all the things normal seniors in high school must talk about. Well . . . they talk and I mostly just listen, because I'm not sure what exactly I have to add to the topic of exams and parents and college applications.

"You coming sledding with us this week?" Taylor asks me. "We're going on Tuesday, when break starts."

"Uh, yeah," I say, surprised she's inviting me. Surprised she's being so nice to the girl dating her maybe-girlfriend for the holidays. "That sounds fun. I haven't been sledding since . . ." I trail off as Caroline looks over at me. "Well, for a really long time," I finish.

"Well, the coast should be clear now. We better head out before they lock us in the school," Maya announces, tossing her napkin into the trash.

"Maya, Levi stole my car today and dropped me off here, because his is in the shop. Can you give me a ride home?" Caroline asks, but Maya shakes her head.

"Ugh. I would, but I've gotta pick up my sister from a gingerbread house contest at Clara's Bakery. Maybe Taylor can drive you?"

She looks pointedly at me as she says it, and I can see Taylor starting to nod.

"I can do it," I blurt out before I can stop myself. Everyone turns their heads to look at me.

Caroline looks between me and Taylor, then shrugs. "It's on Arden's way home," and for some stupid reason I feel like I won something.

As we say our goodbyes to everyone, Austin pulls me into a hug, holding me for an extra second to whisper in my ear. "Sure this is fake, Arden James? You looked like a whole cherry tomato when you held her hand."

I startle, but when I pull back to look at him, I don't show it, chuckling casually instead. "Yeah, right. I'm wearing face paint."

"Your ears aren't," he says with a mischievous grin, tapping his.

I pull my keys out of my pocket, ignoring him, but I'm sure that they're probably red again right now.

We head out to the parking lot and separate at the cars. Caroline shivers as I start up the Volvo and crank the heat up to full blast.

I shift into drive, and Caroline pulls out her notepad and flips it open.

"Question time?" I ask.

She nods, stealing a pen from the center console. "What was it like going to a high school basketball game as someone who never got the chance to experience high school?"

I tap on the steering wheel anxiously as Caroline touches on what I've been thinking all night. Suddenly I'm remembering why my interviews are always vetted, personal questions pulled long before I'm miked up. Because I can't stand the idea of *everyone* knowing *everything* about me. But, surprisingly, I don't mind it as much as I usually do. Even though my answer will go public at Christmas, right now it's just Caroline asking me.

I exhale slowly, thinking how to put it into words. "It was strange. Surreal. To sit in the stands with a group of people I could have been friends with, at the school I would have gone to, cheering for the team I would have cheered for or maybe even played on. Since I never really went to high school and just had on-set tutors, I guess I didn't know what I was missing. These past four years have been so busy, so wild, and I've been so lucky that I told myself I couldn't miss what I could have had. What *you* have."

"Your lifestyle in LA doesn't really convince me that you'd

be remotely interested in living a normal life," she says, like she knows anything about my life. And this time, instead of guilt, I feel frustration prickle.

"Caroline. It *isn't* my lifestyle," I reply. "Well, it wasn't *supposed* to be, anyway. It started just to get me attention, better roles, whatever I wanted in that town. And then, well . . ."

Her head swings up at that, eyes glimmering with interest. I focus my attention on the road ahead, not wanting to dive any deeper. "It's not important. But, honestly, after tonight? I do wonder what my life might be like with some normalcy. Math tests and prom. Best friends you eat hot dogs with and then laugh until your abs are sore. Cheerleaders crushing on you." She gives me a look as she writes, and I grin. "Don't include that last bit, obviously, but I do envy it. I envy *you*, in a lot of ways, Caroline. I didn't know how much until I came back here."

"You're acting like it was taken away from you, though. You could have had it!" she says, exasperated. "Normalcy. The generic high school experience. All of it."

"And miss out on my dream?"

"Who said you had to go so all-or-nothing, Arden? I was still here. Edie was still here. You had people here who loved you, who supported you, who could have given you a bit of normalcy whenever you wanted."

She pauses and I notice. *Loved. Supported.* Past tense.

When I don't say anything, she adds, "Was it really worth the sacrifices you had to make?"

I glance over just long enough to see her face made up of shadows and darkness before I fix my gaze back on the road, which makes it easier to answer. "Not all of them," I say quietly.

Caroline nods and puts her notepad away without a word, and then we're both quiet the rest of the way until I put the car in park outside her house.

"Thanks for the ride. I guess I'll see you tomorrow?" she asks.

"I'll see you tomorrow," I reply.

She pushes open the passenger door, and I watch her walk up the drive to her house. She's almost to the door when I unbuckle and stick my head out of the car. "Hey!" I call after her. She turns back around to look at me, eyebrows raised expectantly. "Congrats on the win, LeBron."

A smile creeps onto her face before she turns and heads inside. I slide back into my seat as the door closes behind her.

The whole drive home, I think about her questions, her friends, her hand in mine on the court. This article is supposed to show the world that I really am a small-town girl, but if I can't even get Caroline to buy into it, how am I supposed to convince everyone else?

I've got ten days left.

Ten *dates* to prove it to her.

CHAPTER 13

CAROLINE

DAY 3

I don't hear from Arden all morning. My gaze flits to the doors of the diner or down at my phone every few minutes during my shift, even though we're noticeably busier than usual.

Maybe it's because of the group of teenage girls in the corner booth, who have been camped out for the entire morning, that I can't stop thinking about her. There were New York plates on the car they rolled up in, and one of them is sporting a *September Blues* shirt. Not to mention the fact that they giggle with their heads pressed closely together every time I walk by, which is a little disconcerting.

I feel torn that this busy diner and the Arden fan club in the corner *are* proving good for business. I mean, I *knew* things were going to get more public. I guess I just didn't expect so many more visitors to town so soon.

And, as the girls watch me leave at the end of my shift, faces pressed against the glass, Arden nowhere to be found, I can't help but wonder *what* exactly got them to drive all the way to Barnwich.

When I get home, I launch myself onto my bed and try to think of Austin's upcoming hot chocolate competition, of what I should get Riley for Christmas, of what I should get Levi for Hanukkah. Of anything but *her* . . . but my curiosity gets the better of me.

I grab my phone and open Instagram, thumbs hesitating over the search bar. When I finally tap out *Arden James*, her blue checkmark profile appears with a tiny picture of her wearing sunglasses and red lipstick, a colored circle around it letting me know a few unwatched Stories are waiting for her 10.6 million followers.

I can't resist. I need to know what on earth could have motivated the girls in the corner booth to drive *all the way* to Barnwich.

First, there's a video of Finn grinning as he paints Arden's face. Then a picture of her holding up the GO CAROLINE sign, followed by a close-up of me taking the court in Melanie's sweaty jersey, which Arden took the time to add a heart-eyes emoji to.

I frown, hating how much she's committing to this role. If I didn't know better, I'd believe it myself.

Small-town girl at a small-town basketball game with her small-town girlfriend.

Me.

I roll my eyes when the next story is a stack of Edie's signature pancakes, piled high and loaded with butter and syrup, followed by a picture with the group of girls from the corner booth, because *of course* Arden decided to show up just after I got off.

Groaning, I flop onto my back. "Really, Caroline?"

I feel annoyed at myself for being bothered that I missed her at Edie's. Annoyed at myself for even *thinking* about her in the first place.

I swipe out of Instagram and go to text Austin and Maya to see if they want to meet at Barnwich Brews later, but stop short when a message pings in.

I'll be at your house to pick you up at 5:50

dress warm.

How exactly like Arden to text just when I'm about to give up. I think about replying that I have plans, that I wasn't just *waiting around* for her to text me, but my Columbia acceptance might be riding on this. Like it or not, I need this article too, so instead I send back a thumbs-up emoji, then chuck the phone onto my bed, resolving not to look up anything *Arden James* for the two hours until she gets here.

I take a shower and plunk down in my desk chair with a cup of tea to study for my last final tomorrow. Thankfully, it's calculus, and it's hard for my mind to wander when I need every brain cell I've got to commit the formulas to memory. Math has never been my strong suit.

After my millionth yawn and my millionth attempt at the same practice problem, I tap my phone, my eyes widening when I see it's already 5:35.

"*Shit.*"

I tumble out of my desk chair and grab an oversized button-down from my closet, before tripping into a pair of jeans as I run to the bathroom to do my makeup, since who knows what she has planned, and who knows how many people are going to see whatever we do tonight.

Riley pops her head out of her room to see what all the commotion is.

"You good?"

"Arden's picking me up at 5:50. I lost track of time."

She leans on the bathroom door, crossing her arms over her chest. "Your socks don't match."

I glance down mid–mascara application to see I'm wearing one floral short sock and one long white one. Groaning, I quickly finish the mascara and book it back to my room to find the second long white sock. Thankfully, the doorbell doesn't ring downstairs until six o'clock.

I head down, still pulling on my right sock. I pause in the entryway, my hand on the door handle, and take a deep breath to collect myself, wanting to make it seem like I was ready the whole time.

"You said five—" I say as I throw open the door, but I trail off when I'm greeted instead by Edie and a crew of older women, all regulars at the diner: Shirley, Ruth, Clara, and Josephine. All of them instantly burst into a rendition of "We Wish You a Merry Christmas," complete with Ruth absolutely ripping it on a cowbell.

I slip into my coat, and Arden's head pops up from the very back, giving me a mischievous grin.

"Wait!" Shirley says mid-song, and their shrill voices cut out. "Honey. That is *not* warm enough."

They all bustle just inside, and Riley watches with a great deal of amusement from the bottom step as they wrap me up in extra scarves, squish a wool hat onto my head, and conjure a pair of mittens seemingly out of thin air.

Finally, they all stand back, nodding their approval.

"You're ready," Josephine says, and I barely have time to shove my feet into a pair of boots before I'm pulled out the door and into the snow.

"For your 'little friend,'" Clara says to Arden, stealing two hand warmers from her pockets to give to me with a wink.

Then Ruth calls out, "Always knew you two would end up together!" That sends the whole group of ladies giggling as Arden's cheeks turn bright red. Only Edie glances back with a knowing look.

Meanwhile, I try to resist the urge to steal Ruth's cowbell and whack Arden with it.

Thankfully, her teeth chattering from the loss of hand warmers and her delicate LA body shaking like a leaf from the cold feel like punishment enough.

"Told them you were one hell of a soprano," Arden says, handing me some jingle bells. I glare at her as I take them.

"You also told me five fifty. I was waiting for like fifteen minutes."

"I said five fifty instead of six because I know you're always late. Or did you just want to show me you don't know how to button your shirt?"

I look down in surprise to see my last few buttons are mismatched.

Fuck.

I fix them as I glower up at her, but she just nudges me. "Come on, Caroline." She jingles the bells she's holding, grinning. "Time to spread some holiday cheer."

Caroling is far from unusual in Barnwich, especially in the lead-up to Christmas. From December 1 to the big day, you can usually hear the faint sound of people crooning somewhere in town if you just stick your head outside your front door in the evening.

That being said, I am *not* one hell of a soprano, so *I've* never done it before. And what's more, *we've* never done it before. Me and Arden. Maybe that makes it better, though, because it's not something wrapped up in or tainted by what used to be. Like our dance is.

As I walk next to her, though, on the same snowy Barnwich streets we've walked hundreds of times, it's hard not to still that familiar twinge of melancholy. The one that's gotten worse since the town started to struggle. Since . . .

I cast a sideways glance at Arden. *Since she left,* I hate to admit. And I feel even more *melancholy* over the fact that it's come to this. Two strangers putting on an act.

As we clamber up the steps of my next-door neighbors' house, I'm tempted to just turn around and go back to my cozy room. From here, I can still see the glow of my desk light through my window, my basketball career last night probably about as much performing as I can handle. But then Edie turns around to hiss, "'Jingle Bells'" at the group with so much intensity it roots me to the spot until the door swings open to reveal Mr. and Mrs. McHugh.

Edie and her friends burst into song, all starting at different times before coming back together by "in a one-horse open sleigh."

I kind of mumble along, house after house, and after a while my melancholy lifts just enough to begin to see why people around here do this so much. The good-natured messiness of the singing, the people in the houses lighting up when they pull open the door, offering us hot chocolate and cookies, everyone giggling as we shuffle off down the street.

It's so . . . *Barnwich*. The good and the bad. The joyful with the bittersweet. The girl who caused so much of my souring for the season standing right next to me, and, well, the other part that always sits deep in my chest. Being part-Jewish in a town like this, so filled with Christmas it doesn't feel like it has a place for that part of me.

I feel it as we stand on the steps of the Bernsteins' house, Dr. Bernstein flashing me a commiserating smile over her daughter's head before she closes the door. As we walk down the street, I find myself wishing I could figure out a way to make *them* feel seen too. To share and spread the joy I feel with my family at Hanukkah to all my neighbors, the way singing about a reindeer with a glowing red nose does.

Arden bumps her arm lightly into mine as we sing on the porch of the fifth house, breaking my train of thought like she can tell I'm spiraling. Reflexively, I actually almost *smile* at her. But when I glance up at her, I notice something.

She's just *mouthing along* instead of actually singing.

"Unbelievable!" I say, whacking her with the jingle bells as we head down the steps.

"What?" Josephine asks.

"Arden isn't really singing!"

Arden laughs, rubbing her arm as all the old ladies converge on her, pushing her down the block to the next house while I jog along to keep up.

"That means you get a solo!"

"'O Holy Night'! From the top!"

"A duet!" Arden says hastily, grabbing Edie's arm as the door swings open, and when Edie beams up at her, Arden's face breaks into a real *Arden* smile that only Edie could pull out of her.

The two of them start to sing, and for the first time all night, I feel myself slowly but surely getting swept up in it. Seeing the two of them, happy together after all these years, it's hard not to.

While neither of their voices is particularly great, Margo, the tenth-grade cheerleader who opened the door, is too starstruck by Arden to care. She whips out her phone to record, blue eyes glowing, and I feel the moment deflate like a balloon.

I think of the girls looking for Arden earlier at the diner and the freshmen chasing us last night at the game. And when my gaze travels back to Arden's face, sure enough I see that the glimmer of the Arden I know is gone, a smile that doesn't quite meet her eyes taking its place. But something in her expression is still familiar enough for me to know that this constant scrutiny bothers her.

And that surprises me. She's in the tabloids so much, I just assumed she *liked* the attention.

Looking at the girl standing in front of me, though, I see that couldn't be farther from the truth. She has to just stand here and *let it happen*, like a bug underneath a microscope.

The sudden urge to protect her resurfaces, completely blindsiding me. I want to reach out, to lower Margo's phone, but I swallow the urge, and once the song ends, Arden does it herself with far more ease and charm than I would have.

"Hey, if you promise not to post that, I'll take a picture with you."

Margo nods eagerly, and Edie takes the phone and snaps a couple of quick shots before we head back down the road.

"Jesus," Clara says, her white bob bobbing as she shakes her head. "Back in my day, the actresses used to know how to sing."

"Judy Garland?" Ruth says. "What a talent!"

All the ladies nod in agreement, roasting Arden about how Judy would've knocked way more socks off caroling with them tonight.

"Way to rat me out," Arden says, shooting me a fake glare as we walk side by side down the sidewalk behind them.

"Such animosity," I say, and place a frozen hand over my chest. "Judy would never."

Arden smirks, and I hold out one of the half-used hand warmers in truce. "Why weren't you singing anyway?"

She grabs it from me and rolls it between her icy fingertips, stalling. "It's ridiculous," she mumbles finally, but my journalistic instinct kicks in and I press her on it.

"Come on. Why?"

"Just like . . . let's say that girl posts the video, right? Not only can the tabloids and social media turn it into a million things it's not, but it can impact my entire image. How people in the industry see me. Some small moment like that could change my career. Could change my *life*." She laughs. "It sounds absurd, but I haven't spent the last few years pretending to be . . ." Her voice trails off, and she motions to herself. I think about what she said last night in the car, but she continues without elaborating, ". . . just for a Hollywood exec to see that and never offer me a role in the next *Moulin Rouge!* or *Mamma Mia!*"

"Well, I mean, that's probably for the best," I say.

She laughs, but before I can ask any follow-up questions, we're heading up another driveway.

I guess tonight feels a little off for both of us.

"You know what?" Arden says, tapping my arm as we watch

the ladies giggle their way to the front door, Ruth a little too giddy to rock out on that cowbell again. "Maybe we should just like . . . *go for it*."

"Go for it?"

"I mean, look how much fun they're having," she says, motioning to the group, her thoughts echoing my own. "Maybe we could have as much fun if we just . . . get out of our heads and let ourselves."

I nod as the door swings open, and I can't help but think of her and Edie smiling at each other at the last house. What tonight could be like if I let myself get swept up in it.

Arden shrugs at me as Clara counts us off, kick-starting a rendition of "Frosty the Snowman."

"Fuck it," I mumble before joining in at full throttle, Arden tossing me her jingle bells with a laugh. By the time we get to "that old silk hat," I can feel the good beginning to outweigh the melancholy.

We go to another house and then another, and soon not even Margo popping out of a bush with a professional camera could sour this evening. With every door that opens, I find myself actually having *fun*. Getting swept up in the songs and the joy and the chocolate chip cookies.

The best is seeing how happy it makes Edie, though. When Arden slings her arm over Edie's shoulders, I pull out my phone, wanting to snap a quick picture of the two of them underneath the streetlights.

But something stops me.

Whatever frustrations I might have with her, tonight I want to just let Arden be here, able to live in the moment without a camera infringing on it.

After another three houses, and a subpar "Deck the Halls," Ruth grumbles out, "Don't know how much more my god-damned knee can take."

You'd think one of them got run over by a reindeer with how fast the holiday cheer disappears. All the ladies take turns complaining as we scuttle back down the street toward my house, caroling officially over for the night.

"I'm pooped!"

"My arthritis is flaring up."

"Does anyone need a throat lozenge?"

I grab one from Clara, and when I pop it into my mouth, the cherry menthol and the cold air make my eyes water. Soon they're all giving me quick hugs before clambering into the bright red rental Corvette to take a load off. But Arden stays behind, nodding up to my front door.

"I'll walk you."

As we head up the steps, I glance over at her, hating how pretty she looks underneath the glow of the porch light, her nose rosy from the cold.

"You really crushed 'A Holly Jolly Christmas,'" she says, and I shake my head as she leans against the beam of the porch. "You got a question for me?"

Oh right. The article. I don't know how I feel about the fact that I almost forgot.

I dig into my jacket pocket, pull out my notepad, and flip it open. My eyes scan my list of questions until I find the one I want for tonight. I think of her talking about "pretend-ing." Her laundry list of fears about being under a microscope. And how, even when she's working, her every movement is still being recorded. "What role were you most scared to play?"

I look up at her, her eyes dark in the dim light, and see that same expression from when we sat in front of the Christmas tree looking back at me. The familiar one. "Honestly? This Bianchi role. It terrifies me. Maybe because it's so much more real than anything I've ever played before." She lets out a long sigh. "There was this moment at the end of my audition where I had to get emotional. And it just . . ." I watch as she shakes her head. "Wasn't happening. It's not something I have to do for a lot of my roles. Anyway . . . I thought that was it. All the months of prep I did, alone in my room, were about to be for nothing. But then I thought of Barnwich, of one particular image, one particular moment, and that—"

She stops and runs her fingers through her hair, a tell that she's anxious about what she's about to say. That whatever it is will be pure, unfiltered Arden.

And that makes me anxious too. I feel my heart stutter in my chest.

Instead, she puts the wall up again, vulnerability and the Arden I recognize disappearing into a lackadaisical shrug. "And it worked."

"What was the moment?" I press.

She shakes her head again.

"Seriously?"

When she doesn't budge, I roll my eyes at her. "Arden—"

"It's not important," she says, frustrated. "The thing that makes this role so scary, Caroline, is how much I'll have to dig down to the realest parts of myself in order to make this character become real too."

The *realest parts* of herself?

I don't know if I should laugh or cry. If I should believe her or call bullshit.

I want to push her off the porch into the snow. I want her to take down the damn wall, to be *real* with me.

I want to never see her again.

I . . . *want my best friend back.*

It's a thought I can't believe is actually crossing my mind.

She frowns, just for a second, before continuing. "But maybe if I can't do that, if I can't get this role, then my dream isn't worth anything after all."

I let out a long exhale as I look up at her. I didn't realize when she asked me to write the article and pretend to be her girlfriend that this role meant more to her than just a hefty paycheck and fame.

Or how nice and how hard it would be to stand on a porch across from her and hear that Barnwich was the most real thing to a girl who spends her entire life pretending.

"I hate you," I say with a pathetic laugh.

"No, you don't," she whispers.

And I hate the fact that she knows that. That despite what I've told myself, I could never. I might hate parts of her, I might hate what she did, but I could never hate Arden.

We stare at each other for a long moment, neither of us talking.

I'm about to concede the point when a horn honks loudly. Both of us jump and turn to see the windows of the Corvette roll down and heads pop out.

"Any day now, James!" Ruth calls, Shirley cackling beside her. "Not getting any younger!"

"Stop flirting and let's get going!" Clara shouts.

Arden laughs easily, waving them off.

"Night, Caroline," she says, reaching out to tug gently on the corner of one of my scarves before heading down the steps.

"What was the moment?" I call after her, and she skids to a stop. I watch her exhale, see the swirl of white smoke.

"I thought of the day I left," she says, glancing back at me before climbing into the backseat.

There's too much to say, so I don't say anything. I just watch from the porch until the car fades from sight.

CHAPTER 14

ARDEN

DAY 4

"Dear Lord," I groan, straining to push the overflowing cart of stuff from Restaurant Depot out to the Volvo, while Grams quadruple-checks we got everything on her list.

"Oh, stop your whining."

She swings open the trunk and I watch as she struggles to lift a fifty-pound bag of flour into it.

"All right, let's not give ourselves a hernia on a Monday morning," I say, before wrestling it from her determined grip and plunking it into the bottom of the trunk.

"Don't be ridiculous," she says, as proud as ever.

"You do this alone every week?" I ask, frowning as I watch her fight to throw the second bag into the trunk to prove her point.

"Always have, always will."

"I'm sure Caroline or Harley could—"

She waves a dismissive hand in my direction. "You gonna blab or help me empty this cart?"

I clamp my mouth shut and get to work before she does it all herself.

As I finally slam the trunk shut and start to wheel the cart back, my phone buzzes in my back pocket.

"Hey, Lillian," I say as her face appears on my screen in her familiar white desk chair, an abstract painting just over her shoulder.

"A few photos of you and Caroline popped up on my feed," she says in lieu of a greeting.

"Yeah?" I slow to a stop in the middle of the parking lot. "Why do you sound unhappy about that? Isn't it part of our whole scheme?" I feel a little weird about calling it that, even though that's exactly what it is.

"Well, it's a photo of the two of you at some kind of sporting event." She whips over to her laptop to take another look. "What the hell is on your fa—*anyway*." She reappears in frame, shaking her head and pushing a pair of thick black glasses up farther on her nose. "The two of you aren't looking very smitten."

I roll my eyes and start pushing the cart forward again, then send it ricocheting into the cart return. "Lillian, can you not?"

I swipe out of our FaceTime and go over to Instagram, double-checking that Caroline's profile is still private and safe from prying eyes and trolling comments. *I wonder if she'd accept my follow request now?* My thumb hovers over the blue follow button for a few seconds before I swipe back to FaceTime.

"Look," Lillian says as I come back to our call. "I just don't want this all blowing up in your face when Bianchi sees right through your bullshit. You're an actor, Arden. So *act*."

"Lil, I got it, okay? Thanks."

I hang up and let out a long breath, kicking up gray slush as I walk back to the car. I glance to the side to see a guy with a worn baseball cap looking at me intently, and I pull my hood up before sliding into the passenger seat.

"All good?" Grams asks.

I nod and press my forehead up against the cool glass of the window while she pulls out of the parking spot. As we drive, Lillian sends me the post from the basketball game this past weekend. In it, I'm holding Caroline's hand, but both of us are looking away from each other.

I press the side button until the screen goes dark. If I was Bianchi and I saw that, I'd be thinking the same thing as Lillian too, but it's total bullshit. Even if our relationship *was* real, does it mean that if we aren't giving each other googly eyes every second, we're not really together? Do I have to perform in my personal life every second too, *just in case* someone is out there taking a photo? I know the answer is yes, I've known for a long time, so why is it suddenly bothering me so much? That's my reality right now, so if I need to pivot the plan so the public can snap and upload some cozy photos of Caroline and me, then that's what I'll do. I haven't come this far to let a few lukewarm, invasive photos stand in the way of me and Bianchi's movie.

It's as simple as that.

I make eye contact with the baseball cap guy as Grams drives past, and sure enough, he snaps a photo. I'm not here to fix things with Caroline, even if it does feel good that she doesn't totally hate me now. I'm here to *pretend* to date Caroline. And, like Lillian said, I'm an actress. I have to—*we* have to—make it believable. Because somone is *always* watching.

We drive the thirty minutes back to the diner on snow-covered roads, fresh flakes landing on the windshield faster than they can be swiped away. I'm so far inside my head that I don't even hear Grams trying to talk to me until we're back in Barnwich.

". . . because I'm moving to Florida next month," she says, and I look over at her with my jaw practically on the floor of the car. She throws her head back and laughs. "Just seeing if you're listening."

I shake my head at her.

"What's eatin' ya, kid?" Grams asks, turning down her Christmas hits crackling through the FM radio.

"Everything." I let out a big sigh, not sure where to begin.

"Could you be a little more specific?" she asks, but I can only shrug as we turn into the diner parking lot. "Does it have anything to do with a certain strawberry-blond waitress?"

"I don't even know, Grams. It's just . . ." I think about when I first got here, how I came in all ready to act my way through these twelve days. I thought I could just jet back to LA when it was all over and forget again about all the pieces of my heart that I left in Barnwich. "It's more complicated than I thought it was going to be," I say finally as Grams stomps a little too heavily on the brakes outside the back door of the kitchen. She looks over at me, throwing the car into park at the same time.

"You thought showing up on your best friend's doorstep unannounced and uninvited after four years of not speaking to her and then asking her to be your fake girlfriend, was going to be *simple*? That it wouldn't dredge anything up?"

I cover my eyes as a chuckle escapes my lips. "Okay, well, when you put it like that . . ."

"Arden, why is it all so important to you? Why did you cut Caroline out of your life?"

I shake my head and let out an exasperated sigh. I can already tell by her tone that she thinks it's all ridiculous, but she's waiting for an answer, so I start thinking back to what started it all.

"In the beginning my agent, Lillian, thought it would be best for me to cut ties with Caroline to stay focused on work. And I mean . . . she was kinda right. If I had stayed connected with Caroline, it would've made it that much harder to stay out there long enough to get where I am now. This is what I've *always* wanted. It's what I've spent the last four years working toward, even if I didn't always know it, even if it's lost me things along the way," I tell Grams. "Anything worth doing takes sacrifice," I add, remembering Lillian saying that to me during my first shoot, when she found me crying in my trailer on Caroline's fifteenth birthday.

"Arden. You aren't a kid anymore, and no one can force you to make these choices. You don't have to live this life just because it's what you wanted when you were fourteen."

"That's very wise, Grams, but I didn't get to stay a kid for very long," I reply.

"Your mom and dad . . . They didn't—" Grams starts.

"Come on. The ice cream is going to melt," I interrupt, reaching for the door handle. I don't need to hear Grams pathetically attempt to defend my parents like she used to.

"This is important," she says from behind me, but I pull the handle anyway and start to step out.

"Arden, sit down!" Grams raises her voice at me, something I've never heard her do in all the years I've been alive. "Now I know you went and got too big for your britches, but I'm still your grandmother, and when there are things I want to say to

you, you will listen." I hold her eyes as her chest rises and falls rapidly. "Please," she adds, more softly.

I nod, feeling a wave of anxiety crash into me as I plop back into the seat and pull the door shut.

"Your parents never liked being stuck in one place. So when you got the opportunity, I thought it would make things better and that the best thing for you was to be with them. But it all happened so fast, and I thought you'd all come back a lot. So . . . I let them take you. Twelve hundred miles away from here. From your home. From me. It's been the greatest mistake of my life."

"Grams—" I start, surprised, wanting to tell her that none of it is her fault, but she holds up her hand to silence me.

"Let me finish." She turns in her seat to face me better. "I wish I could say that I didn't think your mom would ever fully abandon you, but I think maybe deep down . . . I *did* know. I just didn't want to believe that I had failed so badly in raising her. Arden, I want to tell you . . . I've always wanted to tell you . . . that . . ." A soft sort of whimper escapes her quivering lips, making me so fucking angry at my parents for the first time in a long time. I reach over and take her hands, my thumb tracing circles over her skin, thin and blotchy from years of working in the kitchen. Her eyes are so filled with tears that I can hardly even see her pupils. "I'm sorry," she finishes, and I immediately pull her into a hug so tight that I can barely breathe.

"I love you, Grams. But you aren't the one who needs to apologize. I'm okay. I *will be* okay," is all I reply, because if I were a grandma, that's probably all I'd want to hear from my granddaughter right now. All this time, I didn't come home because I've been too scared of what she might think about me, what she might say. And all she's wanted is to give me an apology for guilt that's not hers to carry. It makes me feel even worse than the first night I arrived, about all this time I've wasted, all the pain I've caused. Just like Mom and Dad.

Eventually, we both release our grip and straighten up in our seats, wiping a couple of tears out of our eyes. Once she gets herself back together, I decide to ask the question. The one I only let myself think about when I'm alone in my big empty house, the reason I try so hard not to be.

"Grams, am I like them? Like her?"

"No, sweetie." She shakes her head fervently. "She was *always* restless. Never really content. It was like she was always searching for something, even when she was a little kid. She just never seems to find it." She squints through the windshield.

"You think she rubbed off on me?" I ask, and she shakes her head again, a soft smile spreading across her face.

"In some ways, yes. The bravery. The ambition. But you've always been like a tree, Arden. Wherever you are, you stretch out your roots. You make your presence felt." She looks over at me. "Callie is like a breeze, here one minute, gone the next, so quickly you're not even sure she was there at all. But you? I think it pains you more than you let on to be uprooted. To be unsettled. And I know we all feel it when you're gone."

I meet my own gaze in the reflection of the window, thinking of hundreds of moments in the makeup chair, a person I hardly know looking back at me. And now, being back home . . . I don't know. I almost feel like I can see myself instead of a stranger in my reflection.

"I can see that this role means something special to you, that it's different from all the rest. I don't expect you to give up on your dream, and I wouldn't want you to. But you have an opportunity here to do things differently. You're right. Anything worth doing should take sacrifice, but it shouldn't take *everything* from you."

I think of my fifteen-year-old self crumpled into a ball in my trailer, knowing exactly what Grams is getting at.

"All right, honey, get that ice cream in the freezer before it's a gallon of garbage," she says, patting my leg twice and then stepping out of the car.

We work together to unload the supplies, carrying them into the kitchen, and all the while I wonder why Lillian wouldn't let me take a minute to call my best friend on her birthday. Like one phone call would've brought down my whole career.

My phone buzzes as I drop the last bag of flour onto the floor, but for once, it's not her.

Hey it's Austin. hot chocolate competition today at 5:30 at barnwich brews. everyone's going to be there so if you need an idea for your fourth "date" . . . you should come :)

and i do mean EVERYONE in Barnwich

My mouth is already watering at the idea of pounding hot chocolate for an hour straight, and I think I could use a night of just hanging out with everyone.

Plus! Hot chocolate making screams kitschy holidate, and if everyone is going to be there, it could be a perfect opportunity for some more . . . romantic photos that I know I need if I'm going to get this part.

I'm about to say yes when another message comes in, a picture of Caroline, her hair half-up, half-down, chin resting on her hand while she writes away in her notebook, oblivious.

your girl is looking cute today btw

I tell him I'll be there, then shake my head, smiling to myself as I pocket my phone and finish helping Grams unload. He's not wrong. Maybe making some romantic photos look believable is going to be easier than I thought.

CHAPTER 15

CAROLINE

DAY 4

I feel a weight lifted off my shoulders as we clomp down Main Street to Barnwich Brews after our last final before break. While I check my phone, Maya laces her arm through mine so I don't run into anyone. The streets have been busier the last two days, and it's hard not to admit that Arden was right. Her presence and the steady flow of Barnwich Instagram stories are slowly starting to have an effect on tourism.

"Arden text you?" Maya asks as she pulls me out of the way of a group of people lugging ice skates to the rink in the park.

"No," Finn says, reading off my screen from my other side, because fake dating Arden James apparently means I have no privacy.

I glare at him and pocket my phone. "Just want to make sure she'll be here so this article gets done. For Columbia."

"Mm-hmm," Maya says.

"Seriously. I couldn't care less about Arden."

"Mm-hmm," Finn echoes, and the two of them exchange a look.

"Aren't you *Team Taylor*, anyway?" I hiss back, and Maya groans.

"Yes, but . . ." She frowns. "Ugh. It's just . . . Arden spent like half the basketball game asking me about art school and looking at pictures of my most recent projects. And not in like a bullshit appeasing way. In like a genuinely interested way. And as much as I hate to admit it, she—" She shakes her head. "She really grows on you, doesn't she?"

"Until she doesn't."

As we get closer, I catch sight of Arden leaning casually against the side of Barnwich Brews, looking way too cool for Barnwich in a black shearling jacket, a pair of sunglasses dangling out of her mouth as she taps away on her phone.

"Arden!" Finn calls, and she glances up, smiling and pocketing her phone and sunglasses.

It's when she pushes off the wall and our eyes lock, though, that I feel my heart flutter like last night and I know Finn and Maya are right. I'm full of shit.

"Hi," I say, moving to follow everyone inside while I try to get this flutter under control again. Have I never seen a beautiful girl before? Jesus.

But she grabs my wrist and pulls me aside, down the small alleyway, out of earshot of the rest of the people heading to the hot chocolate competition. She turns to face me, casting a quick glance over my shoulder to make sure the coast is clear. "My agent called me this morning and said we need to make things . . . more believable."

"Nice to see you, too. My day was good, thank you for asking."

"*Caroline.*"

I cross my arms over my chest, frowning at her. "More believable? What does that even mean?"

"I don't know," she says, letting out a long sigh. "There was a picture or two from the basketball game put online, and we're not exactly looking like we're in the throes of some epic romance." She lowers her voice. "I definitely don't want to do anything you're not comfortable with, but can you just like . . . ?"

She holds my gaze as she takes a step closer, enough for me to see that tiny scar on her chin that she got from falling off the handlebars of my bike when we were ten, for me to see her chest rising and falling, for her knee to lightly knock into mine. Close enough that my gaze falls without thinking to . . . her lips.

She reaches out, fingertips trailing down my arm and into the palm of my hand, and my breath hitches. "Pretend you're in love with me?"

That's not the hard part. I *was* in love with her once. But it's scary to just . . . blow off the dust on those buried-away emotions, to pretend they never even existed.

To act like I feel them now just to put on a show.

Especially with her standing here, right in front of me, looking like she's going to kiss me.

Wait. *Is* she going to kiss me?

"Fine." I turn my head to look down the alleyway, breaking the moment. "But no kissing," I say to regain some sort of control over myself. I may not hate Arden anymore, I might even want her to get this part, but it doesn't mean I trust her yet. And it certainly doesn't mean I'm going to fall in love with her again.

"No kissing," she confirms with a nod of agreement that makes me wonder if I imagined the moment altogether.

We head inside to rejoin the group, and the wave of warm, sweet, chocolatey goodness that hits us as we walk through the door helps me collect myself. This is one of Barnwich's signature events of the season, and the room is accordingly packed with people, milling about the six stations set up for the finalists. Austin's at the very end on the opposite side, and he has his brow furrowed as he churns out tiny sample cups. During the qualifying rounds, everyone was required to make regular ol' hot chocolate, but now they can add any flavors they want, which I have a feeling will go both ways tonight.

I notice a couple of heads turn as we come in and remind myself to turn my body toward Arden instead of away, like I *want* to be close to her. We slow to a stop alongside Finn, Maya, and— shit, *Taylor*, who must've shown up while we were talking outside.

"Your ballots," she says, holding out two yellow papers and a tiny pencil to me and Arden. I notice her eyes flick down to our interlaced hands, and I have to look away as Arden takes them from her and turns to tuck the tiny pencil behind my ear.

Despite the awkwardness, I keep hold of Arden's hand as we head to the first station, where Mr. Horowitz, a science teacher at the middle school, is churning out a mint hot chocolate.

Arden grabs a tiny cup and takes a big swig. She once again proves she's a damn good actress, because I only realize something's wrong by the subtlest eye twitch as she swallows it. While the rest of our group is making various grimaces of disgust, her expression transforms into a big, toothy smile.

"Wow, Mr. Horowitz!" she says. "That's something!"

"Let me try it," I hiss as I pull her off to the side and grab the cup from her, taking a tiny sip.

"It's like if spoiled milk and Listerine had a baby," she hisses back through her teeth, still grinning as I fight to swallow it because that assessment is maybe being generous.

"What a way to start," Taylor groans, gargling with a cup of water as we head to the next station.

"One less competitor for Austin," Finn whispers as Ruth, our caroling buddy and the returning champ, offers us a plain old classic hot chocolate.

"No frills," she says defensively as we accept our cups. It's easy to savor the warm, rich, sweet hot cocoa, though, after Mr. Horowitz tried to take us and half of Barnwich out in one minty blow.

"Oh shit, that's *gotta* be first," Arden says, nodding as she fills in her ballot. "Or maybe second," she adds hurriedly, changing her *1* to a messy *2* when she catches Finn narrowing his eyes at her.

The next, a way-too-sweet white hot chocolate version from Alexis, one of Riley's middle school soccer buddies, is a shoo-in for fifth position. We follow it up with a much better cinnamon orange from a Barnwich Brews employee, and then a not bad red velvet from a tourist who made the trek just to compete.

Arden holds up the red velvet cup. "Oh, this has gotta be *at least* third."

"Absolutely not." I turn to face her. "*That* is better than the cinnamon orange? You're kidding yourself." I notice she has some whipped cream on her upper lip. "You've also got . . ."

I reach up and use my thumb to wipe it off. Then she glances down to my lips. I let my hand linger against her smooth cheek.

Obviously just to sell the moment a bit more, like she asked.

"Oh my gosh, get a room," Maya says, fanning herself with her ballot, a mischievous glint in her eye, while Taylor gives me a searching look from next to her. I'm surprised when Arden pulls quickly away, like she's clocked it, disguising the sudden movement by throwing the cup into the trash can next to us, and I feel . . .

I don't know. *Disappointed?* I grimace at myself.

Really? Disappointed? Just the possibility of that scares me. Even if it's pretend, it's dangerous to play with fire. Especially when that fire is Arden.

Thankfully, we head to Austin's booth, and I refocus on the most important reason we're here. Supporting him. He lifts his head as we cheer his name, and I snap a couple of pictures of him hard at work. I nearly melt into a puddle when I see he's making salted caramel hot chocolate, Finn's favorite, even though Austin *hates* any and all things caramel.

To see them so in love, always thinking about the other, whether it's hideous red gloves or warm winter drinks, makes the lie I'm swept up in sting just the tiniest bit more.

We all take a sip, and it's pretty easy to make a big show over how good it is. The decadent hot chocolate. The smooth sweetness of the caramel adding another depth of flavor. The tiny, crunchy bursts of salt.

"Holy Mother of God," Taylor says, going to swipe a second cup, but Austin slaps her hand away. "I need everyone else's votes too!"

"This is unreal," Arden says. "You can tell how hard you worked to balance all the elements perfectly."

Austin blushes at her compliment, pleased that she noticed.

"It took me three months alone to figure out the right amount of caramel. Don't even get me started on the salt."

Three months? I look over to see pre-measured condiment cups of salt, weighed to the very last granule. I'm his best friend and I had no idea he worked *this* hard on it.

And Arden showed up and just . . . *knew*. Made him feel seen.

I could maybe fake kiss her right now.

She nods. "I'm sure. You made the best hot chocolate here by a landslide." She hesitates and runs her fingers through her hair. "I don't want to make things weird, but if you have like a barista Instagram page or something, I could post about it. Or share it? I don't—"

"Oh my God, yes," Austin says, eyes wide with excitement.

Arden relaxes instantly and pulls out her phone to let him type in his handle. I down the rest of my hot chocolate and try to get my feelings, *whatever they are*, under control, then join Taylor in gazing mournfully at the sample cups on the table. And Arden somehow sees that too, because she holds the rest of her cup out to me while Austin hands her phone back.

I take it, hating how right Maya was. *She grows on you.* Whether you want her to or not.

"Seriously, Austin," I say after another perfect sip. "I think I hear a choir of angels singing."

"Probably just a sugar high," he says modestly, handing Finn a second cup, topped with extra whipped cream this time.

"Favoritism," Taylor mutters as we all head off to the side to drop off our ballots at a table where Sheila and Margie, two of Edie's Saturday-night card-playing pals, are frantically tallying everything up.

As we await the results, I try to gaze adoringly at Arden, which feels particularly difficult because . . . I don't know. I'm finding it hard to fully look her in the face after what just happened with Austin. Like if I do, I'll see too much Arden there and not enough *Arden James*.

"Holy shit," she whispers, head dipping down, cheek brushing up against mine. She nods across the room, letting me know it's not a move. *"Look."*

I follow her gaze to see Ruth puttering around the ballot table, pretending to drop off two cups to the ladies counting. When she thinks no one's looking, she digs into her purse to pull out a handful of yellow ballots, scattering them quickly onto the table.

"Ruth is *cheating*," I say, horrified. But then it gets worse. I watch as Sheila grabs the ballots with a wink, passing them over to Margie. "And they're helping her!"

This is practically a crime in Barnwich. Cheating in the annual hot chocolate competition? You might as well just kill someone.

This would make for a damn good article, but I can't stand the idea of Austin losing just so I could get an exposé.

When Ruth digs around in her bag for another handful, I hear my voice call out, "She's cheating!"

The entire room freezes. Ruth's eyes go wide as she swings her head up to look at me. She recovers quickly, putting on a performance of almost Arden caliber. "*Me?* I was just dropping off some hot chocolate for our hardworking judges. I wouldn't call that cheating, now, would you?"

"What's in the purse?" Arden calls, putting an arm around my shoulder. A united front.

Ruth reaches innocently into her bag and pulls out . . . the fucking cowbell from caroling.

Arden rolls her eyes. "What else?"

Ruth's gaze flicks quickly to the exit door, and before Mr. Lee, the owner of Barnwich Brews, can confiscate her purse, she's running through the crowd, dodging people with the agility of a D1 football recruit, tampered ballots trailing after her.

"She's loose!" Mr. Lee shouts. A few people try valiantly to catch her but fail. She makes it to the door without being apprehended and pushes through it, shooting Arden a middle finger through the front window before disappearing into the night.

I gape at Arden in disbelief, and then the two of us burst into laughter in a way that's hauntingly familiar. Soon, the entire room joins in as we all try to process what just happened.

"When she pulled out the cowbell—" Finn wipes tears from his eyes.

"When she gave Arden *the middle finger*," Taylor adds, cackling.

It just keeps getting funnier the more anyone says anything, so Arden and I lean into each other as the laughter doubles us over.

Mr. Lee is definitely not laughing, though. He goes straight into damage-control mode, removing Sheila and Margie before hopping up on a table to survey everything, chewing his lip as he comes up with a plan. After everyone has had a chance to sample, the whole room quiets and waits for him to talk.

"Merry Christmas!" he calls, and everyone choruses it back.

Except for Riley. "Happy Hanukkah!" she calls back, meeting my eye, and the two of us grin.

"Well, I want to thank everyone for coming out to our sixtieth annual hot chocolate competition! It certainly was a memorable one." He sighs, and the room responds with cheers and whistles and laughter. "With the voting being tampered with, I feel like the only fair way to find our winner is to let all of you decide as a group, right here, right now."

I cast a sideways glance at Austin to see that his fingers are crossed behind his back, teeth gnawing on his lower lip. A win would not only put a thousand dollars into his pocket, but it would be another thing he could add to his résumé. Another thing to help him on his path, his dream, of one day owning his very own coffee shop.

Just like this article is for me.

I look down to see that Arden's fingers are crossed too.

"So, I'll go right down the line," Mr. Lee says, motioning to all the tables. "And when I say the name of a competitor, if you think they should win, *cheer as loud as you can!* Okay?"

Everyone claps in agreement.

"First up, we have Mr. Horowitz, with his one-of-a-kind mint hot chocolate!"

You could hear a pin drop.

Someone coughs over by the bathrooms, and it sounds like thunder in the silence.

His own wife doesn't even clap for him. Brutal.

"Uh, all right," Mr. Lee says, scratching his chin. "Better luck next time, Mr. Horowitz!" He motions to the next table. "How about Alexis Piccadillo with her white hot chocolate!"

Alexis blushes as a bit of scattered applause sounds through the room and her middle school friends shriek like banshees, led by one Riley Beckett. She's a good friend, because I know she *hates* white chocolate.

Mr. Lee smiles and shakes his head, motioning for them to quiet down. "Okay! We've got a couple of fans of Alexis and her white chocolate. Well done!"

One of the middle schoolers lets out a final shriek of support, and then Mr. Lee moves to the next contestant.

"What about Mrs. Walters's *delightful* cinnamon-orange hot chocolate?"

The crowd cheers louder than for Alexis, but nowhere near as loud as the applause that follows for the out-of-towner, Abigail Darcy, and her red velvet hot chocolate. Abigail beams and waves as Austin looks on nervously.

Arden leans closer to me, her chest grazing up against my shoulder, voice a whisper on the back of my neck. "Told you it was better than the cinnamon orange."

I scoff in protest, trying to ignore the goose bumps running down my arm.

"And last but not least . . . Austin Beck"—Finn whoops before Mr. Lee can even finish saying his name—"er with his salted caramel—"

But the rest of the crowd starts to go wild too, his voice drowned out as all of us start hooting and hollering. Austin buries his blushing face in his hands as the noise crowns him the clear winner.

It takes Mr. Lee a full minute to get everyone to quiet down enough to make the official announcement. "And with that, Barnwich Brews' very own Austin Becker is the winner of Barnwich's sixtieth annual hot chocolate competition!"

The cheering starts back up again as Finn scoops Austin up in a hug and spins him around. He only lets go long enough for Austin to pose for a picture with Mr. Lee for the local newspaper.

As the crowd slowly begins to disperse, Finn stays behind to help Austin clean up while Taylor gets pulled into a conversation with someone from the cheer team. The rest of us head outside, following the flow of people, including Riley and her friends who are giggling down the street. We're barely through the door, though, before Maya makes up an excuse about a school project that I know doesn't exist, leaving me and Arden standing alone underneath the Barnwich Brews sign.

"We made quite a team today," she says, an eyebrow ticking up. "Single-handedly saved the integrity of the hot chocolate competition."

I laugh. "Our names will be in Barnwich history books."

Arden smiles at that, so genuine and so pretty I have to look away. The two of us fall silent as snow starts to drift down between us, sparkling in her dark hair.

"I'll . . . I'll text you the question for today," I say, something about this day of pretending suddenly feeling like too much. I glance in the direction of my house, just two blocks away, wanting to put space between us. "I'm gonna . . ."

I turn to leave, but she calls out, "Wait . . ." and grabs my hand, pulling me into a hug. I squeeze my eyes shut as my arms wrap around her waist and my face burrows into her neck, her skin smelling the same as it always has.

But to be this close to her feels so . . .

Strange? Different?

No. *Intimate.*

Four years ago it was just a quick hug, the graze of a hand, our knees touching under the table, me always silently aching for more.

The only time it ever felt like this was the winter before she left, when she jumped into the lake before it froze over, wearing only her bra and underwear at Jacob Klein's house for fifty dollars. She shivered as I held her in my arms, using my body heat to warm her back up.

Now I can feel her heartbeat through her shirt again. Feel the weight of her against me, just like I did that night.

After all the pretending we've been doing since she got home, this is the first time the closeness has felt real. And that knocks me off-balance.

"To make it believable," Arden whispers into my hair. "There's someone taking a picture."

It makes my stomach sink. But when I open my eyes, there's not a phone or a camera in sight.

She's lying. But why?

We pull apart without another word, and I turn, walking as if in a daze down the empty street. After only a few steps I glance back to watch her head in the opposite direction, my hand resting flat against my stomach like it can suppress the army of butterflies threatening to burst through my skin.

That night after dinner, I lie on my bed staring at the ceiling, my heart still pounding in my chest.

And not just because I drank an obscene amount of sugar.

"Just do your job, Caroline," I mutter, finally getting up the courage to pick up my phone, swipe into my text thread with Arden, and tap out today's question.

I might be a bad actress, but I know for a fact I'm a good journalist.

where do you see yourself in 10 years?

I watch as almost instantly three dots appear. And then stop. Over and over again. I try to picture what I think she'll say, flashes of Arden in flowing designer dresses at award shows, drinking champagne somewhere chic with a great view, strolling casually along a cobblestone street in a pair of sunglasses.

oscar? emmy? a different city every night? I prompt when the dots disappear again.

Her reply comes in quickly this time.

lol no

Then:

I mean an oscar WOULD be nice, but ever since I left barnwich, she writes, I've felt like I've been on a speeding train, like I can't slow down or turn around or get off. I'd hope by 28 I'd be able to feel like I have some control, that my life was more than just a career, than some bullshit image that was constructed for me, you know? I just . . . I want the simple things. friends, family, somewhere to call home, something constant I can count on when this industry is always trying to kick you out on your ass

I think about our conversation from a couple of nights ago after the basketball game. About normalcy. The part of her that envies the ordinary and the mundane. My phone buzzes again, the screen lighting up.

maybe somebody to come home to

I swallow, my previous image of an older Arden shifting drastically. The same fancy dress, but instead of the glamorous red carpet, she's come home early, not even changing before curling up on a big leather couch under a cozy blanket, someone's hand in hers, an Oscar on the mantel.

It shouldn't surprise me. Four years ago that was word-for-word exactly what I would have thought she'd say. But it does.

It still feels so strange to hear from her about what the past four years have been like instead of just guessing, trying and failing to reconcile the Arden I knew like the back of my hand with the one I read about on magazine pages. It also feels strange to think about what it would've been like had I been there in real time to hear about it from her, to experience some small part of it, instead of being left behind. There's so much I just assumed about her life from the internet, assumed about her and her reasons for not getting in contact, because she wasn't there to tell me differently.

It's hard to hold both things in my head, especially when I still feel the hurt of being the girl in the pink jacket she drove away from.

Three dots appear again, followed by,

you?

I hesitate, knowing this is an opening to let her in or shut her out again. I bite my lip, still thinking of standing on the curb and watching her go all those years ago, and then . . . *today*. Her arms around me outside Barnwich Brews, the way her face felt underneath my fingertips.

And I start to type, giving in, figuring that some Arden, if even for a little while, is better than no Arden at all. The only way I'm going to heal from this is if we actually start talking instead of me keeping her at arm's length.

a successful career in journalism, living in new york or LA, with a dog and a girlfriend taylor hill? she asks, and I hesitate, unsure what to say.

A few days ago I thought maybe those feelings would come, but somehow, frustratingly, even mad at Arden I can feel more for her in our fake relationship than I do for Taylor. We've practically stopped texting because I'm so swept up in Arden's orbit.

I sigh and tap out a diplomatic response: I don't usually like blondes.

can't say the same

I stare at my phone for a long moment before tapping the side button, letting the screen go dark as I lay it flat against my chest, resolving not to look at it again.

It buzzes, and I flail as I sit up to read the message, an instant liar.

The text that comes in is from Riley, though.

you're trending

I frown, tapping the tweet she's sent me to see it features a picture of me and Arden at Barnwich Brews. There's a small smile on my face as I wipe the whipped cream off her lip, and Arden's face is soft as she looks at me, her gaze . . . adoring. One note from her agent and she's got a new submission for her Oscar reel.

Then I scroll down to see—*Jesus Christ*.

24,000 likes in an hour?

I scroll through some of the comments. People wondering who I am, saying we look cute together, complaining that it should be them Arden's looking at instead of me.

Or just being plain mean.

I search her name and see the picture has been reposted a hundred times in way more tweets. So have more shots of us at Barnwich Brews and some from the basketball game a couple of days ago. I keep swiping, images flying past, only stopping when I come across a blurry picture of us talking outside just a few hours ago, snow floating down around us, moments before she hugged me.

I guess . . . I didn't really think about just how big this part of our little deal is.

The part where Arden is *Arden James* and this isn't just one article or a simple byline tucked into my portfolio. It's not black-and-white like the other stuff I've done. I'm part of the story. My face is all over social media now, for better or worse. I'm no longer just an invisible person behind the words I write.

They might not know who I am now, but they will when the article goes live. Shit, I mean they'll probably figure it out by midnight tonight.

It's . . . overwhelming. And I'm just getting a small taste of what she gets every day.

No wonder she wants normalcy. No wonder she wants simple, constant things.

I hope that one day she gets it. Ten years from now, when she actually wants it. When all the partying, and the girls, and the late nights get old. Not for a role, or to tell people what they want to hear, or to rebrand her image. But something real, with someone real.

I roll over onto my side and put my phone down to stare out the window, thinking now about how I'll eternally be known as *the girl who dated Arden James that one Christmas*.

And even though I didn't, even though I'm not, even though it makes me hate myself, part of me still cares about her enough, still feels *something* enough, to think it's worth it if it means I'll have a few more days getting to know the girl I've never been able to completely forget, again.

CHAPTER 16

ARDEN

DAY 5

"Incoming!" I call as I dive headfirst onto a red sled and rocket down a snow-covered Cemetery Hill on the first day of Caroline's break. The wind stings at my eyes and bites at my ears as I lean to the right, aiming straight for the ramp that Antonio and L.J. made out of snow. I hit it dead center, and my stomach jumps up into my throat as I soar through the air before slamming back down onto the ground.

Despite the rush of adrenaline, I dig my toes into the snow to slow down before I hit the tree line at the bottom, knowing from past personal experience that there's an iced-over creek just on the other side that *will* crack open if you hit it hard enough and *will* make your snow pants feel like they weigh about thirty-nine tons.

I've barely come to a stop, though, before I hear Caroline yell, "Arden!" and a second later she slams right into me, using my body as a human guardrail.

I groan as the two of us attempt to untangle our mess of limbs. I roll onto my back, and her head pops into my field of vision against the gray sky, warm brown eyes searching my face as a few loose strands of her strawberry-blond hair escape from underneath her wool hat.

"You good?"

"Think you punctured a lung," I say, but I sit up, remembering my own hat in my jacket pocket. I pull it out, my icy ears practically sighing in relief as I pull it onto my head.

"Wait . . ." Caroline sits up and reaches out to tug at the edge of the beige hat just below the blue stripe. "Is that the hat I made you? I can't believe you found it at Edie's!"

"No." I shake my head. "I brought it from LA. Wear it every winter, even though it never snows."

She meets my gaze, her full lips not fighting pulling up into a smile this time. A thought about kissing them floats across my brain, and I quickly chase it away.

God, I'm getting a little too into character.

"You grew into it," she says.

I'm about to ask her if she's saying my head is as big as Levi's now, when Austin shouts down to us from the top of the hill.

"Hey! Lovebirds!" We swing our heads over to look up at him and the rest of the crew, decked out in puffy jackets and snow gear. "Get the fuck out of the way!"

I laugh and shake my head, but grab my sled and Caroline's hand, pulling her to the side to begin the trek back up. Even though the hill is pretty empty aside from us, I don't let go when we get to the top.

Neither does she.

I hate how happy that makes me feel, especially when I catch sight of Taylor Hill eyeing our interlaced fingers yet again.

We stay like that, watching Finn wreck it, Austin miss the

ramp completely, and L.J. go down standing until the sled slips out from underneath him, sending him sliding on his ass the whole way to the bottom. Only Taylor and Antonio manage to coast down together perfectly.

"Coming?" Caroline asks, tugging me toward the edge again.

"I think I'll hang back this round, give my ribs a chance to recover from you crashing into them." I shove her playfully in the side before she hops on the sled to follow everyone down the hill.

"So," Maya says, sipping hot chocolate loudly from a thermos, clearly here to socialize instead of sled. "You two seem to be . . . getting along."

"Well, I'm a professional, and Caroline was all three wise men in our school play that year everyone was out with the flu. So she's obviously got some talent in the acting department too," I reply with a laugh, but Maya only narrows her eyes at me.

"I saw you two outside Barnwich Brews after the contest yesterday, Arden James. You can't stand there and try to tell me that was all fake."

"What, are you rooting for me now? I thought you kinda hated me," I say, looking away so she can't read my thoughts.

"I don't hate you. I just didn't trust you . . . like at all."

"And now you do?" I ask, nudging her playfully until she uses her shoulder to knock me away a foot or two.

"The jury's still out. I just want Caroline to have what she wants."

"Caroline is getting exactly what she wants. An article in *Cosmo*."

"Arden, be for real," she says, seeing right through my evasive reply. "And whatever does happen, if you're going to show her off online, you better be there to protect her for the breakup, too."

"Is she okay? With everything last night?" I ask, thinking about the millions of notifications I had overnight, everyone freaking out about the two of us. *I'm* used to it, obviously, but . . . Caroline. She's not used to being thrown to the wolves, the endless scrutiny of the internet.

"Why don't you ask her?" Maya replies, motioning to Caroline and the rest of the crew, huffing and puffing as they make their way to the top of the hill.

"Arden! I dare you to hit that jump full speed!" Finn shouts at me.

I force out a fake laugh, but take the opening to end this conversation I'm not ready to have. "Maybe later. Caroline, you want to go down with me?" I ask, pointing to a sled big enough for two. She nods.

I hold it at the top, the snow crunching as Caroline plops into the front. I give us a push and then hop in the back, trying not to think too much about how close I am to her right now. We fly down the hill and then skid to a perfect stop at the bottom.

"Hey, Caroline. You're, uh . . ." I stand up and dust myself off as she looks up at me. "You're good, right? I checked your Instagram a few days ago and saw it was private, but I know the posts last night were . . . a lot. I get it if you're having second thoughts about the article or whatever. I don't want you—"

"Arden." She stands and pulls me over to the side by my jacket sleeve so Antonio doesn't bowl us over. "It's fine. I mean, it's not. It's like . . . ridiculous that you have no privacy and people treat you like a spectacle. I don't love having my face plastered all over Twitter, but I'd do just about anything to get into Columbia, so . . ."

She shrugs and I nod, pretending like I don't feel the teensiest sting that no part of her motivation is just getting to spend time with me. That Maya was wrong and that hug outside Barnwich Brews last night meant way more to me than it did to her.

Shake it off, Arden.

We walk back up to the top, where Caroline crunches over to Maya, steals the thermos, and takes a swig. I give them some space and head over to Finn, who nudges me, a wide grin spread across his face.

"Race you to the bottom?"

"I don't know, I mean—"

I sprint toward the edge, launching myself face-first on a sled for the head start. I hear Finn laughing as he chases after me, the two of us flying down the hill, neck and neck. When we skid to a stop at the bottom, practically even, he hops up and holds out his hand to me.

"I think that was a tie," he says, raising an eyebrow. "Although the start was a little questionable."

I grab his hand and he pulls me up, and then the two of us talk and joke the whole way up the hill.

God. It's been so long since I've done something like this, something an eighteen-year-old *should* be doing with her *actual* friends. I forgot that hanging out with your friends doesn't have to require paparazzi, money, and drinking, let alone things that are so much worse.

Needing to leave this small town was such a given to me when I was growing up here, but now . . . it almost feels like I have to dig for that feeling. I thought being here would give me a little added inspiration for my role in Bianchi's movie, but it doesn't remind me of all the reasons I couldn't stay like my character. Instead, it's reminding me of what I could have kept if I did.

Maybe that's not a bad thing, though.

Maybe Grams was right, and I'm meant to keep some roots planted here, even if I can't stay.

I go down a few more times over the next hour, always acutely aware of Caroline. When she's sledding, when she's talking with Maya and Austin, when she's walking past me.

"Caroline!" Taylor calls to her, motioning to the front of her sled. "Do you want to ride with me?"

"Sure," Caroline says, tossing aside her orange disc to hop right on.

I clutch my sled tighter, my jaw locking as I try to ignore the jealousy that swims into my stomach when Taylor's arms wrap around her waist, her legs sliding around to straddle her.

"Arden, if you don't get over here right now . . ."

I look over to see Austin motioning to the front of his sled. He gives me a small smile and I return it, nodding and hopping on as Taylor and Caroline push off, giggling away.

"Running start!" Finn shouts, suddenly pushing us from behind. L.J. and Antonio join in, legs churning, and the sled begins to fly, faster and faster.

"Holy shiiiiit!" Austin screams as we pick up more and more speed, rocketing down at a breakneck pace. "Finn, I'm going to kill you! Oh my God, oh my GOD! Arden, what the fuuuuuuck!"

I can't help laughing, even as my eyes water from the speed.

"Nope! I'm out!" he says, and he rolls off the sled and onto the hill in a puff of white powder.

I think about bailing too until I catch sight of Caroline and Taylor, all smiles, pressed close together on the sled ahead of me.

So instead, I lean forward and hit the ramp.

Hard.

I'm pretty sure nobody in the history of Cemetery Hill has ever gotten this much air. Time slows around me and I swear my entire life flashes before my eyes.

Then I slam into the ground, and my ass splinters into a thousand and one pieces on impact. I roll off the sled, flailing around, pain reverberating through my entire body.

"I think I broke my ass!" I say to uproarious laughter from the top of the hill. "Is it possible to lose a cheek? I think one's missing!"

I lie facedown in the snow, waiting for the pain to subside.

"Well, at least it wasn't the ol' moneymaker," a voice says, and I pop my head up to see Caroline standing there, arms crossed, Taylor nowhere in sight. She taps my sled with her foot. "Get on. I'll pull you back up."

Groaning, I roll onto the plastic sled, and Caroline grabs the string and slowly but surely, one inch at a time, pulls me back up the hill. Everyone claps when we reach the top, and I raise my hand and wave dramatically, while Caroline rolls her eyes at me as she huffs and puffs.

"You had to have been six feet off the ground," Finn says in awe.

"It was siiiick," L.J. adds, nodding enthusiastically.

"It was definitely high enough for me to pee a little."

While everyone tries to top my run, Caroline drags me over to Finn's pickup truck and snack station and dumps me out into the snow. As I struggle to sit up, she fiddles around with a gigantic thermos on the tailgate, then plops down beside me, sipping coffee from a paper cup.

"So," she says, digging around in her snow pants to pull out her handy-dandy notepad.

"Oh my God, Caroline. Do you carry that thing everywhere?" I swipe the coffee from her and take a sip but grimace when it hits my tongue. *Way* too much sugar and cream for my taste, but the warmth of the liquid overrides her horrible proportions.

"Pretty much." She swipes the coffee back and flips through the pages, eyes scanning her notes. "You've been working nonstop since you turned fourteen years old, one movie or TV show after the next. So what do you do for fun . . . when I'm not around?" she adds with a wink.

"Fun?" I ask, squinting at her. "Everyone in America, yourself included, knows what I do for fun. That's kinda the whole problem." My mind flashes through dim rooms and salt-rimmed glasses, strobing lights and pumping music, girls that I forget faster than I learned their names. Cast members I'm close to for a few months and then only know as a flash across my Instagram feed.

Maybe it was fun at first. Or at least better than the alternative. But after a day like this? None of *that* feels particularly fun to me.

"But like . . . you've gotta do stuff other than that. I mean like actual fun you can remember. Like this," she says, and I shrug.

"Caroline, I don't really get to do stuff like this. Like . . . ever."

"Yeah." She nods. "Not a lot of snow in LA."

"I don't mean sledding. I just mean . . . *this*," I say, motioning to us, to the rest of the group.

"What?" She frowns, trying to understand. "You're telling me you don't ever just hang out with friends? I've seen a thousand photos of you out with a thousand different people. You must be friends with some of them."

"Yeah, I mean, I *have* friends. But they're mostly co-stars, or people I know from the industry. And the people I meet out . . . well they're usually much older than me or I only see them one night," I say, looking away to squint out at Cemetery Hill. "So . . . yeah . . . I don't know. Maybe I *don't* really . . ."

"Arden," she says, and her voice sounds like me not having friends causes her physical pain. "Isn't that . . . lonely?"

"I—I don't know." I shrug again.

I'm about to leave my answer right there where I always do, before I can actually tell her about the things that eat away at me and keep me up, that Lillian would never want the readers of *Cosmo* to hear about. But then I remember what Grams told me the other day in her car, that I am not my mom, and that I'm not a kid anymore. I can decide for myself what I do and don't want.

And I don't want to spend these last eight days with Caroline an arm's length away.

"Caroline, every day after work, I come home from set to a dark, empty house. I have to fall asleep to shitty reality TV shows flashing across my flat-screen just so I don't have to hear the ringing in my ears all night long. I spend weekends drunk, lying awake in my bed with a stranger just to forget. I never meant for it to become my life, but somewhere along the way I just . . . lost myself. Everybody thinks I must be surrounded by people who love me all the time just because I'm a celebrity. But the truth is . . . I've been alone since the day I left." I finish, my eyes watering from the cold sting of the wind and the truth as I finally bring myself to look over at her.

"You could have . . . ," Caroline says, the sympathy and her own hurt fighting in her voice.

"I know," I reply. She doesn't press; instead, Caroline scooches closer and links her arm in mine, laying her head on the shoulder of my puffy coat. I don't know what exactly will come at the end of my time here. I don't know if Caroline and I will be able to keep up a long-distance friendship this time, but I don't really want to think about that right now. Right now, I just want to enjoy whatever time we have left.

"So I'll just write 'has no friends' in the—"

I smack the notepad out of her hands, and she scrambles to get it, laughing. I finally breathe, thankful for a break in the tension.

I barely finish having the thought when a snowball smacks me square in the face and I whip my head over to see Finn laughing before *he* gets hit in his. "Okay. *That one* got me right in the moneym—"

I gasp as Caroline dumps a handful of snow on top of my head before leaping to her feet and running for the group, only glancing back at me long enough to shout, "Come on, Hollywood!"

Hollywood?!

Oh, it's on.

I hobble after her, holding my broken ass the whole way.

CHAPTER 17

CAROLINE

DAY 6

I think I've changed my outfit six times already.

Maybe seven.

I let out a long sigh, turning right and then left, inspecting my latest option of jeans and a cardigan in the mirror, my long hair pulled half-up, half-down.

"You look nice," Riley says, coming into my room and plunking down on the bed with a bag of Doritos. "For your date."

I meet her eyes in the mirror. "It's not a date."

"Mm-hmm."

"It's not."

"Okay!" she says, sliding a chip into her grinning mouth, eyebrows wiggling. "You sure are spending a long time getting ready for it not to be a date."

I roll my eyes and swipe a necklace off my bookshelf, putting it on along with a spray of the perfume my mom got me for my birthday, the smell sweet and floral.

"Whatarrryuurevemdouing?"

"What?"

She swallows her mouthful of chips. "What are you even doing?"

"I don't know," I say, shrugging as I grab my phone and check the time. 7:58. "She just said she'd be here at eight."

"Got it, got it." Riley nods. "So you spent like two hours getting ready, you're done early for the first time in your life, and it's *not* a date."

"Yep." I pocket my wallet and phone, then flick off my bedroom light and head down the hall.

Riley hops off the bed, following me. "Do you wish it was?"

"Wish it was what?"

"A date."

I stop on the top step, glancing back to give her a look. *"Riley."*

She tosses another chip into her mouth innocently, waiting for an answer I won't give. I ignore her and head down the steps.

"That's not a no," she says, as the doorbell rings. Eight on the dot.

I glare at her before pulling open the front door. Arden looks perfect as usual in a black leather jacket and a pair of boots expensive enough to put me through college, a baseball cap tucked onto her head, out of place with the rest of her outfit. *Is it to hide her face?*

She gives me a once-over, the corner of her mouth pulling into that lopsided grin.

"You look nice," she says like she means it, and I feel my cheeks grow warm.

I hear a loud crunch and turn my head to see Riley standing next to me. "Caroline says it's not a date."

"I mean, technically, it *is* a date," Arden says, leaning forward

172

to grab a chip and pop it into her mouth. "Since we're, you know, *fake dating*."

I grab my jacket, pushing her out the door in the direction of her car. "Bye, Riley!"

"Bye!" Riley calls back. "Have fun on your date!"

I slow to a stop outside the Volvo, fingers around the icy door handle while I wait for Arden to unlock it.

Instead, she makes a sharp left turn, heading in the direction of town.

I jog after her, grabbing her jacket sleeve. "Where are we going?"

"You'll see," she says, and I quickly rack my brain for all the places in town we could walk to from here, places we used to go, Barnwich holiday events happening tonight, trying to figure out where she's taking me.

"Bookstore?"

"No."

"Clara's Bakery?"

"Nope!"

"The pinball arcade?"

"No . . . but . . . ." She hesitates, frowning as we turn the corner onto Main Street. "That would've been fun too."

I scan the street in front of us, signs hanging underneath strings of glowing lights. "Taste of Italy?"

"No."

I hope she's not thinking of the little pottery studio on the corner where we used to go as kids, because that closed a couple of years back.

Suddenly she skids to a stop outside Beckett Brothers. She

pulls open the door, and the sound of a girl shrieking out Adele nearly blows my eyebrows off.

Karaoke night.

"Oh no." I take a step back.

"Oh *yes*. We're doing this. Figured it might be fun to do something for the article that's not *so* holiday-centric, and give your brothers some promo while we're at it."

Right. For the article.

Arden grabs ahold of my hand and pulls me inside the dim bar, lit only by a neon sign with the name on the wall, some modern pendant lights I helped put up, and a spotlight on the stage in the corner, where Jessica O'Reilly from Levi's class is squawking like an injured seagull. Arden guides us around the surprisingly crowded tables and chairs to the red leather stools in front of the bar. My brothers are hard at work making drinks behind it, in front of their wall of alcohol. A few heads turn as Arden passes by, but not nearly as many as usually do in broad daylight. I watch as she confirms my earlier suspicions by reaching up to adjust the baseball cap, clearly still conscious of it.

Arden motions to a free stool and I slide onto it, then swivel it around to face Miles. My breath hitches when she moves close enough for her chest to press lightly against my shoulder.

"Hey!" he says, when he glances up from the gin and tonic he's making and sees us.

"Miles! This place is awesome," Arden says, and he beams proudly as he slides the drink across the bar to Mr. Green, who must be fresh off his shift since he's still in his Santa costume, hat hanging limply off his head.

"What can I get you two?"

"Two beers, please," Arden says innocently, her breath tickling my neck, making my stomach flutter. Miles snorts and plunks two root beers onto the wooden counter in front of us instead, then swings a bar towel over his shoulder.

"Miiiiles," she groans. The guy sitting on the stool next to us gets up, and the part of me that can't be quieted protests as she moves away and takes the open seat.

"Don't Miles me, Arden James." He raises a dark eyebrow before moving down the bar to take a few more orders. Thwarted, Arden swivels around to face me and I do the same, my knee grazing hers.

"So," she says. "Do you come here often?"

"Is that a pickup line?"

She gives me an amused look, taking a slow sip of her root beer.

I shrug. "Not really. Sometimes I'll stop by after school. The first month or two we all came every day it was open. Some days we were the only customers. But now . . ."

I motion to the modest crowd of people milling about as Mr. Green hops up onstage with his fresh G & T to scattered applause and whistles.

Maybe it's partially the Arden effect, but part of me also thinks it's that they're the only place in town willing to stray from tradition. Willing to try new things instead of doubling down on the old. Trivia and singles night and karaoke, elf costumes not required.

Maybe Barnwich needs to try something new too.

Arden peers around, taking everything in while I take her in, her face glowing in the red neon light.

Then Levi's head suddenly appears between us, cutting off my view of Arden. He swaps the root beer bottles for two actual beers with a wink, holding a finger up to his lips.

I laugh, and Arden holds out her bottle to me. "Cheers."

I clink it against hers, and the two of us join in as the bar sings along with Mr. Green's rendition of "Piano Man," people swaying to and fro in their seats.

As karaoke night continues, some performances are better than others. We sit awkwardly through a recently divorced Erica Miller crying her way through "Shallow," followed by some passable Shania Twain by a tourist in from somewhere down South. But things get a real lift from an *impressive* "Bohemian Rhapsody" belted out by our elementary school janitor, Mr. Stukuley.

"Holy shit!" I grab hold of Arden's arm as Mr. Stukuley rips out *the* high note, sending a few people whistling in admiration.

"Heard him singing once when he cleaned the second-floor bathroom," Arden says with a laugh. "Knew he had it in him."

Our eyes meet, and I'm not sure which is making me dizzier, the beer or her hand sliding down to my wrist and then my palm, until her warm fingertips finally close over mine. I catch sight of two girls just over her shoulder, sitting at the end of the bar, heads pressed close together as one of them pulls out her phone and snaps a picture of Arden.

I can't help but wonder if she's doing this because she's already clocked them.

I think of Arden's fake smile on Margo's front porch and everything I saw on Twitter two nights ago, and my grip tightens around her hand. I fight off the urge to drag her out of here, to protect her. But this is a *fake date*. We need, *Arden* needs, to be seen.

So instead I just let go to stop myself, disguising the movement by putting both hands on the bar and leaning forward.

"Miiiiles!" I call out, and my brother pops into view. "Can we get some fries?"

He narrows his eyes at me. "Did Levi . . . ?"

He catches sight of the empty beer bottles and lets out a long sigh. "Yeah. I'll get you some fries."

It isn't long before the red-and-white boat appears in front of us. Our hands crash together as we both go for the same perfect fry, lightly salted, impeccably crispy. Arden surprises me by pulling her hand away, motioning for me to have it. Instead, I break it into two and hold out half to her. Her lips pull into a small smile as she leans forward and bites it out of my hand.

I roll my eyes at her to cover the blush creeping up my cheeks, then look back at the stage, where a woman about Edie's age is rocking out to some Cher.

"You want to do it?" she asks playfully.

"What? *Karaoke?* Absolutely not."

Arden pops a fry into her mouth, a mischievous glint in her eye as she stares at the stage. "I'd crush it."

"Says the girl who was lip-syncing Christmas carols."

"Ouch." She clutches her chest. "But fair." She takes a swig of the replacement beers Levi has provided, apparently not daunted by Miles's threats, then nods in the direction of the bathrooms. "Gotta pee. I'll be right back."

I'm so busy watching her go, I almost don't notice Levi sliding onto her unoccupied stool, plastic bin under his arm. "So," he says, brown eyes crinkling at the corners. "What's the deal?"

I glare at him and eat another fry. "What do you mean, what's the deal?"

"You and *Arden*." He leans forward conspiratorially when he says it. He stole my diary when I was in eighth grade, so he knows all too well about my deep, all-consuming crush.

"There is no 'deal.' Not a real one, anyway. You know that. There never has been a deal with me and Arden." My crush is in the past; this is just the ripple effects, the fake dating calling them up. Arden has always been the maybe. The what-if. If anything, this little game of pretend feels like finally getting an answer to it so I can just . . . move on.

"She's here for seven more days. And then she'll just . . ." I shrug, munching on a fry, a little too much of a lightweight not to be honest. "Forget about Barnwich again. Forget about me again."

"Mmm." His gaze flicks past my head, though, and a huge grin appears on his face as the whole room starts to clap and wolf-whistle.

I spin around to see that Arden has hopped up onstage and is taking the mic from the Cher crooner. "Hey, everyone," she says into it, and a few phones rise in anticipation, the excitement palpable. She clears her throat. "This next song goes out to *my girlfriend*."

Oh God.

Her eyes lock with mine, and the moment that perfect, annoying smile of hers appears, I know exactly what she's about to do.

"Jesus Christ," I mutter, resisting the urge to crawl underneath the bar as the opening notes play.

"*Where it began . . . ,*" Arden starts, and immediately the whole bar turns to look at me.

As she sings, she hops off the stage and starts weaving her way around the tables, doing crowd work the whole way, letting people sing into the mic, taking a quick sip from someone's glass with a wink, even slinging an arm around Mr. Green.

Whatever her voice lacks, she makes up for tenfold with charisma, and by the time she gets to the bridge, what seems like the whole bar is singing along, swaying right and left in time with her.

She reaches out and a sea of hands reach back at her, a few fingertips grazing hers.

And it'd be all too easy to just . . . give into it. My what-if with Arden James. To imagine what it would be like if I really was hers, watching as she serenaded me at karaoke or got Austin *ten thousand* more Instagram followers or listened to Maya talk about art school. Maybe it's good it isn't real, because I'm not sure my heart could handle falling in love with one person so many times in a day.

She spins around and clambers onto the end of the bar, but this time she holds my gaze like there's nobody else in this entire room.

"*Sweet Caroline.*"

"*Bum, bum, bum!*" everyone adds in as she whips her hat off and chucks it into the crowd, sending people diving to catch it.

The whole room chants as she walks closer and closer to me, making my heart pound so hard in my chest I feel dizzy.

Soon she's in front of me, stooping down until we're face-to-face, so charming that even though I still can't tell what's real and what's not, I'm not sure I want to anymore.

She offers me a hand, one eyebrow ticking up in challenge as everyone cheers.

"Full stack or bust," she mouths, but somehow I know the challenge is more than just about karaoke. I let out a long exhale and finally, I do give in. I let her pull me up onto the bar. I let myself slip fully into the lie. And even though this is all so far out of my comfort zone, something about the way she's looking at me makes me less afraid, just like it always has.

We sing the next verse into the mic together, and one person holds up their beer bottle, and then *everyone* does.

She smiles out at the sea of bottles, the whole room of people, during the verse, but when we get to the chorus again, it's back to me, only me, her eyes shining in the glow of the neon sign, the same eyes that held my own when we stayed up late whispering secrets to one another, and drank milkshakes at Edie's, and ice-skated until we could barely feel our feet. The same eyes I fell in love with so many times, it makes me realize that what I thought was a scar was actually just a scab.

The song ends to uproarious applause, and Arden lowers the mic until there's nothing between us but air. Her eyes flick down to my lips, and for the smallest moment, a heartbeat, it feels like we're going to kiss. This time I don't deny it to myself. I *want* to kiss her.

I *want* it to be real.

But instead, she blinks and looks away, grinning out at the crowd as she hops down off the bar, then offers me a hand. She helps me climb down before heading back to the stage to hand the mic off to the next person.

As I watch her go, Levi leans over to whisper in my ear, "It doesn't seem like she forgot about you."

And I can't help but hope that maybe she could want it to be real too.

CHAPTER 18

ARDEN

DAY 6

Eventually, we giggle our way out of the bar and onto the sidewalk. The Barnwich winter chill feels less biting with the two beers Levi snuck us in my system.

"Sweeeet Caroline," I sing as we walk back to the Becketts' house under the orange glow of the streetlights.

Caroline laughs as we turn onto her street, then immediately gasps as she slips on an icy patch, arms and legs flailing. I grab ahold of her to keep her upright, and her fingers curl into my jacket, but it's no use. The two of us end up in a heap on the concrete, Caroline on top of me.

"My buuuutt," I groan. "It's still sore from sledding!" We burst into giggles again, and I notice for the hundredth time tonight that she smells warm and sweet and *good*, an unfamiliar scent I still haven't placed mixed with the same blue-bottle shampoo she's used since sixth grade.

Maybe it's not the beers keeping me warm after all.

"God, it's been so long since I've had a night this good. I

forgot it could be like this," I say, taking it all in.

"Yeah, it . . ." Her voice trails off, eyes searching my face for an answer. "It kinda feels like—"

"Old times," I finish, and she nods.

We push ourselves back up onto our feet, careful not to eat shit again as we head back to her house.

By the time we make it up the front steps, it's after midnight, and everything around us is still and quiet. "I have to pee before I go," I tell her.

She grabs the sleeve of my jacket and pulls me up the steps. I watch her fumble with her keys, dropping them three times before managing to get the right one in the lock.

"Butterfingers," I whisper as she somehow manages to drop them one more time while pulling it out. She's clearly a lot tipsier than me, but I'm feeling drunk on something else tonight. When the two of us finally tiptoe inside, Blue thumps his tail from the entryway mat in hello.

I use the hat rack in the corner to stabilize myself while I go to take off my *way* too tight and blistering boots, but the whole thing starts to topple over. Thankfully, Caroline catches it before it hits the ground.

"Arden," she hisses, and I grin at her.

"What? How was I supposed to—" We hear the floor creak upstairs, and she presses a hand against my lips, our heads swinging to peer up the dark steps to the second floor. I look back at her pale face, illuminated in the moonlight that's creeping in through the window, her eyelashes casting shadows against her cheeks as she searches for the source of the sound.

The shadows disappear as the light flicks on above us, revealing Mrs. Beckett standing at the top of the steps in a pair of striped pj's, arms crossed.

We pull apart quickly, and I lift my hand in an awkward wave, squinting against the blinding entryway light.

"Good morning!" Caroline says, and I snort, but Mrs. Beckett drops her arms to slap against her legs, instantly sniffing her out.

"I'm going to kill your brothers."

"Mrs. Beckett, they only gave us one beer," I say, and she gives me a look. "Maybe two. She's just a lightweigh—"

Caroline elbows me in the side to get me to shut up.

"They can get in a lot of trouble. And *you* should know better," she says to Caroline. Both of us hang our heads in an attempt to look remorseful until the hatstand just behind us slowly topples over with a crash, and we burst into laughter.

"All right. You two are in for the night." She points at me as I tilt the hatstand back upright. "Arden, tell Edie you're staying over."

I hold up the keys in my pocket. "I can just . . ."

If looks could kill, I'd be dead. "I didn't think you knew better, but I sure as hell hoped you did."

Ouch.

She clomps down the steps to swipe the keys out of my hand, reminding me more of the moms I've had in movies than my own. "You'll get these back tomorrow. I'm going to bed. Caroline, we can talk in the morning." In a way it feels like I've been slapped, but in a way it also feels . . . good? Like she actually cares if something happens to me.

She flicks the light back out, and the two of us stand there in the dark for a minute until we hear the bedroom door close down the hall.

I clear my throat as Caroline and I look at each other. "You still got that snack drawer?" I whisper sheepishly, stalling and waiting for Caroline to start freaking out about what just happened.

"Obviously," she says instead, and then heads into the kitchen.

"Wait, that's it? You're not upset?" I ask, as I follow her.

"You mean my mom?" She scoffs. "She'll get over it. I mean, it's not the first time I've had a beer, Arden. Plus, is it really *my* fault if my *older* brother gave it to me?" She smirks. "Levi will probably get into more trouble than me."

"Still playing the little sister card." I shake my head as Blue trots after us, following the glow of Caroline's phone flashlight into the pantry. It's filled with perfectly organized cereals, soups, pasta, and canned goods, and . . .

The Drawer.

Caroline pulls it open to reveal a sea of snacks. Hostess products, candy, Pop-Tarts, fruit snacks, you name it.

The Becketts *always* had the best snacks. Mr. Beckett used to pack the kind of lunches that had every kid at Barnwich Elementary trying to trade for theirs.

We grab a bunch and run up the steps to her room, just like we used to, collapsing onto her bed after we make a pit stop to go pee. Caroline flicks on her small bedside lamp and the single bulb glows a dusty yellow, but shadows still linger in the corners of the room.

"Look at us," I say, popping a sticky Gusher into my mouth

as we stare up at the ceiling. "Having a sleepover. Even more like old times than I was expecting."

"Well, this time, technically, you're paying me to hang out with you," she says through a mouthful of cinnamon-sugar Pop-Tart.

I laugh. "Technically, *Cosmopolitan* is paying you, not me."

She takes another bite, grinning before it turns into a quiet laugh.

"You probably don't even remember, but I was just thinking of that time when Jacob Klein paid you fifty dollars to jump into the lake behind his house."

"It's kind of hard to forget almost getting hypothermia," I reply. "And then once I dried off, we left the party early and spent it all on snacks and nail polish from Walmart."

"That was my favorite nail polish for like two years."

"What ever happened to him?"

"Jacob?" Caroline asks, pulling out her second Pop-Tart. "He went out to LA too. Was in a failed pilot for Amazon."

"Really?" I whip my head over to look at her.

She snorts. "No. He's going to Penn State in the fall."

I grin and shake my head as I crumple up the Gushers wrapper. Then I pick up a bag of Flamin' Hot Doritos.

"Give me one," she says, reaching toward it.

"You hate spicy stuff," I say, confused. "Remember when we tried sriracha on our eggs instead of ketchup? I thought I was going to have to throw you on my back and run you to the hospital."

She laughs. "Yeah, well . . ." She reaches out for a chip again, snapping her fingers at me. "My taste buds changed. Not everything stays the same after four years."

As I hold the open bag out to her, I chew my lip, debating if I want to possibly ruin all this forward progress. Singing to her in public is one thing, but talking here in her bedroom, just the two of us, is a whole other level of vulnerability.

Still, something tells me it's worth a try.

"Well then, we should ask each other questions," I suggest.

Caroline holds the rest of her chip between her teeth and digs around in her back pocket to pull out her notepad. She flips to a page and is about to ask me something when I swipe it from her grip and chuck it over my shoulder onto the floor.

"Hey!" she says, glaring at me.

"No notepad. I mean like . . . questions to get to know each other. You know, who we are now. For real. Off the record."

I watch as she considers, her eyes moving across the ceiling. I hold my breath the whole time until finally . . . she nods. "Okay."

"Okay?"

"Ask me again and I might say no." She fixes me with a look, and I seal my mouth shut. "Worst thing about living in LA?"

"The traffic," I lie, off to a great start. "Who's your celebrity crush? And you can't say me," I joke, and her face immediately turns red, so I know it's going to be good.

"Andrew Garfield."

I give her a confused look. "Aren't you a lesbian?" I ask.

She just shrugs and shakes her head. "Yeah, but . . . the heart wants what the heart wants, I guess. And this heart wants a British cinnamon roll. If you weren't an actor, what would you want to be?"

"A high school teacher." I pop another handful of chips into my mouth.

She cocks her head, intrigued. "Me too. I mean, if journalism doesn't pan out, it'd be cool to teach a writing class or something."

"Who's your favorite sibling?" I ask.

"I love them all the same," she replies, but then clamps her hand over her mouth, clearly blocking a smile until "Levi" slips through the cracks in her fingers.

"I like Riley," I say.

"Only because she worships the ground you walk on."

"She's got good taste. What can I say?" I shrug, and Caroline throws another bag of Gushers at me.

We spend the next hour asking questions back and forth. I find out she still listens to music to fall asleep and religiously keeps a vegetable garden with her mom every spring. That she goes to Maya's family's beach house for a few weeks each summer and that she went to every football game with Austin but only to keep him company as he cheered on Finn. That she works at the diner mostly to check in on Edie, and when I tell her about Restaurant Depot, she says she'll go with her from now on.

She finds out about me, too. That the coolest place I've been to for filming was Croatia and the worst was an overnight at an old mental hospital. That I wear a wig and a pair of sunglasses and go to the movies alone every other Friday. That I watch *When Harry Met Sally* every New Year's Eve like I used to with Edie, even if I get home from a party well after midnight. That I adopted a toothless senior dog named Neil two years ago, and we had a great six months together before he passed.

I tell her all the things that I never talk about in interviews when I'm on press tours. Things that feel too . . . well . . . personal to open up to everyone else's judgment.

"What's the worst thing about high school?" I ask.

"Cafeteria food," she says, then hesitates. "And having to get up at seven."

"Oh my God. I *wish* I could sleep in until seven during the week." I groan. "On shooting days, I've gotta be on set at like five most days. It sucks."

Caroline laughs and falls back onto the bed, staring up at the ceiling. "I couldn't even get you out of bed in the morning for Edie's pancakes when we were little." She pauses, both of us quiet while we think of our next questions. I roll onto my back too, staring at the fan going around and around above us.

"What happened with your parents? Where are they?" Caroline asks finally, her voice soft.

I shrug and let out a pathetic laugh, knowing I could turn this into some kind of joke.

A cruise down the Rhine?

A cabana in the Caribbean?

Six feet under the ground somewhere?

A big part of me *wants* to, because if I don't, I'm afraid I'll just cry instead. But telling Caroline about how lonely LA is after we went sledding—without the world ending—makes me not want to hold back from her anymore. For once, I want someone to actually see me.

So I take a deep breath and start, "Remember how we thought things would get better after I went out to LA?" I ask. "That they'd finally stop fighting . . ."

She nods.

"Well, it worked. But only because they weren't actually there anymore. They started using my money to run away from any responsibilities. Well, their *only* responsibility. Me. So I figured if they wanted not to be parents to me anymore, *fine*. But I wasn't going to let them keep stealing my money. I got emancipated when I turned sixteen, but really I was on my own long before that," I say, still staring at the ceiling.

"I don't understand how they could just . . . *leave*," Caroline replies, as I try to swallow the lump rising in my throat.

"I don't think my mom and dad were ever really meant to be parents," I admit finally. "Not like yours. A dad who makes pancakes every Tuesday. A mom who works her ass off but somehow still makes it feel like she always has time for you. Who yells at you for coming home with a buzz and takes your car keys right out of your hands." My back is too warm against the bed, and I wish the fan was spinning faster. "Parents who . . . who really love you," I finish, trying to let the rest of my breath out quietly before any tears can slip out.

But then Caroline's hand moves down the bed between us. Her fingers slide along my palm and intertwine with mine. She's not doing it for the article or because somebody might be watching. She's just doing it for me. And after that, there's nothing I can do to stop the tears that roll down my face.

"I'm sorry. You deserved better," she says, squeezing my hand.

"Most days, it doesn't feel like that's true. It seems like I'm always making the wrong choices," I reply, shrugging.

"Arden . . . ," she starts, turning onto her side to face me, but I motion that I'm ready to move on to the next question. She's quiet while I take a sec to get myself together a little.

"Why journalism?" I ask when I can, hoping she'll answer me this time.

She frowns, nose wrinkling, and for a moment I think she won't, that it's something she still doesn't want to share with me. But finally, she lets out a long sigh, lets go of my hand, and rolls off the bed onto the floor to dig around for something underneath us.

She emerges with a worn, dusty shoebox, which she plunks down in the space between us. I sit up, and she nudges it toward me, so I flip it open to find it filled with articles and carefully cut newspaper clippings.

I pick up one, then another, and my stomach falls when I realize they're all about . . .

Me. My first year in Hollywood.

BARNWICH GIRL ON THE SILVER SCREEN

ARDEN JAMES: A STAR IN THE MAKING

REDEFINING METEORIC?

I look at Caroline. Her strawberry-blond hair is finally freed from the claw clip that held it all evening, and her gaze is focused on one of the articles in her hand.

"I read *so many* articles the year you left. Some good, some bad. I was just . . . searching for you in all of them. Any familiar trace of you. But I couldn't find that in *any* of this, and that made me think about what makes a good writer. A good journalist. How you should be able to capture the person within the story you're trying to tell, make them come alive for the reader. Honest and real, not a collection of SEO words."

She shrugs, but the paper crinkles in her grip. "Anyway, it made me want to do that. To be a journalist who *could* do that. And, well, I didn't want to admit it at first, but I guess in some small way this *Cosmo* article is my first chance to make a real impact with something like that."

She goes to put the clipping back, but I grab ahold of her hand and her brown eyes flick up to meet mine.

"I'm sorry. I'm sorry I didn't call, Caroline. I'm sorry I didn't come back. And I'm sorry I haven't given you any good reason to forgive me, but sometimes it's hard for me to talk about, well, feelings. Why I . . ." I look into her eyes and she looks back into mine and . . . I just . . . can't seem to articulate it. Or maybe I can and just don't want to, because the truth is those feelings still scare the shit out of me. Before I can finish my sentence, Caroline blinks quickly, breaking eye contact.

Then the springs of her bed creak as she stands. "I forgot my phone downstairs. I'll be right back."

I watch her go, letting out a long sigh. Then I look back at the box and carefully close the lid.

When she returns, she yawns a little too big, not much of an actress.

"You ready to hit the hay?" she asks, climbing into bed and turning down the other side of the comforter.

"Sure," I reply, even though I wish we could stay up and talk like this all night like we used to. I wish I could have gotten the words out. I wish . . . Well, it doesn't matter. I probably shouldn't push my luck anyway. So I lie down next to her, her sheets smelling just like her shampoo.

It takes a while, but she falls asleep first, one earbud in, listening to her Spotify sleep playlist. Her eyes are closed, her lips slightly parted, her breathing slow and soft. I reach over to pull the earbud out, and the music hums as my fingertips linger on her cheek for a stolen moment.

This feels so much like the old days, and yet I can still feel the four years sitting between us. I don't even know if I can erase them by telling her the truth now, by telling her *why* I didn't call and *why* I never came back. By telling her how I feel. And then I think of how fast she bolted from the room, not even waiting to see if I could finish the sentence.

Maybe it's too late. Maybe it's a question Caroline doesn't want the answer to anymore.

CHAPTER 19

CAROLINE

DAY 7

The first thing I see when I wake up is Arden's face.

I burrow deeper into the covers, taking in all her familiar features now that her makeup has been wiped off. Sharp nose, soft lips, that small scar on her chin. Somehow she looks even more attractive without her signature eyeliner, and something about it missing makes her feel even more like, well . . .

My Arden.

Especially after last night and her apology. Even though it was still lacking any sort of explanation, I could feel how much she meant it.

And I can't really hold it against her this time. I left before she could give it because, well . . . I was suddenly scared. Scared that I couldn't take knowing the answer, in case it wasn't one I wanted.

She stirs, and I try to act like I wasn't just staring at her as her dark brown eyes slowly open, her hand reaching up to rub at the right one.

"Morning," she grumbles.

"Morning," I say, rolling over to grab my phone off the bedside table. I frown and sit up when I see the screen filled with notifications and tap on one from Instagram. My eyes widen when I see—

"*Ten thousand* follow requests?"

"Oh boy." Arden sits up to peek over my shoulder. The two of us watch a grainy video from the bar last night that found its way onto TikTok. The song name and Arden's little dedication at the beginning must have made it pretty easy for her fans to track me down.

I scroll through screenshots, fans shouting, *ARDEN HAS A WHOLE GF* with cry emojis in the comments. There's even an article entitled "Ten Things to Know About Arden James's New Girlfriend." I tap on it to see that half the things are incorrect, from being down a sibling to claiming I'm an "aspiring basketball player." But without a doubt the worst part is that my ninth-grade yearbook photo somehow makes an appearance. My heart hammers in my chest as I try to process it all.

I mean, I *knew* this day would come. It's just . . . a lot sooner than I expected. I thought with the article that I'd be able to do it at least a little bit on my own terms.

"Holy shit," I say, slamming my phone down on the mattress when I see someone posted two screen grabs from the very end of the song, from *that* moment. Arden leaning forward, my cheeks burning when I realize her eyes are focused on my lips.

It feels so strange to see it from the outside. To see how unfiltered I was and how, well, obviously *into her*.

I wonder if it was obvious to Arden too, or if she just thought I was getting better at pretending.

We sit there in silence for a long moment, shoulder to shoulder.

"Are you sure you're still—" Arden starts.

"Do you want to hang out today?" I cut her off, looking over at her. "Like we used to. Without people watching. Without fake dating. Without all . . ." I motion to my phone. "We could make cookies and watch—"

"Love Actually," we both say at the same time. Our favorite movie from back in the day. We must've watched it a hundred times, even when it wasn't Christmastime, but I don't think I've watched it since she left.

"Absolutely." She nods. "So cookies for breakfast?"

"Cookies for breakfast."

Arden borrows an abandoned oversized T-shirt and sweats from Levi and Miles's old room, since all my pants would be capris on her, and we head into the hall. I peel a sticky note off my door-frame left by my mom: *WE'LL TALK LATER* in bold Sharpie.

My parents are at work, which puts my mom's speech off for a few hours at least. We're not even at the bottom step, though, before I hear Riley crunching her cereal loud enough to be heard all the way at Barnwich Brews.

"Well, well, well," she says, leaning back in her chair as we approach. "Looks like the date went well."

She holds out the box of Lucky Charms she's keeping next to her for easy refills, and Arden takes a handful.

I don't reply with my usual *it wasn't a date*, because . . . I don't know anymore.

Instead I head over to the pantry to get the ingredients for my dad's chocolate chip cookie recipe. When I come back out, Arden is sitting on the counter, tossing cereal pieces into the air for Riley to catch in her mouth.

"When's Hanukkah?" Arden asks, nodding to the menorah sitting on the windowsill.

"It starts super late this year," Riley says, swaying left to catch another piece while I turn on the oven to preheat. "On Christmas, actually. But we've got the family Hanukkah party this Saturday because Grandma and Grandpa are going on a trip to celebrate their fiftieth wedding anniversary." She munches noisily, grinning at Arden. "You should come."

"Oh, I don't . . ." She casts a quick glance at me, and I shrug.

"You can if you want." I add brown sugar, flour, baking soda, and salt into a bowl. "I mean, no pressure, obviously."

The doorbell rings and Riley jumps up, throwing her bowl in the sink as she bails on the awkward moment she created. "Gotta go. Hanging out at Sammy's house today." She's out the door in a flash, calling goodbye to Arden (and not me) on the way.

Arden hops off the counter and tosses the rest of her handful of Lucky Charms into her mouth. "You sure it's cool?"

"Best brisket you'll ever have," I say with a nod, like it isn't as big a deal as it feels. "Besides, my grandma really liked *Operation Sparrow*. She watches it like once a month."

She laughs, reaching over to crack an egg, our arms brushing lightly against one another. "Grams hated it."

"Edie . . . may have better taste in movies than my grandma."

We move like clockwork, as we have hundreds of times before. I add vanilla extract, milk, and shortening. Arden adds the dry ingredients and then dumps in a boatload of chocolate chips.

"I think it would be cool to have a little bit of Hanukkah in the article," she says while she mixes. "Everything in Barnwich is so . . . *Christmas*. It's kind of messed up that there isn't anything for people who celebrate other holidays, people with other faiths."

I look up at her, surprised that Arden clocked what I feel. What no one else seems to see. "I wish Barnwich had something for us too. I just don't know how it would . . . fit. Into a town like this. I know sometimes I don't even feel like *I* fit," I admit.

"Well, you and Levi and Miles and Riley and your mom are a part of this town as much as me and Edie and your dad are. And you're not the only Jewish people here." She shrugs. I think of a few kids from school I know, Sarah and Heather and Jake and Zoey, the Goldbergs who live two blocks over, and the Bernsteins from caroling, just a few houses down, as she continues. "Maybe we can find a way to . . . I mean, maybe it's what Barnwich needs. What's been missing. Instead of just doing *more* of the same shit and expecting a different result, maybe it needs something *new*. More . . . diversity."

I give her a long look while she grabs two spoons from the silverware drawer, holding one out to me like she didn't just echo every single one of my secret thoughts.

"Let's keep thinking about it. In the meantime . . . we obviously have to try it," she says, gesturing to the bowl of cookie dough in front of us.

I nod and take it from her, then scoop an overflowing spoonful as she does the same. "Will your fans hate me if you get salmonella?" I ask through a mouthful. The cookie dough is sweet and smooth and delicious, the brown sugar standing out just like I remember.

"Absolutely," she says, flicking a chocolate chip at me. "You think you're trending now? Just wait."

I groan and take another bite as we scoop the cookie dough

onto the pan, which Arden then slides into the oven. It doesn't take long for the kitchen to start smelling incredible, and we spend a few minutes cleaning everything up. The scent follows us down the hall to the living room, where I get the movie queued up from next to her on the couch. It's jarring when an ad for a TV show Arden did last year pops up before it starts.

"So serious," I say as Arden mimics the photo, arms crossed, eyebrows furrowed. I push her over, and she smiles, brow softening.

"I had the biggest zit that day," she says, pointing to her chin in the picture, where I only see smooth perfection. "Someone must've spent at least two hours airbrushing that baby off."

"Too many sour gummy worms?"

Arden only got zits on her abnormally perfect skin when she ate an enormous amount of candy. Sour gummy worms were her weakness.

She looks over at me, defensive. "I got ten of the big bags for *five dollars* when the pharmacy by my house went out of business. Can you believe that?"

I toss the remote onto the couch as the timer dings from the other room and Arden trails after me, continuing her justification. "Were they a little stale? Sure. Did I finish two whole bags by the next morning? Definitely."

We pile the cookies onto a plate and grab two glasses of milk, before heading back to the living room.

As we press play and settle under the same blanket, all at once I can't decipher the past from the present. I'm suddenly fourteen again, and all I can focus on is her leg, barely an inch from mine, the plate resting between us. It takes half a dozen cookies and halfway through the movie, Hugh Grant dancing around the halls of 10 Downing Street, for me to actually be able to pay attention.

In some small way, once I lose myself in it, the movie makes me think of Barnwich again. My conversation with Arden, and what I hope this town could be. All these different stories and people intersecting. Embracing every person and every perspective, all the different celebrations that bring us together.

My train of thought is broken, though, when we start *13 Going on 30*. With the plate now on the coffee table, Arden lounges close enough to my lap for her head to be lightly grazing my hand, and I force my fingertips to resist the urge to tangle in her hair.

"Ugh," she says, handing me half of another cookie when the Seven Minutes in Heaven scene happens and Matty is pushed out of the closet. "This part always stings. He's got the *biggest* crush on her!"

"It all works out in the end," I say, and she snorts, glancing back at me.

"I guess you're right. I mean, I had *such* a big crush on you back in the day. And look at us now! Instagram's sweethearts."

I nearly choke on the piece of cookie in my mouth. *"What?"* I manage to gasp out.

Arden had a crush on *me*? I feel lightheaded. There's no way—

"Well," she says with a shrug. "Maybe not a crush."

"Oh. Okay." I resist the urge to roll my eyes, because *of course* Arden didn't have a crush on me. That would be ridiculous.

"It was more than that," she says with a laugh, eyes shifting to focus on the TV as the piece of cookie shoots straight back down my windpipe. "I was so lovesick over you that sometimes I thought I was going to die or something. Silly, right?"

I sit there, too stunned to say anything.

Finally, she shoves the rest of her cookie into her mouth like she didn't just completely upend my world in less than a minute, and swings her legs over the seat of the couch before I can even figure out how to reply. "I gotta go to the bathroom. I'll be right back."

I watch her go, fingers curling into the blanket as I try to process what I just heard. The door Arden just opened and then slammed shut.

Could Arden actually have been *lovesick* over me?

I think of all those moments that meant so much to me that I was sure she didn't even notice. Our hands brushing against one another as we lay out in the snow watching the stars, sleepovers where we'd stay up so late talking only to wake up curled into each other the next morning. That night she jumped into the lake at Jacob Klein's party, her body pressed against me, her face so close to mine. How much I wanted to kiss her.

None of it was one-sided?

Arden was on the other side, suffering just as much as I was? Maybe wanting to kiss me as much as I wanted to kiss her?

But how could she feel the same way I did and just . . . cut off the connection, as quickly as she stood up to go to the bathroom?

Should I tell her? Should I—

My head whips around as she comes back into the room, but her eyes are on her phone and her mouth is pulled down into a frown.

"There was a leak in the kitchen at the diner. Whole place

is closed down for the rest of the afternoon. Rest of the night if it's part of a bigger problem," she says, hesitating by the couch, rubbing her face. "I can tell Grams is worried." She looks toward the door. "I should go over there."

"I can come," I say, and she nods. The two of us get changed before we head out to her car, and just like that, once again, I'm left with more questions than answers.

The drive is short, but Arden chews her lip nervously for most of the ride.

Without thinking, I reach out and grab her hand off the center console, squeezing it. She looks over at me and gives me a small smile as our fingers lace together.

When we get there, despite Edie's being closed, the parking lot is *packed*. We exchange quizzical looks until we pull into a spot and see what looks like half the town inside, mopping or carrying out furniture to dry. I can even hear the Christmas music pumping through the closed windows as Arden parks the car.

This time when we look at each other, we're smiling. *"Barnwich,"* we say at the same time, laughing as we hop out and head over to find Edie.

The turnout is incredible. So much so that Tom's even set up a little tent with a grill and is churning out burgers and hot dogs for everyone there in his usual stained white T-shirt, even though it can't be much above thirty degrees out. Luckily there's a hot chocolate table set up right next to him.

It feels like what I was thinking about during *Love Actually*, and it makes me wonder if the town *would* embrace something if me and Arden just tried.

We find Edie there in the middle of it all, accepting cookies and well-wishes and directing her sea of helpers. The two ladies who run the card store in town are even setting up the rest of Edie's dust-covered Christmas decorations, Arden's favorites, rescued from the closet. I watch Arden crane her neck to look at our wreath, now hanging proudly on the diner's front door, before she refocuses on the task at hand.

"All good?" Arden asks, tucking Edie under her arm after Mr. Green leaves for his Santa shift, already decked out in his costume.

Edie nods, patting Arden's side. "I mean, no, but . . . it will be. It's a big repair, but the plumber said we should be back up and running tomorrow, thanks to all the help."

"You'd let me know if you need anything. Right, Grams?" Arden asks. Edie smiles but doesn't answer the question. We both know, though, that missing out on a day of business in an already slow peak season is no small loss. The whole town knows; that's why they're here.

When Edie shuffles off to help Tom at the grill, I head over with Arden to join the hot chocolate line.

"Just how slow has it been this year?" she asks.

"You were right about Barnwich," I admit, looking out at all the people here to help, all of us fighting to keep the place going. "There has been a bit of a drop-off from the holiday crowds we used to have. I didn't want to admit it before, but just you being here *has* started turning it around."

I think of Main Street, the diner, even the bar last night. More people than Barnwich has seen in a while have been trickling in these last few days, thanks to her Instagram stories and the news articles that follow.

Arden's about to respond but stops when we reach the front of the line, shocked to find that Ruth is the one dispensing the hot chocolate.

"Did you spit in it?" Arden jokes, as Ruth hands her a cup. I laugh, but Ruth only glowers at the two of us. Clearly she still has not gotten over the incident at Barnwich Brews. So we take our hot chocolates away quickly and lean against the vinyl siding of the diner.

Arden takes a long sip of hers, her face thoughtful. Meanwhile, my phone buzzes noisily in my hand, the entire screen lighting up with even more notifications.

"*Caroline,*" Arden says, grabbing ahold of my arm. When I look up, I see her face is glowing with excitement. "You work tomorrow, right?"

"Yeah, six to noon."

"Grams won't take money from me, *but . . .*" She holds up her phone. "What if I work your shift with you tomorrow? I could post about it today, and I bet it would drum up some business."

I nod, catching on. "Yes! Like a 'pancakes with Arden James' kind of thing."

"Exactly!" The corner of her mouth pulls up into a lopsided grin. "We should take a picture for the post."

"*We?*"

"I mean, not to exploit you any further than I already am, but . . . *we* are trending. If you're in the picture I post, people will be even more eager to come and see our relationship in person. I mean, hell, I'll serve the paparazzi some pancakes myself if I know the money is going into Grams's pocket."

She has a point, but I glance down quickly at what I'm wearing. A vintage crewneck and a pair of leggings underneath an enormous puffy jacket. Nothing particularly flattering. "Can I at least go back to my house and change?"

"You look fine," Arden says with a shrug. "Beautiful, even." The words come out so easily, just like admitting her crush barely an hour ago, but they floor me just as much. "Besides, people will love how 'real and natural' the picture is. You know, 'home-grown.'" She smirks. "Bianchi-style."

For the first time since we left the bar, I can't help but wonder again if that is all this is to her.

She steps close enough for me to feel the warmth radiating off her body and holds up her phone, Edie's sign in the background. I lean into her and smile as she snaps a couple of photos. Still snapping, Arden turns her head to look at me, and my eyes drift to her face too.

I could just lean up, could just *kiss* her. A part of me wants it so badly again that it makes my bones ache.

But Arden said that she *was* lovesick. Not that she is now.

So, instead, I look back at the camera, and Arden does too. After a final snap she moves away, taking the warmth with her. I shiver, despite myself.

Arden notices, eyes flicking up from reviewing the photos. "I can take you back," she says, and I nod, my head still spinning from every conversation and moment we've had since she picked me up last night. "No sense in the both of us freezing our butts off today."

As we drive, I fight the urge to tell her, to shout that I felt it too. That all those years ago, I loved *her*. I want to ask why she didn't tell me. Why she kept it a secret.

And, most of all, why *did* she never call if that was really how she felt?

It takes until she's halfway back to her car after dropping me off at the door for me to actually say anything at all.

"Wait!" I call out, and Arden spins around to look at me with those dark brown eyes, with that face that I haven't been able to get out of my head, out of my *heart*, for years.

"I . . ." I hesitate, the words getting caught in my throat as she walks slowly back up the porch steps. So instead of telling her how I felt, how I'm starting to think I could feel again, I pull the notepad out of my jacket pocket and hold it up. "I forgot to ask you your question last night. So I've got two questions for you today."

She rests her head on the pillar of the porch while I look down at my notepad. "You really do *always* have that on you."

"Yes."

"Even when you sleep?"

"You didn't see it? Tucked into bed last night?"

She laughs as I flip through the pages, but everything blurs together, words jumping out at me but not making any sense. Finally, I close it, letting out a long exhale as I look up at her and prepare to ask the closest thing to what I want to know. "What was the easiest part about leaving Barnwich?" I ask, easing into it.

"Chasing my dream. Seeing my parents actually happy, even if I wasn't really a part of it."

"And . . ." I steady myself. "The hardest part about leaving?"

"That's an easy one," she says, flashing that perfect lopsided smile of hers. "Leaving you."

And with that, she's gone, heading down the porch steps to

her car. The engine grumbles to life, and she sets off to get back to Edie's. I watch the blue Volvo until it fades from view, my head spinning as I slide down onto the cold pavement of the top step.

All I hear is her voice saying it over and over again.

Leaving you.

Leaving you.

Leaving you.

But all I want is to ask the same question I was scared to hear the answer to last night. The one I'm still scared to hear the answer to even now.

Then why did you?

CHAPTER 20

ARDEN

DAY 8

"Arden, what the hell are all these people doing here?"

I grin at Grams as we pull up to the diner the next morning. The sun isn't up yet, but the parking lot and the street around it are packed with cars, and a line of people braving the cold for some flapjacks spills down the sidewalk.

Well, not just for flapjacks. My post last night clearly did pretty well. I put up the photo of me looking at Caroline, her smiling at the camera, with the caption: *We're serving up pancakes from six to noon at Edie's Eatery in Barnwich, PA! Stop on by!* Then I ignored about a million calls and texts from Lillian, bitching about how it ruined my edgy Instagram aesthetic with all my professionally shot photos that look nothing like me. And I feel vindicated because it accumulated more likes than any post since my Teen Choice Award a little over a year ago.

Which honestly makes me wonder if I ever even needed to create my public persona in the first place. People seem to be loving just regular old Arden from Barnwich, and I've kinda been liking her too.

"Hey, guys! Thanks for coming out!" I say after rolling down the window of the Volvo, the crisp air stinging my eyes as I wave to the line. A few screams of excitement follow when people recognize me, and phone cameras start flashing in the dim light. I sit back as we whip around to the rear entrance, and Grams gives me a look when the window squeaks closed.

"What? It's just a little extra business."

"Mm-hmm. I shoulda known y'all were stirring something up when you were awake at five asking to come to work with me."

She parks the car, and we head in to see Tom, Harley, and Caroline peering through the serving window at everyone waiting outside. The place already smells like heaven, twenty carafes of coffee and a whole pile of bacon waiting and at the ready.

"This is gonna be something," Tom grunts.

"Yes, it is. Thanks to these two, I suspect," Grams says with a smirk, her eyes flicking between me and Caroline. The three of them turn around, but only Caroline meets my eyes. Her flushed cheeks made all the more obvious since her hair is pulled away from her face.

With only fifteen minutes until open, Edie goes into business mode, setting tasks for all of us to get things as ready as we can before we unlock the doors.

Tom starts on the pancakes, while Harley and I line up coffee mugs and plates. Halfway through there's a knock on the back door and Caroline pushes it open, letting in a gust of cold air along with Maya, Austin, Finn, and Taylor, who stumble inside, bleary-eyed.

"Moooorning," Austin says with a sleepy wave, while Finn gazes at the bacon longingly.

"Figured we could use a little extra help," Caroline says, and Grams nods gratefully as she furiously mixes up more batter.

"Y'all can grab some coffee. Harley will give you the rundown."

Harley hops up onto the bar, chewing a pink wad of gum noisily as she divides the group, giving everyone a task: from busing and dishwashing, to taking orders, to helping Tom back in the kitchen.

"One minute to open!" Grams calls out, eyes on the clock.

"Here," Caroline says, tossing me an apron from off the rack.

I tie it on and pull my hair into a ponytail, stomach churning slightly. I squeeze my eyes shut and take a deep breath, steadying myself as we head out to the front, where people are peering through the windows like I'm a rare exotic animal in an enclosure. Pointing and taking pictures and pounding on the glass to get me to look at them.

Oh.

What. Have. I. Done.

Suddenly I remember why I never talk to the public about this. About this diner and Edie and Caroline and my life before all the fame. It wasn't *just* to keep up some sort of bad-girl image. I did it because Barnwich was the one place that could always remain *mine.* Untouched by the world outside. Even by me. If I never came back, I couldn't ruin it like everything else.

But now I've invited them here, into a life that's starting to feel real and mine again, putting people I really care about under their microscope.

"You good?" Caroline asks, eyes studying my face curiously.

"Yeah. I'm fine . . . just a little nervous. Why?"

She shrugs. "I didn't think you got . . . you know, nervous. This was your idea. I just thought you were comfortable doing it."

"How could I possibly be comfortable with constantly being scrutinized by people who know nothing about me?" I ask, motioning to the crowd. Caroline cocks her head slightly, her eyes searching my face for something. "But I'm not going to sit back in the kitchen and hide. This is the life I chose . . . right?"

"When you were fourteen," she says.

"What's it matter now?" I huff out a pathetic laugh. "It's my life."

I tear my eyes away from hers and plaster a smile on my face. I wave and point at people with a wink, my muscle memory kicking in even as my feet still feel frozen to the floor.

Then Harley reaches out to turn the lock.

"Hold on to your asses," she calls out, and pulls open the door. Immediately, people pour in eagerly, running to stake claims to booths and stools, entirely ignoring poor Austin at the host stand, who was going to seat them.

Maya and Taylor come bustling out of the kitchen with coffees and waters, and suddenly it's a blur of taking orders and signing autographs and delivering pancakes and posing for pictures. Even when it threatens to overwhelm me, with each ding of the cash register and Grams's increasingly rosy cheeks as she hustles around the kitchen, I feel better about my decision again, more grateful.

"Can I get one of both of you?" a girl with braces asks as Caroline moves to slide past with two stacked plates.

"Oh, I don't—" I start to say at the same time Caroline starts talking.

"Sure," she says, readjusting the plates. My hand finds the

small of her back like a different muscle memory, goose bumps prickling up my arm.

But then, in a literal flash, she's gone as quickly as she came, heading to the very last booth to drop off the pancakes.

Tom rings the bell, and I head to the back to grab another order but run into Taylor by the serving window.

"Thanks for coming to help out today," I say.

"No problem. Always loved Edie's," she says, nodding. I'm about to head back out when she unexpectedly grabs ahold of my wrist. "Hey, Arden?"

She glances behind her to check that the coast is clear, that no one is close enough to hear her, before leaning forward.

"Listen, I know you guys are doing this whole *thing* for the article, but . . ." She pauses and lets out a long exhale as her gaze moves past me to where Caroline is across the diner. "I can tell Caroline has real feelings for you. So I want you to be aware, okay? Of how much you string her along before you up and disappear back to your real life and leave her here heartbroken. Especially when she has someone right here in Barnwich that wouldn't."

I open and close my mouth, trying to process her words. "Caroline doesn't . . . We're *barely* friends again. . . . She . . ."

She rolls her eyes and grabs a few mugs and a fresh carafe. "Arden. Be fucking for real."

I watch her go, then see Caroline heading over, scribbling on a guest check.

"How the hell can you have a sunny-side-up egg without the yolk?" she mutters as she tears out the page and slaps it onto the ticket rack. Finn immediately grabs it from the opposite side as I try to process what Taylor just said.

Caroline has feelings for me.

Caroline has feelings for me.

I search for a sign in her expression, her movement, but I don't see anything in the look she fixes me with as she scoops up three waters to bring over to a new table of customers and whispers, "Your fans are ridiculous."

I told her about my childhood crush yesterday thinking that if she ever felt anything for me, if she feels anything now, she'd say something, *anything*. As much as my heart wanted her to feel the same, though, there was a part of me that was relieved when she didn't. Because if she did, things would get incredibly complicated. I meant what I said when I answered her question yesterday. Leaving her behind was the hardest thing, next to leaving Edie, maybe. But leaving again knowing she has feelings for me would be almost impossible, and staying isn't an option. So, her not saying anything meant everything was simpler. The only hurt would be my own.

But if Taylor's right . . . If Caroline is feeling the same way about me as I'm feeling about her, then . . . we've got a prob—

"Hey," a voice says, and I whip my head over to see Finn, who now somehow is matching Tom in an identical bandana. "Your order is getting cold." He points at three plates of pancakes with his spatula.

"Right," I say, in a bit of a daze. "Sorry."

I smile and charm my way through the rest of the morning, which feels like the only thing I know how to do right now. I keep trying to make eye contact with Caroline, trying to find some answer to a silent question, but she's so busy she hardly looks my way.

She ends up finding me, though, a while later as I'm digging around in the storage closet for more straws.

"We'll swing by to pick you up at three for the Hanukkah party tomorrow," she says as she leans past me to pluck more napkins off the shelf I'm staring at. She notices my struggle and points to a box in the upper right-hand corner that is literally labeled STRAWS.

"Sounds good," I say as I reach up to grab it. When I look back down, I see she's already halfway out the door.

"Caroline," I blurt out before I can stop myself. She turns around, eyes wide, but the rest of what Taylor said stops me in my tracks.

Stringing her along.

Leaving.

I've kept her in my heart for so long, she probably has a permanent home there. Somewhere just above my right ventricle.

But *my* home isn't here. It hasn't been for a long time. I have a whole life a world away from here, where the role I've been working toward for what feels like years is waiting for me. It's something I've sacrificed literally *everything* for.

Even twelve amazing days can't erase that. And in six days . . . I'll be leaving.

"What should I wear?" I ask instead.

She shrugs. "Whatever. It's casual, not like a movie premiere or anything."

I nod as I follow her out of the storage closet and watch as she disappears around the corner, always just a little bit out of reach.

Always by my own doing.

I sigh and lean against the wall, surprised when Edie pops up in front of me.

"What's with the dilly-dallying?" she says as she taps the box of straws I'm holding. "Not used to working this hard? Used to the cushiness of Hollywood?"

I laugh and shake my head. "Hey, I do a lot of twelve-plus-hour days! No, it's . . ." I glance past her to see everyone preoccupied in the kitchen, Maya ferociously cleaning the dishes loud enough to drown out our conversation. "Taylor said Caroline has feelings for me."

I wait for Grams to react, but she just stands there staring at me like I just told her the grass is green.

"You knew?" I gasp, and she rolls her eyes.

"Arden. A rock on the damn sidewalk could tell that girl has feelings for you."

"What—for how long? When did you—"

She shrugs. "Always."

"Always?"

"Arden. Listen to me." She grabs my face in her worn hands, her dark eyes holding my own. "Don't play with that girl's heart, okay? Intentionally or not. I taught you better than that. Your actions have consequences. Leaving, staying. Here, there. Pretending is fine, but don't start something real if you're not sure you can finish it."

I think about this past week. It started with Caroline pushing me into a snowdrift and ended with us lying in her bed, holding hands. It took coming back here to understand the damage I did to her heart when I left four years ago. This whole time I thought we've been healing our friendship, but actually we've been growing something completely different. Something so much bigger and scarier. I had planned on keeping in touch when I leave this time. I was going to call often and visit any chance I could. But now . . . . I'm starting to remember the reason everything played out the way it did the first time. And maybe that *is* the only way to truly protect both of us. Because I can only imagine how she would feel if I let our relationship keep growing into something more serious this time.

I nod at Grams to show I understand, and she gives me a smooch on my forehead before nodding to the bustling diner. "Now get out there before we have to start reusing straws."

I plaster a smile on my face and get back to work, shutting down my feelings to showboat my way around the restaurant. The Arden James special.

Finally, as noon ticks closer, I clear my throat and hop up on the bar, calling out, "Hey, everyone!"

Heads turn and Grams appears from the back, smacking me with a menu to get me down. "What is it with you and standing on every damn bar in Barnwich?" she says, whacking me a second time in the kneecap. A few people laugh.

"This," I say, motioning down to her, undeterred, "is my grandma, Edie. She's run this diner here in Barnwich for the past *thirty-five years.*" There's a smattering of applause while Grams gives up on trying to get me to ground level in favor of ducking her head in embarrassment. "I can't tell you the number of times I was at a shoot or traveling overseas or at an awards show, and all I could think about was being right here, in one of these booths, eating my Grams's pancakes."

Grams cracks a smile at that, eyes teary as she looks up at me. And I realize I don't think I've ever told her that before. I wish I would've before now.

"Anyway, I just want to say that I am really grateful for all of you showing up today to help support this place and to help support my Grams. I know some of you traveled pretty far to be here today to see me." I flash a quick smile to a table of old ladies who loved *Operation Sparrow* and did a whole overnight road trip from Boston to meet me and are now making plans to enjoy Barnwich in all its Christmas glory. "But I hope you'll come back again and again for the pancakes. It really means everything to me." I motion to Grams. "Now, can we give it up for Edie?"

The room breaks out into cheers and applause, and with a boost from Finn that overcomes Grams fighting against me, I pull her up onto the bar. I throw an arm around her shoulder, and a guy with a camera at the end of the bar snaps a picture.

"Now, I won't be in Barnwich that much longer, but I hope you'll take good care of her when I'm gone," I say, eyes flicking over to meet Taylor's, something silently passing between us.

By the time I finally bring myself to look for Caroline, she's already disappeared into the kitchen.

It's just as well. Standing in the spotlight right now in front of all these people, all these cameras, reminds me of why I'm really here.

Grams and Taylor are right. I have to be realistic. I have a job that I love that I need to focus on. Or at least a job I could love this time.

Complete the article. Land the role. Make my life in LA worth it.

Stop wanting things I can't have.

CHAPTER 21

CAROLINE

DAY 9

"Stop bouncing your leg," Riley says as we drive down Main Street toward Edie's house to get Arden. Levi glances in the rearview mirror at me as Riley leans across the backseat, inspecting my face.

"What?"

"Are you nervous?"

"No."

I lightly push her back over to her side of the car, looking out the window at the crowded streets, a blur of wool scarves and hats and familiar black coffee cups from Barnwich Brews, the melancholy less biting as I watch them. They came for Arden but stuck around for Barnwich in all its holiday magic.

I'm not nervous. I'm . . .

Confused, maybe.

I guess that's a good word.

I think about Arden mentioning an old crush one minute, then standing on top of the bar at the diner the next, saying, *I won't be in Barnwich that much longer.* How Austin's hand wrapped around my arm in the kitchen as she did, Maya peeking out just behind him. How Arden left right after with only a quick wave of a goodbye and I typed a question in our text thread over and over, before finally asking her, What's your fondest memory of Edie's Eatery? instead.

Just when I started to wonder what it would be like to have her stick around, or if she might feel the same way, she confirmed she never will, closing that car door shut again.

I watch Cemetery Hill roll by, and then Levi's old Jeep slows as he turns onto Edie's street and into the driveway. Arden steps out the front door and my insides combust as she walks toward the car.

I feel Riley's hand press into my shoulder. "Get out. I want Arden to sit in the middle."

With a frustrated exhale, I push open the door and come face-to-face with Arden. "Hi," she says, and smiles at me, eyes crinkling at the corners. But something's different. She looks like the movie star she is again, *Arden James*, and it knocks me off-balance the tiniest bit.

"Riley wants you in the middle," I blurt out.

"Cool," she says as I look down to see she's wearing a brown leather bomber jacket. Is it . . . ? It is. The same one she wore in *Operation Sparrow*, patches and all.

"You're kidding me," I say, touching the American flag patch on the shoulder. "My grandma is going to pass out."

Arden glances down at it. "Oh yeah. I had my agent over-night it when you said she was a fan of the movie."

For the millionth time in my life, I resist the urge to either push her or kiss her.

This girl is such a walking contradiction. She'll say she's leaving and then do something meaningful and thoughtful like this. She'll say she had a huge crush on me but then leave and never keep in touch. It's beyond confusing.

"We're gonna be late!" Riley calls from inside, and Arden immediately slides past me into the middle seat.

I heave a sigh and wave at Edie before getting in myself.

Miles turns on some music, but Riley is already talking Arden's ear off. I try to distract myself from how close her knee is to mine, reminding myself, over and over, that she's leaving again. In four days our fake dates will be over. In five days she'll probably be gone.

We park on the street just outside my grandparents' house, my relatives' cars lining the curb, including my parents' Toyota. Grandma and Grandpa live just outside Pittsburgh, and the skyline is visible in the distance.

I love coming here for the Hanukkah party every year. I remember playing with my siblings and cousins in the backyard when I was a kid, snow coating the grass as we sledded down toward that skyline until the smell of latkes called us inside. Even though we don't really do that anymore, I still feel the same anticipation just being here. It's the good kind of nostalgic, unlike what I've felt driving through Barnwich the last few holiday seasons.

We hop out and walk along the hedges in single-file, Arden bringing up the rear. We're about to turn up the steep driveway when I glance back to see her chewing her lip, arms crossed over her chest.

I slow down, and the two of us fall into step.

"Are you good?" I ask. "You seem kinda quiet."

"Just hungry," she says, which I definitely understand. I can practically smell the latkes and brisket from here.

I just don't think it's the truth.

We keep walking anyway, speeding up to catch my siblings, who are already crossing over the threshold, my family's voices pouring out from inside.

"Hello!" my grandma calls, snow-white hair perfectly sprayed into place, a stark contrast to her black sweater and floral scarf. "How was the drive?"

"Good! No traffic," Miles says as she hugs him and then Riley, then beams at me.

"Caroline!" she says, smooching me on the cheek, leaving a lipstick stain, I'm sure. "How is the application to—"

She freezes, looking past me, eyes going wide.

"Arden James," she says.

"Thank you for inviting me today—"

"Oh, you're even prettier in person," my grandma says, squeezing Arden's face. "I just *loved* your movie *Operation Sparrow*. And—" Her eyes turn into two perfectly round circles. "Is that . . . the *jacket*?!"

"Do you want to try it on?" Arden asks, sliding it off.

"Oh! I couldn't possibly!" Grandma replies, but she's already got her arm through one of the sleeves.

"David! You have to come meet Caroline's girlfriend!" she calls to my grandpa.

"Grandma, she's not—"

She shushes me, turning right and left to inspect herself in the hallway mirror, while my grandpa lumbers over in a striped button-down.

"What's this now?" he says, wrapping an arm around my waist.

"Hi, Grandpa," I say, his thick beard scratching my face as he kisses my cheek. He reaches up, smiling warmly, to wipe my grandma's lipstick stain off.

"Someone take my picture!" my grandma says, clomping off to the living room, where a group of my aunts and uncles are lounging on the white couches, a few little cousins running around them, excited for presents later. My dad winks at me from an armchair, while my mom is in an animated conversation with her sister, their heads pressed closely together while they giggle away like she didn't read me the riot act two nights ago about the drinking. Riley trots over to them, getting in someone else's business for a change.

The rest of us head into the kitchen to get drinks. As we pad across the red terra-cotta tiles, I notice my cousin Hannah, a freshman at NYU, leaning against the wall next to her older brother, Ethan, both clutching plastic glasses of Coke.

"No way," Hannah says, immediately standing up straight. "Arden James?"

"Hey," Arden says with a small wave. Her usual charm, her way of making you feel like the only person in the room, is non-existent, an Arden I can't fully read taking her place. She's not even attempting the slapped-on bravado from the diner.

Something is off. Like she's already miles away, even though she's right here.

"Are you two *really* dating?" Hannah asks bluntly as Arden pours some soda into a glass at the antique minibar in the corner of the kitchen. Levi winks as he adds a splash of whiskey into it before Miles swipes the whole glass, muttering something to him about having gotten them in enough trouble with Mom over the two beers at the bar.

"How's college going?" I ask Hannah to deflect, pouring Arden a fresh drink.

"Oh," Ethan says, laughing. "So it's like that."

Arden doesn't laugh. She doesn't say anything. She just grabs her drink from me and avoids my gaze.

We talk about school and the bar and Ethan's cool new job as a travel writer as we pick at the appetizers on the wooden kitchen counter.

"You working on anything new?" Ethan asks Arden eventually, and she nods.

"I have a Netflix movie coming out this summer. And I just auditioned for a pretty cool role before I left LA."

"If the movie coming out this summer is *Operation Sparrow 2*, Grandma *will* have a heart attack," Hannah says, and everyone laughs in agreement.

"Is she still wearing—" Levi starts just as she bustles into the kitchen with her sisters Paula and Linda to slice the brisket and to fire up the stovetop for latkes, indeed still rocking Arden's jacket.

"You might not get that back," I say.

"You think she'll sleep in it?" Arden asks, and all of us nod as my grandma motions for us to help carry the food over. A few minutes later everyone else filters in as the smell of the fried potatoes drifts out to them.

"You hungry?" my mom asks as she puts an arm around Arden, who nods, eyeing the pan over my grandma's shoulder.

"Definitely."

We scoop up plates and utensils, Arden following just behind me. I roll my eyes when my grandma plops an extra latke onto her plate with a wink, and then we stop in front of the bowls of applesauce and sour cream. Arden looks back and forth between them.

"Applesauce," I say, adding a spoonful onto one of her latkes. "Trust me."

"She's lying to you," Riley says, putting sour cream on the other.

We grab seats in the living room and dig in. Arden lets out a low whistle after her first bite of brisket. "This is unreal."

"Right?" Miles says, his plate piled high with food. "I used to have her make it for me instead of birthday cakes."

Arden looks to me for confirmation, and I nod.

"It's true. Candles and all. Every year."

Arden narrows her eyes, looking between me and Miles. "You're lying."

We burst out laughing, and she shakes her head but grins, the first genuine smile I've seen from her all day. "You almost had me for a second."

"Arden," Levi says through a mouthful of food, "when are you going back to LA?"

"Uh." Her expression changes, the guard coming back up. She shrugs and takes another bite. "I don't know just yet. I think my agent wants me back the day after Christmas."

Five days.

I shift in my seat, ignoring the look Levi throws at me in favor of focusing on my carrots, cutting them into tinier and tinier pieces until the conversation moves on to when the next wave of snow is coming in, Arden's favorite places to eat in LA, and how annoying Hannah's roommate is.

As we finish and go to throw our plates out, Arden leans into me, my skin prickling as she whispers in my ear, "Applesauce was the right choice."

"I know," I reply.

At sunset, we all crowd into the kitchen, where my grandparents pull out their assortment of menorahs, all various shapes and sizes and styles, our celebration far from orthodox. Every family unit has one that fits their personality, from the more traditional gold tree-of-life menorah to the highly sought-after banorah (a menorah in the shape of a banana). And it changes from year to year, as kids get older, or babies are born, or Aunt Lauren elbows you out of the way for the beautiful green ceramic one.

"Arden! You have to light one!" my mom calls, and everyone scrambles to find her the right pick. While people hold up green dinosaurs and intricate pieces of pottery, debating over each option, I see her gaze land on a cute VW bus menorah I know Grandma probably snagged from a yard sale. She doesn't say anything, doesn't fight, though, when Ethan shoves a gold bird into her hands, making some comment about *Operation Sparrow* that apparently wins consensus.

But when everyone's attention shifts, I quickly grab the VW bus and slide it in front of her. Ethan's head turns, his mouth opening to protest, but I hold out the gold bird to him.

"You want to light it so bad, it's all yours."

He grins and shakes his head, turning his attention back to the prized mushroom menorah he's fought tooth and nail for ever since he was fifteen. Arden's fingers lightly graze mine, and I look up to see her flash me a grateful smile.

"How many are we lighting?" my uncle Jared asks as we pass around a box of candles. With Hanukkah not starting for a few more days, we don't exactly have a guidebook. We never do, except for coming together to celebrate every December.

"All of 'em," my grandpa says, and everyone cheers in agreement as he flicks out the lights.

I help Arden load up the VW bus, my family all around me, and as I do I can't help but feel . . . I don't know. Whole. *Proud.* I look at everyone and I feel the part of me that's been missing this holiday in Barnwich slot back into place.

And even though something isn't right with Arden, I'm still glad she's here to share this moment, one we've never had before. I'm glad that the article, our twelve holiday-filled days together, will include her lighting a menorah in my grandparents' kitchen. That it feels like whatever I write will now show more of Arden *and* more of me.

My thoughts are interrupted when my little cousin Danny gets pushed forward by his mom. "Danny! Tell the story of Hanukkah. He learned it in Hebrew school."

Danny looks absolutely mortified as he stumbles, beet-red, through a shaky retelling with some minor prodding from Aunt Lauren. Everyone claps when he's done, and his dad lifts him up onto a stool to light the candles as we say the blessings in Hebrew, then in English. I point to which candle Arden should take and the direction she should light them in. Arden's eyes widen as the entire countertop is ablaze with candlelight by the end.

And I watch her soften, whatever mask she's had on since we picked her up falling away as she looks on.

"You think the fire alarm is gonna go off?" Uncle Jared asks abruptly.

"Maybe," Aunt Lauren replies, eyeing the one in the corner.

My grandpa waves a hand. "The batteries died in there a year ago."

"Dad!" Uncle Jared and Mom say in unison, and in a flurry of movement, the moment is over. My mom digs batteries out of their junk drawer, and Aunt Lauren holds a kitchen chair while Uncle Jared climbs on top of it to get the fire alarm in working order.

Eventually we shuffle off to the living room again for presents. The younger kids sift through a pile, determined to find their names and identify Great-Aunt Paula's wrapping paper. She's famous for giving the best gifts.

I get a Barnes & Noble gift card from my grandparents and a hundred-dollar bill in a card from Great-Aunt Paula, who hands it to me with a wink. "Take your girl out somewhere special," she says, drifting off before I can protest.

Riley plucks the hundred out of my hand and holds it up to the light. "Yeah, Caroline," she says, giving me a mischievous grin. "Take 'your girl' out somewhere special."

I swipe it back from her with a glare, and she trots off to get her own gift.

But maybe I will. I only have *five days* left with Arden.

And, even scarier than that, it feels like a part of her is already slipping away.

"Fine. Tomorrow," I blurt out, turning around to face Arden.

"Tomorrow what?"

"*I'll* plan what we do tomorrow," I say, waving the money before I pocket it. "I mean, I'm sure I can do better than stealing a Christmas tree."

Arden laughs before nodding. "Okay."

CHAPTER 22

ARDEN

DAY 9–10

"I think you maybe gave my grandma the best Hanukkah gift of her life," Caroline says as we clomp out to the Jeep after the party. I rub at my arms, the cold biting without my jacket, which is now permanently in the possession of Caroline's grandma.

"Needed some space in my suitcase anyway, with all the food Grams is going to try to send me home with."

We get to the car, and Caroline motions for me to go in before her.

"You do know sitting in the middle seat with long legs is really—"

She pushes me forward and I tumble inside, laughing despite my mood.

We drive in silence other than the steady hum of the radio. I'm assuming everyone must just be in a food coma, but when I cast a quick glance over at Caroline, I see her brow is furrowed.

"Hey, guys," she says, leaning forward, a wave of her floral shampoo washing over me while Levi turns down the music.

"Do you ever think about doing something . . . I don't know . . . Hanukkah-related in Barnwich?"

Miles shrugs, but Levi nods. So does Riley. "I mean, I know the place is practically run on Santa's *ho ho ho*, but it's always glaring to me every holiday season, and especially after the Hanukkah party, that something's missing," Levi says.

"What if we did like a first night of Hanukkah event at the bar?" Caroline says. "We could light the menorah, and—"

"On *Christmas?*" Miles asks, turning in his seat to face her. "Nobody would come."

"We're not the only Jewish people in Barnwich," Levi says, giving him a quick look.

"And besides, nobody does anything the *night* of Christmas, Miles," Riley chimes in from next to me. "Everyone just opens presents and eats food, and there's nothing to do in Barnwich because everything's closed."

Miles considers this, nodding.

"It could be fun. Maybe Barnwich needs some new traditions," I say, and Caroline turns her head to look at me. "I mean, worst-case scenario, it's just us hanging out together."

"If you plan it, you can do it in the bar," Miles says finally.

"Deal." Caroline grins at him as she sits back in her seat.

"I'll help," I announce. Caroline lets her head fall to the side to look at me.

"It'll be your last night here," she whispers, reminding me of what I already know, but I nod anyway. We keep looking at each other until she pulls out her phone. Her face glows as she types something, then holds the phone out to me. Today's question.

The role in this movie, Hollywood, LA, being an actress . . . Does it still make you happy?

I chew my lip as I look out at the road in front of us, glowing in the headlights of Levi's Jeep.

My immediate answer should be *Yes! Of course!* I mean, it's the entire point of this article. And when I look at it from the outside, it still seems like the best job in the world. I get to basically play for a living, and I get paid insane money to do it.

But I'm not sure it's the truth.

I just spent the whole party watching Caroline be surrounded by her family, a core group of people who love her, who will *always* love her. I think maybe that's something I've been missing in my life. It's something I haven't been able to find in LA, and that's why I let all the other stuff consume me. To try to fill the hole I carved out of my heart when I left.

So when I take her phone, I write, Parts of it.

My thoughts start to run a bit wild and my thumbs tap away.

I like the challenge of becoming someone I'm not for a few months and that sometimes pieces of a character stick to me long after I'm done shooting. I love being able to dig deep into myself and pull out the kind of emotions that I rarely let myself feel in my real life. It gives me an outlet to release some of the pain I felt when I left home and when my parents left me.

But I'm realizing acting can't fill the hole left behind, not totally.

For a while it's felt like I'm doing something wrong, over and over again. Like something is missing even though I wouldn't want to do anything else, but I couldn't stop the train long enough to figure out what and get it on the right track. So most days I haven't been happy.

And yeah I think this role in Bianchi's movie would be a good start. A launchpad to turn my career in the direction I always wanted it to go and make acting more fulfilling.

But being back in Barnwich is showing me that what's actually been missing this whole time isn't on a set or a screen. It's being in the place where every corner holds a memory, where I left my childhood, the town that I love, with the person that I . . .

I stop when her head droops onto my shoulder.

I look down to see that she's fast asleep, eyelashes casting shadows on her cheeks, red lips slightly parted.

I watch her for a long moment, my heart beating steadily because being so close to her is starting to feel scarily comfortable. I could finish typing that last word and leave it for her to find. Tell her the truth. Tell her how I feel, not just how I felt. I could change everything.

But then I remember how far away I'll be in just a few days, and Edie's warning I've been trying to keep in mind all night.

I remember what Taylor said about Caroline being able to live a normal life out of the spotlight with a normal girlfriend who would actually be here.

I have feelings for Caroline and she might have feelings for me, but . . . I'm not the right person for her. My life, despite this brief break from my reality, is still a mess. And I'm not about to drag her into it. I'm not about to make a mess of her life too.

Don't complicate things, Arden.

I delete the last few sentences and tap the side button, letting the screen go black.

Then I just sit in the dark while she sleeps, trying to figure out how to balance the rest of my time here. I know I can't let her get too close. I shouldn't have even offered to be a part of the Hanukkah party at the bar, but . . . it feels impossible when every fiber of my being so badly wants to just soak up every second I can with her.

I wake up the next morning to a FaceTime from Lillian. My thumb blindly swipes across my phone screen until I hear her voice. "Arden? Hellooo?" I push myself up on my elbow, the bed in Grams's guest room squeaking underneath me.

"Lillian," I say as I squint at the phone. "It's only six *here*. Do you ever sleep?"

"Power naps and espresso, baby," she says, taking a sip from a coffee cup for good measure. "Arden . . . I've got some great news for you."

"You're going to hang up so I can get some more sleep?"

She gives me a look. "Better. Bianchi saw you and Caroline's pancake-serving thing at your grandmother's diner. I mean, hell, just about everyone saw it."

Lillian sent me a ton of articles yesterday before the Hanukkah party, pictures of me and Caroline, me and Grams on the diner's counter, me with a few fans. Funny that once it was a success, she immediately changed her tune.

"Anyway, he wants to invite you *and* Caroline to his annual Christmas Eve party here in LA."

I sit bolt upright.

"What?"

"I'd be shocked if he doesn't give you the role by New Year's. This whole small-town-girl bit was the best fucking thing you could've done for your career," she says, and I immediately bristle.

"Lillian, it's not a bit. I *am* a small-town girl. Or at least I *was* before . . ." I sit up in bed, frustrated. "Why are you making it sound like I never needed to take on this whole party-girl persona in the first place, when you're the one who told me that was the only way I'd get noticed?"

"Does it even matter now? Everything we've done has led us here. We're going to make so much fucking money."

"Who cares about the money? How many millions have I already made you?" I raise my voice as I throw the covers off, then hop out of bed. "I lost almost everyone I've ever cared about, not to mention myself because of your advice. I couldn't just *pretend* to be someone like that. I had to become it, and then you had the audacity to judge me for it, all while dragging your feet on helping me fix it. If Bianchi hadn't said what he did, you'd never have agreed to this."

"Arden, I don't know what you're complaining about. You were basically begging for me to make you a star, and I *did*."

"I was *fourteen* when I signed with you! I was just a kid. I'm *barely* an adult now!" I move to the window and curl my fingers around the frame. "Do you know what people my age do around here? They eat hot dogs at basketball games and go sledding and enter hot chocolate contests."

"Arden—"

"I was fifteen the first time you got me invited into private clubs to party with people twice my age. I mean . . . what the fuck, Lillian?" I ask, my blood boiling, but she just lets out a long sigh on the other end of the line.

"What do you want me to say, Arden? I'm sorry you didn't get to grow up eating your grandma's pancakes and became incredibly famous and rich instead. But this time you need to hear it. I am not your mother. Nobody wanted *that* job. I nurtured your career, which was *my* job. And now you're going to do yours. I'll forward you the invite," she says, and then I hear the click of her hanging up on me.

I throw my phone onto the bed, feeling like I've been slapped, and then lay my forehead against the cold glass of the fogged-up window. I think of everyone it would leave high and dry if Caroline and I go to this party. Riley, and Levi, and Miles, and Caroline's parents, and Grams, who's downstairs right now.

But despite how angry I am at Lillian and how much I don't even want to go right now, I know I have to at least show up if I want this role. I have to show Bianchi that he takes priority, because he does. . . . He has to. For me at least.

So I'll ask Caroline to go, but I won't push her into it.

I groan and pull the covers back over me, but I can't go back to sleep. I just stare at the ceiling fan, listening to Grams rustling away in the kitchen downstairs and thinking about how much I don't want to get on a plane to LA in four days, let alone two. How much I don't want to leave my grandma again. Leave Barnwich again.

"You're late!" Caroline calls out to me the following afternoon, leaning against the wall of Barnwich Brews, looking especially pretty in a pair of faded blue jeans and a cozy winter coat, her long hair lightly curled.

"That must be the first time you've ever said that to anyone," I say, and she responds by tugging my beanie down over my eyes.

I pull it back up, tilting my head to look at the now-familiar coffee shop. "Wow. *Very* exciting destination. *This* is what you have planned? Are we stopping another scandal?"

"No," Caroline says, grabbing my hand and pulling me inside. "This is the *start* of what I have planned. We're just here for a warm drink. My treat, obviously."

I grab a table while she orders two of Austin's winning hot chocolates. I plop down in the booth and watch her at the counter. She peels off her big winter coat to reveal a skintight turtleneck underneath that accentuates all the parts of her that have uh . . . changed.

When I see her start to turn toward me, I force my eyes down, pretending like I see something incredibly interesting on the floor.

"You good?" she asks, giving me a weird look as she sets our drinks on the table and looks around on the floor for whatever I'm looking at.

"Yeah. They, um . . . installed some new tile after I left, huh?" I ask, finally looking up at her face, hoping she can't see how red mine is.

Smooth, Arden.

She shrugs and laughs it off, digging around in her back pocket for something.

"Here." She slides a little homemade paper book across the table to me. "I read the answer to my question that you left on my phone last night about feeling something missing. So I want to give you something to hold in that empty space when you leave." She sips her drink while I inspect it.

It's a Barnwich passport that she's made using stapled-together printer paper and colored pencils. As I go to flip through it, she reaches her hand out and clamps it over mine.

"Wait! We're supposed to do it one page at a time. So each destination is a surprise."

I nod and she slowly releases her grip, letting me open up to page one.

"'Hot chocolates just like the old days.'" I squint, looking up at her. "I thought you said it was supposed to be a surprise. We're already here with our hot chocolates."

I watch as she fishes around in her coat pocket.

"Surprise," she says with a smile as she takes out two giant marshmallows from a bag and plops one into each drink.

"Oh my God. I forgot!" I shake my head, laughing. We used to bring our own giant marshmallows with us when we were kids, because we both always hated the mini ones.

"Okay, flip to the next one," she says, pointing to the little book that holds our destiny tonight.

I do as she says and read the next page.

"You're kidding me," I say, shutting the book. "We're writing letters to Santa, Caroline? What are we, ten?"

"We used to be," she replies, slipping back into her coat as she stands up from her chair and then picks up her drink. "Come on. It'll be fun."

After a big sigh, I grab my hot chocolate too and follow her toward the door. She makes a stop by the bulletin board and pulls a bright blue flyer out of her pocket, an invitation to the Hanukkah party at the bar.

"We're also going to hang these up where we can along our route," she tells me as she pins it up there. Then we step out into the cold.

"You're not going to ask Santa for a plate of spaghetti and

meatballs with two pieces of garlic bread, are you?" I joke as I take a few long strides to catch up with her on the sidewalk.

She bumps her shoulder into mine.

"You ask Santa for something to eat *one* time when you're seven and you never live it down."

"He did deliver, though, didn't he?"

"Woke up to an Olive Garden gift card in my stocking. We went the next day. Remember?" she asks.

"I remember," I reply. "Pretty sure we got our twenty-five dollars' worth in breadsticks alone."

We make our way through the crowded streets, people far too busy looking at the lights and the shop windows to pay any attention to me tonight. We ascend the steps to the post office, a small historic building with a mailbox labeled NORTH POLE sitting out front. Caroline hands me a pen and paper from her apparently bottomless coat pocket, but then I just stand there frozen, with pen to paper.

My list when I was a kid used to cover the front *and* back. Now I can buy just about anything I want. I try to use my height to peek over Caroline's shoulder at her list in progress, but she catches me in the act.

"Hey. No peeking!" she yells, and shields her paper from me.

You're cute, I want to tell her, but instead I swallow it and settle for staring at my blank sheet. There's only one thing I could write down. One thing I can't buy. The one thing I want but can never have.

Caroline.

"Okay, ready?" she asks, looking up at me as she folds up her paper. I stare at her name scrawled across my paper, then quickly fold it up before she can see it.

"Uh, yeah," I reply, plastering a smile on my face. She holds out her hand, takes my paper, and then drops them both into the mailbox.

"What did you write?" she asks as we walk back down the steps to the street together.

"That's between me and Santa," I reply.

Our next stop is the used bookstore at the corner of Main and Maple. Bells ring above us as we enter, and Mrs. Graham, a regular at the diner, waves hello from underneath an absolute blizzard of paper snowflakes that hang from the ceiling.

We walk past a table of books of all sizes. Each is wrapped in red-and-green paper, with a brown tag giving a very short, mysterious description. A sign above the table reads COZY CHRISTMAS BOOK DATE.

"Remember when we used to come here like every Wednesday when my mom would pick us up from school?" Caroline asks as we meander up and down the narrow aisles. Her fingers drag along the different-colored spines, and I have to resist the urge to reach out and hold them in my own. Just like the night in her room. No one watching, just for me and Caroline.

"Yeah. You'd always, without fail, find a new book to buy even though you hadn't read the last one," I reply.

"And you'd flip through that same cookbook every time. What was it?" she asks, crouching down to scan through the one shelf full of them.

"I don't remember," I reply, even though my eyes immediately picked it out of the lineup the second she mentioned it.

"This one!" She slides it out, the cover showing a familiar

middle-aged woman with blond hair and overalls.

"Oh, yeah. Maybe that's it," I say, turning away.

"Arden James!" Caroline grabs my jacket and pulls me to face her. "Are you blushing?!"

"What? No!"

Her eyes go wide and her jaw drops open as she looks at the book, then back at me a few times. "You totally had a crush on her! Didn't you?" she prods, and with that I finally crack a smile, and she smacks me playfully in the stomach.

"Yeah. She *might've* been my gay awakening. So what?" I joke, stealing the book out of her hands.

"And here I thought I was," she says. Saliva catches in my throat and sends me into a coughing fit, my face no doubt turning even redder. "I'm kidding, Arden. I mean, come on, smoking hot *and* she can cook? I never stood a chance," she says, then turns and heads for the front of the store again, while I force out a natural-sounding laugh.

She stops at the bulletin board by the front door and pulls another flyer out of her pocket.

There's only one open spot, though, and it's at the very top. I watch her jump for it once before stepping up behind her and taking the thumbtack and paper from her.

I reach over her and pin it up there, and then she turns around to face me. I watch her swallow hard as we both pause there for a moment, not a lot of room between us and the wall.

"Come on. There's more Barnwich to see tonight," she says finally, giving a quick tug on my jacket, and I follow her back out to the street.

A few minutes later, with candy canes dangling out of our mouths from the candy store across the way, we pass by the giant tree in the center of the square that a committee is getting set up for the big tree lighting tomorrow night.

"What's next?" Caroline asks, as if she doesn't know. I take out my passport and flip to the next page, where there's a tiny drawing of Santa sitting on a big chair, a beer bottle in his cup holder. I look up, following her gaze to the gazebo to the left, where Santa-fied Mr. Green is sitting on his elaborate red throne, being blasted by a space heater, a line of people waiting to see him.

"Oh, hell no," I say, but she ignores this as she drags me to the end of the line. I shuffle from foot to foot on the red carpet underneath us, shivering in the open air.

When Caroline scooches closer to me for warmth, though, suddenly I find myself wishing the wait was even longer. I should use the time to bring up Bianchi's Christmas party, but how can I when Caroline is literally giving me the Best of Barnwich Tour tonight? I know she said she's doing this because of my answer last night, but I can't help but wonder if the countdown has been on her mind too. If she's showing me all of this as a reason to stay.

If only it were that simple.

Too soon, we're in front of the big man himself.

"Arden! Sweet Caroline!" Mr. Green says with a grin and a forced jolly voice as an assistant teenage elf, looking like he would rather be run over by a sleigh than spend another hour wearing a pair of pointy ears, motions us forward.

"*Santa,*" I say, returning the grin and leaning forward. "How's it going?"

"I need a damn drink," he whispers before plastering a cheery smile back on his face and calling out a "Ho-ho-ho!"

We lean against the throne, letting a second elf with far more enthusiasm snap a few pictures before Caroline pays an obscene amount of money for two four-by-sixes.

"I got it," she says for the tenth time today as she nudges me away and hands over a couple of bills, change from the hundred dollars she got last night.

"You know I don't mind paying—"

She waves me away. "What would my great-aunt Paula say?"

I laugh, an eyebrow ticking up. "So does that mean I'm your girl?" I ask before I can stop myself.

"Yeah," Caroline says with a shrug as we cross the road. "I mean, for the next four days, right?"

I feel a physical pain in my chest at that. If it's such a bad, impossible idea, why do I still want to be hers so badly?

But then I glance down at Caroline's phone and see that she's texting Taylor, and I push all my feelings down even deeper and lock them in the familiar box, where they have to stay.

We stop by the bar next, taking a small detour from the passport. The place is quiet, since it's still early in the evening, and we find Levi cleaning glasses behind the bar.

"Here to get me in trouble with Mom again?" he asks with a grin.

"No. Here to go pee," Caroline says as she shuffles off to the bathroom.

I plunk down on a barstool and slide a ten across the bar to him. "For Mr. Green. On me."

He shakes his head and pops it into the cash register. "Poor guy is a hell of a lot stronger than me. I couldn't sit out there freezing my ass off for a whole month, pretending I'm thrilled about it."

I pull out another ten, sliding it across while Levi laughs.

"So . . . how are things going with my sister?" he asks.

"Good, I guess." I shrug. "I mean, it's been like ten days since she last pushed me into a snowdrift, so . . ." I laugh, but Levi doesn't. Instead he looks over his shoulder to make sure Caroline is still in the bathroom.

"You're not just going to disappear again, are you?" he asks, leaning across the bar.

It would be so easy to lie, to shake my head and tell him that I would never, but when I open my mouth, I just . . . can't. "I don't know, Levi. I don't *want* to," I finally say, the truth.

"Then *don't.*"

"It's not that simple."

"Arden, that's my little sister. I love her." He lowers his head, giving me a look that only a protective big brother could give. "Don't hurt her again."

I'm unable to reply, though, because Caroline is coming back around the corner.

"Ready to get going?" she asks, popping up beside me as I swallow the lump in my throat.

"Where are you off to?" Miles asks as he appears from the back, wielding an enormous box.

"Taking a little tour of Barnwich," she says. "Still got a couple more stops to go."

"Isn't it so nice and warm in here—" I start to say, but Caroline pulls me off the barstool and toward the door. I wave goodbye to Miles and Levi, and we head out of the bar and down the street.

Our next stop according to the passport is the *very* crowded toy store where we spent our allowance hundreds of times as kids. As soon as we step through the door, I spot a giant collection box for the local children's hospital and pull Caroline over to it.

"Hey, I've got an idea. You buy something for me and I'll buy something for you and we'll donate them both?" I ask.

"That's . . . much better than what I had planned. Meet back here in two minutes."

I scan around, and at first nothing jumps out at me. But then on the bottom shelf I see the Statue of Liberty Lego set. It costs more than anyone should ever pay for Legos, but is it Christmas if you're not spending frivolously for the people you love?

It's perfect.

I lug it through the crowd to the checkout and then over to the donation box, where Caroline is already shaking her head at me.

"For when you get into Columbia." I heave it up and over the edge of the box and drop it in.

"Those kids are going to be brawling it out for that, you know," she says, making me laugh. Then, from behind her back, she pulls out the cutest little black stuffed-animal dog that looks just like my boy, Neil. "To keep you company on the nights you can't sleep."

"Thank you," I tell her as I take it, part of me kind of wishing that I *could* keep it. I pause for a second to remember its tiny little face before I place it gently into the bin with the rest of the toys.

"If you don't give that monster truck to me right now, Susan . . . I *swear to God* . . ." A woman's voice carries through the entire store. I look over just like everyone else to see her hand wrapped around Susan's shirt, crinkling her perfectly starched white collar.

"Susan looks like she's about to put the beatdown on her," I tell Caroline, who is standing on her tippy-toes to try to get a view, but it's no use.

"Should we get out of here before they call the cops?" she asks, holding her hand out for me, and despite my better judgment, I take it, following my heart instead of my head just this once.

I nod and let her pull me through the crowd and out the door.

Next on our passport is the neighboring drugstore, where we used to get our snacks. Caroline smirks as we pass the magazines, pointing to one with my face plastered on it. I shake my head at her and flip it over as she buys a pack of Cotton Candy Bubble Yum, our favorite, on the way out.

"Where to next?" I ask, flipping to the last page of the passport, but . . . it's blank.

"Let's just walk," she replies.

We stick to the edge of Main Street and hang a left at the bank, heading down a side street, dimly lit compared to the main drag.

"What do you and Edie have planned for Christmas?" she asks.

"Oh, umm." *Shit.* Here we go, I guess. "Actually, we won't be spending it together this year anymore. Bianchi invited me to his Christmas Eve party back in LA," I finally tell her, looking down at my feet.

"Christmas Eve?" she asks, already looking disappointed. For

her, spending time with the people she loves tops everything. I know the Becketts have their annual ugly sweater party that night. They each draw a name at the start of the month and buy a sweater for another family member. It's their tradition, so I can't believe I'm even bringing this up, but . . .

"He invited *us*, actually. But trust me, Caroline. You don't have to go." I let out a long exhale, meeting her eyes. Mentioning Christmas and Bianchi to Caroline in the same sentence feels almost wrong, like the two should never mix. Oil and water. "I've already asked way too much of you with this article and forcing you into this fake dating thing. I'd hate to take you away from your fam—"

"I'll go," she says.

"Are you sure?" I ask. "You really don't have—"

She waves her hand like it's no big deal, like she's not completely devastated by the fact that we won't be spending the holidays here. "It'll be fun. I mean, who says no to a free trip to LA? Besides, we can't end this article without a Christmas Eve date. And Bianchi certainly won't buy it without me being there. We might as well end things the right way."

End things.

My heart sinks.

I watch our feet hit the sidewalk, falling into sync as the clean concrete squares of town turn into darker, uneven slabs with cracks running through them.

Then Caroline stops and turns. My eyes fall on a small white house. Its vinyl siding is falling off, and one of the windows is covered with plywood, but I recognize it, and the sight makes my heart stop for a second.

My house.

This is one stop on memory lane I want to forget. It's too much.

"Caroline, I don't want to be here," I say, immediately turning in the other direction.

"Wait. Arden, just wait." She grabs me by the arm and tries to spin me around to face her, but I tear myself from her grip and do exactly what Levi told me not to. I start down the sidewalk, back toward town, and leave her.

CHAPTER 23

CAROLINE

DAY 10

"Arden, don't leave me on this fucking sidewalk again!" I call after her, my voice crumbling despite my attempt to steady it.

She skids to a stop when I say that, waiting a beat before whirling around and walking back toward me. "Why did you bring us here? What was the point of this whole night, Caroline?"

"What do you mean?"

She takes another step closer, until her face is lit up by the streetlight buzzing above us. "This whole journey down memory lane, the letters to Santa, the bookstore, the marshmallows at the coffee shop. All the places we used to go together."

"Because we needed something to do for the article." I feel a stir of anger deep in the pit of my stomach as she tilts her head to the side.

"Was it to get me to stay? Or are you still trying to punish me for leaving?"

I cross my arms over my chest and stare her dead in the eyes, even though mine begin to sting with tears. "No, Arden. I'm not trying to punish you for leaving. It's me trying to say goodbye to *you* this time, since you don't seem capable of it. You've been pulling away and you haven't even left yet. We both know part of you is already on that plane back to LA."

She grabs my arm, shaking her head. "Caroline, I'm pulling away *because* I'm leaving."

I rip my arm out of her grasp. "Which makes sense. You've gotten just about everything you wanted out of me and Barnwich," I say, my voice cracking. "And it kills me, Arden, that this was enough for you, because I don't think I could *ever* get enough of you."

She freezes, dark eyes studying my face, snow starting to fall between us.

"That's not true," she whispers, her voice quivering as she reaches out to try to hold me together, but I push her away.

"Then why didn't you come back?" The question I've been waiting four years for an answer to finally spills out of me.

"Because I never would've been able to leave again!" she shouts, running her fingers through her hair in frustration. "I never would've been able to leave *you* again."

I stare at her and she looks away, swallowing, but then she continues. "Did you know that first Christmas I had the ticket booked and everything? My parents were happy to have me out of their hair and back with Edie for a week, and I went the whole way to the airport. To the gate. But I just sat there, watching the plane board, watching it leave. I stayed there for hours, Caroline. *Hours.* Thinking of you and Barnwich and *home*. And I realized it was easier to just . . . never come back."

"How was it easier?"

"The first six months there were *so* hard for me. I got a taste of how cruel that industry can be, even though I was a kid. So when my agent told me that cutting ties with everyone back here was the only way to keep me focused on my career long enough to see it take off, it seemed like she must be right. I knew if I came back and told you what was happening, you and Edie would tell me to come home, and then I'd never see it through. I'd take one look at your faces and stay. I thought once it did take off, though, I could fix it, but then when I booked my first Netflix rom-com, things took off so quickly that I just . . . I lost control of everything. My parents were nowhere to be found, and pretty soon *I* was nowhere to be found. What started out as this pretend curated image of 'Arden James' became *real*. I became the fucking illusion, Caroline. Waking up in strangers' beds, cocaine in every bathroom between Pasadena and Malibu, entire nights I couldn't even remember. And when that happened . . . I knew I couldn't set foot in Barnwich again." She wipes at her eyes with the back of her hand. "I couldn't bring myself to come home because I was too big of a fucking mess to fix."

She huffs out a laugh, but I can see tears clinging to her eyes too.

"And now there's not a single person on this planet who would look at me and not see 'Arden James.'"

"That's not true," I say.

There is someone.

I've always just seen Arden. Skinned-knee, lopsided-smile, small-scar-on-her-chin Arden.

First-best-friend, first-love, first-heartbreak Arden.

Even when she's *Arden James*, I see traces of her. I see it when she's on-screen, chasing down a bad guy like we used to run through the streets of Barnwich. I see it when she's on the red carpet, the charm in every interview like we're in fifth grade and she's trying to convince Mr. Reynolds not to give us homework. I see it when Riley shows me a photo of her stumbling out of some club, familiar eyes hiding something close to pain, close to fear, that only I could see, even when I didn't want to let myself.

She's *Arden James* because she is still Arden at heart, not because of what anyone else tried to make her into.

She looks at me, *really* looks at me for what feels like the first time in days. I step forward, closing the gap between us. My hands slide up the fabric of her jacket to the skin of her neck, until my thumbs gently stroke her cheeks. "I see you."

She leans into them. "Caroline, I . . . *I can't.* You deserve *normal.* Prom and holding hands in between classes and cute coffee shop dates. I mean, you've seen these last two weeks what it's like. My life is *anything* but normal. And it's three thousand miles away. I can't ask you—"

But I'm not asking. Not waiting another second. Instead, I give her an answer of my own as I pull her face down to meet mine. Our lips crash together, her nose cold as it brushes against my skin, and all the years of wanting, and hoping, and longing pour out of me as my fingers tangle in her hair.

It feels like pancakes at Edie's and the warm glow of the menorah at my family's Hanukkah party. Like when a sled picks up speed and your stomach jumps into your throat. Like the first snow beginning to fall outside your window or finding the perfect gift for someone you love. It feels like all of it, every good and magical thing about this season and this place we grew up in, made better. Kissing Arden is the most magical thing of all.

There's a part of me that has been stuck to this sidewalk since she left, waiting for her to come home. Waiting for her to come back to me. And even though she's been here over a week, only now does it feel like she really has come back.

When she finally pulls away, I only let her go far enough that I can focus on her brown eyes looking down at me. Wild. Scared. She opens her mouth, but all that comes out is a swirl of her warm breath in the cold air.

I hold her face in my hands again and look at her like I've always wanted to look at her.

"I want *you*, Arden. That's all I've ever wanted. Can't you see that?"

I love you, I want to say. *I have always loved you.*

But I stop just short as she stares at me, still not saying anything. I'm not sure she could if she tried, but when she pulls me into a hug, it's a hug that tells me everything. I melt into her as snow falls all around us.

"I thought you said no kissing," she mumbles into my hair finally.

"I thought you liked to break the rules," I say back, and she laughs as I turn and kiss her again for good measure.

CHAPTER 24

ARDEN

DAY 10

After dropping Caroline off at her house, I practically float back to Grams's. There is something about dropping a girl off at her house at the end of a date instead of bringing her home to mine that feels somehow more intimate. Especially when that girl is Caroline Beckett. There's a lightness to my entire body that I have never felt before in my life even though I'm full of the anticipation of seeing her again. Of kissing her again. Of growing whatever *this* is into something bigger.

I close Grams's front door and lean back against it, thinking about the way Caroline's fingers felt tangled up in my hair, her body under my hands, her thin turtleneck still feeling too thick between us.

It makes me wonder why I ever spent any time kissing anyone else.

It makes me wonder if I want to kiss anyone else ever again.

"Arden, is that you?" Grams calls from the dark living room.

I shed my winter layer before making my way around the corner to find her sitting alone on the couch with her feet kicked up on the coffee table. An old Julia Roberts movie flashes across the TV.

"You're still up?" I ask, flicking on a lamp before plopping down next to her, jostling a half-full bowl of popcorn I didn't know was there.

"Ah, I got sucked into this damn movie."

"You've never seen *Pretty Woman*?"

Grams turns her head to throw me a deadpan look. "Of course I've seen *Pretty Woman*! But a beautiful face like that on my television screen, how can I turn it off?"

"You've got the hots for Julia Roberts, too?" I ask with a smirk, knowing she was referring to Richard Gere.

She laughs and shakes her head at me, passing over the bowl of slightly black popcorn.

"You're the only person I've ever met who likes burnt popcorn," I tell her, popping a few pieces into my mouth anyway.

She doesn't say anything for a beat. When she does, her eyes look glassy. "Well, this is about the end of your trip, huh, kiddo?" she asks.

"Yeah. I guess so," I reply, and the butterflies that have been fluttering around in my stomach since my kiss with Caroline all fall dead. "Grams, I'm sorry I won't be here for Christmas. It's not how I wanted all this to end," I tell her again, just like I did this morning.

She moves the bowl of popcorn onto the floor and pats the empty couch cushion between us. "Now, I don't want to hear one more apology out of you. Let's just enjoy whatever time we have left together." I smile at her, even though I don't feel like it right now, and scooch under her extended arm. "Me, you, and Julia," she adds, making me laugh as she pulls me in close.

We watch the rest of the movie like that, but by the time the credits roll, Grams is fast asleep beside me. I slip out from underneath her arm and gently guide her feet onto the couch until she's lying down. Then I drape a blanket over her before I head up to my room.

I plunk down on the bed and pull my phone out to text Caroline good night, but I find a text from Lillian waiting for me.

Hey. I'm sorry about what I said earlier. I was just . . . stressed. I just want this all to work out for you, kid. I love ya. And I'm really looking forward to meeting the famous Caroline.

I take a deep breath, and when I let it out, I try to let go of any leftover animosity I feel toward her.

We'll both be at the party. See you soon, Lil, I send in reply.

I lie back on my bed and close my eyes, picturing me and Caroline *together* in LA. Drinking coffee in my kitchen in the mornings and walking the beach holding hands at night. I guess we'd be long distance for a bit before that, though, with her still having half a year of high school left, and if that's going to work, I'm going to have to take charge of my life. I'm going to have to make some changes. But I'll figure it out, because I want to make this work.

And the Christmas party at Bianchi's?

It'll be the perfect trial for us.

CHAPTER 25

CAROLINE

DAY 11

The next evening, I bundle up caroling-style for the Christmas tree lighting, buzzing with excitement at the thought of seeing Arden again.

"You seem happy," Riley says, eyeing me from the stairs, munching away on a bag of Flavor-Blasted Goldfish. "Too happy."

I give her a look while I wrap a scarf around my neck. "What's that mean?"

She chucks another handful into her mouth, still calculating. I try to ignore her, but she's chewing louder than a cow. "Oh my God." She jumps up, bits of Goldfish flying from her mouth. "You kissed Arden."

"What?! No, I—"

"You totally did! You kissed Arden!"

I grab the bag of Goldfish from her hand and bolt down the hall. I don't even make it halfway to the kitchen, though, before she grabs my arm and wrestles me to the ground. Then she sits down on top of me as I twist and turn, trying to wriggle out from under her.

"Jesus Christ," I grunt. "What are they teaching you at soccer? Jujitsu?"

"Tell me the truth and I'll get off."

"I'm not going to—"

"Caroline—"

"Fine! We kissed!"

She smirks and releases me, but not before swiping the bag of Goldfish back. "I knew it!"

I grumble as I sit up. "Happy?"

"Yep." She pops the *P*, clearly pleased with herself. "How was it?"

Incredible. Life-changing. Worth waiting a million years for. At least that's what I told Maya and Austin last night.

But I'm not about to admit that to Riley. I shrug, fixing my jacket and hair nonchalantly in the hall mirror. "It was fine." I meet her gaze in the reflection and can't help but break just the teensiest bit. "Okay, it was . . . pretty great."

"*Pretty* great? This girl has kissed half of Hollywood!"

"Doesn't mean she's good at it," I mumble, though she very much was.

The doorbell rings and I frown, checking my phone to see if I have any new messages, but I don't.

"I thought we were meeting at the—" I say, swinging open the front door, expecting to see Maya or Austin, since Arden is having dinner with Edie, but my voice trails off when I realize it's Taylor Hill standing on my front porch.

"Long time no see, Beckett," she says as she reaches out to tug on the edge of my scarf. She nods in the direction of town, where the festivities are already in full swing for Barnwich's biggest night, the muffled sound of music and voices filtering down the street. "You going to the tree lighting?"

"No, I just wander around the house like this." I motion to my attire, enormous jacket and all, and she laughs, grabbing my hand and pulling me out the door.

"Come on. I'll walk you."

I let go when we turn onto the sidewalk, and Taylor gives me a curious look. "Scared her fans might see you? I'd let go before Main Street."

I shake my head, skidding to a stop. "No . . . I . . ."

She turns to face me, studying my expression. "You stopped replying to my texts. We've barely talked at all when we've seen each other. I know you're busy with the article, and I'm still so fine with waiting for you, Caroline. But I just . . . I guess I just want to make sure I'm still waiting for something."

I feel a wave of guilt. "Taylor, I'm so sorry. It's just—"

"Arden," she finishes.

I nod, and she tilts her head back for a moment, hurt flashing across her face. Finally, she exhales and looks back at me. "I think I should have known from that very first day when she came to pick you up at school. There was . . . *something* in the way Arden looked at you. In the way you looked at her. Seeing you together at the coffee shop and at the diner, how you still orbited around each other even after so many years, kind of confirmed it, but I didn't want to admit it."

I don't say anything for a long moment. Because she's right.

When I do speak, I decide to just tell her the truth. The whole truth. "Taylor, you're *so* great. Truly. When Austin and Maya told me you were interested in me, it didn't even seem in the realm of possibility. I mean, you're *Taylor Hill*. You're the coolest girl at Barnwich High. And once we started hanging out, I liked you so much I really tried to feel a spark, to make it happen. But it's just . . . It's always been Arden for me. And you deserve happiness, someone who feels that for you without even trying."

She nods. "Well . . . fuck. Thanks for letting me know."

She shoves her hands in her pockets as we walk in silence the rest of the way down the sidewalk, slowing to a stop when we hit Main Street and the sea of rosy-cheeked people and twinkling lights. A local band plays Christmas music on a makeshift stage while the tree looms overhead. As I look at her, I can't help but think about what Arden said she can't give me, the future I once tried to picture with Taylor. How easy it would have been. Easy, sure . . . but not magic. Not like last night.

She reaches out to take my hand. "Don't forget yourself, though, Caroline. Okay? Don't lose yourself in her and her orbit and all the pieces she shares with the rest of the world. You're great too. Too great to not get a whole person. To not feel like *you're* a whole person."

I nod and squeeze her fingers.

"I won't," I say, but my stomach churns the teensiest bit. I think of the unfinished article. The application I've hardly thought about in a week. The party tomorrow all the way in Los Angeles, my first Christmas Eve away from my family, away from Barnwich.

No, it'll be fine. Different this time.

"And remember . . . ," she says as she lets go of my hand, walking backward down the snowy street. "If you're ever looking to date a *local* Barnwich celebrity, my cheer team did in fact win states two years in a row."

She flashes me that confident smile of hers, and even though it's tinged with sadness, it makes me feel a wave of relief. That things aren't completely broken between us. I smile back at her, and she holds up her hand to wave before turning and disappearing into the crowd.

"*Caroline Beckett*, smooching Arden James and then holding hands with Taylor Hill the very next day," a familiar voice says, startling me. Maya appears next to me, looping her arm through mine.

"*Quite* a scandal," Austin says, appearing on my other side.

I roll my eyes and elbow them both, relaxing again as we start to walk through the crowd.

"So what was *that* about?" Maya asks. Finn strolls over, chomping on a giant chocolate chip cookie before holding it out to me.

"It was a long-overdue goodbye," I say as I reach out to break off a piece.

"So are you like . . . for real dating Arden now?" Austin asks.

"I don't know." I shake my head. "We haven't talked about it yet."

"Too busy kissing?" Finn asks, cookie bits flying everywhere.

"*Maybe,*" I say, even though the answer is definitely *yes*.

"I can't believe you get to go to LA tomorrow," Maya says with a shiver. "It's so fucking freezing here. If I lose a boob, remember me as I was. . . ." She gets a distant look in her eyes. "The girl with the best tits in Barnwich."

I snort. "I'll make sure it's on your headstone."

"Don't pull an Arden and forget us in the big city," Austin says, and I poke him in the side.

259

"Like I ever could. Besides, I'll literally be back in like a day and a half, in time for the Hanukkah event at the bar. Not four years."

Speaking of Arden, I notice a small commotion coming from the opposite end of the street. Heads turning, phones appearing.

Soon she breaks through the crowd, looking just as beautiful as usual, the prettiest girl to attend any Barnwich Christmas tree lighting since its inception in 1885. The minute I see her, I feel at ease, Riley's and Taylor's and my friends' voices quieting.

"Arden!" Finn calls out, taking his mittened hand out of Austin's to wave, causing even more heads to turn. Her eyes land on me, and her fake smile turns genuine.

"Hi," she says, white teeth flashing, as a romantic flurry of snow falls around us yet again.

"Hi," I say back, and Maya's arm slides out of mine and into Austin's. I pretend not to notice how the two of them exchange knowing smiles and raised eyebrows.

I tug at the sleeve of her very cool but not warm enough denim jacket. "Are you *trying* to get hypothermia?"

She laughs, shivering. "I think I might be? I just wanted to . . ." She mumbles something I can't quite hear.

"What?" I ask, leaning forward.

She shakes her head. "Nothing."

"Tell me."

"Noth—"

"Arden."

"I just wanted to look cute!" she says, and I burst out laughing as her cheeks turn even redder.

I run my hand down her denim jacket. "You would have looked cute in an enormous snowsuit. Which, by the way, would have been a *much* smarter option for tonight."

Our fingers lace together as we walk with everyone through the crowd, stopping along the way to ice gingerbread cookies and make Christmas cards and pet the reindeer that drive the sleds around town. We get hot apple cider from Mistletoe Orchard's booth, and street-roasted chestnuts, before securing a spot with a good view of the tree while Austin, as the contest winner, goes off with Finn to get a rundown on how to light the thing.

With Arden next to me, tonight feels like magic. And I let myself get swept up in Barnwich's charm again.

"You packed for tomorrow?" Arden asks, offering me a chestnut.

I nod. "I think so. I mean, I don't really know what to wear to the party. I'm not sure I have anything nice eno—"

She waves her hand. "Lillian will bring over a couple of options."

"For me?"

Arden nods and takes a sip of her cider. "Yeah. I sent her your sizes to forward to my stylist. If you don't like any of the options, she can always get you something else."

"Your *stylist*," I say.

"I know. I'm cringing at myself. Trust me." She grins and shivers again. Maya was right when she was talking about losing a boob earlier.

"Here," I say, moving closer to pull my oversized jacket around her in an attempt not to have Arden James turn into an icicle on Main Street. That definitely wouldn't be good press for Barnwich.

Her hands slide over my stomach, my hips, clasping behind my back, and my face presses into her chin.

"You're always so warm," she says, ducking her head down to mumble into my shoulder.

"You're always so cold," I say, and she laughs, a rumble in her chest. "I can feel your icy hands through my shirt."

Still, I can't help but smile, shaking my head slightly at how different it feels having her this close. To be able to actually hold her instead of stealing a quick brush or glance.

"What?" she asks.

"Nothing. I just . . . kind of can't believe this is real."

"Me neither," she says, holding me a little bit tighter as the microphone crackles to life and our mayor, Jeffrey Durham, calls out, "Merry Christmas, Barnwich!" The crowd claps and cheers in response, and Austin gives us a little wave from up on the platform. "Now, for those of you who are new to our Christmas tree lighting, it is tradition for me to share the history of the very first time this event was held, over a hundred years ago, right here in this square."

Arden pops her head up eagerly, and all of us Barnwich natives grin in anticipation.

"The year was 1885," we echo along with him, laughing as he dives into the story of how Simon Barnwich, the great-great-grandson of the town's founder, managed to get his hands on an enormous quantity of Christmas lights only a few years after they'd been invented, so when he went to light up the very first Barnwich Christmas tree, people came from far and wide to watch.

Then, of course, there was the Douglas Fir Incident of 1893 that set half the town on fire after a few of the bulbs burst into flame. We've never used a Douglas fir since then, but the lightings continued undeterred.

As he talks about how important this tradition is to our small town, bringing us all together, Arden's hands unlock from around me to curl into the fabric of my shirt, and it becomes impossible to listen. Instead, I squeeze my eyes shut and let myself hold her, her hair blowing against my cheek, everything else fading away.

It feels almost too good to be true.

"One last question for our last date in Barnwich," I whisper, just loud enough for her to hear. "What did you miss most about Barnwich Christmases?"

Her breath catches in her throat. *"Everything,"* she whispers.

It feels like just the two of us, even though we're surrounded by hundreds of people. I pull back to look at her, but her eyes are still fixed on the tree, just past my head.

Everyone shouts, "Three . . . two . . . one . . . "

She looks down at me just as the Christmas tree blazes to life, the lights and colors illuminating her face. As the crowd cheers and the Christmas music swells, fireworks popping above us, her hands slide up to hold my face, thumbs tilting my jaw until her lips meet mine.

And for the first time in a long time, Christmas in Barnwich feels anything but melancholy.

CHAPTER 26

ARDEN

DAY 12

"You coming down?" Grams calls up to me the next morning as I sit on the bed next to my packed suitcase.

I take a deep breath, then lug it down the steps to find her standing in the entryway to greet me, even though it's still pitch-black outside.

"Cup of coffee?" she asks, and I nod, following her into the kitchen.

She pours us both a cup, and I try not to get emotional that it's the last one for a long while that I'll have in the slightly chipped white mug I've been using since I arrived. How long will Grams save it in the back of her cupboard? I swallow a big gulp.

"You were in a good mood when you came home last night," she says, and I raise my eyebrows at her.

"Who, me?"

She gives me a look. "*Arden.* The whole town saw you two kissing. Word gets around fast."

"What?" I say, leaning back on the counter. "*She* kissed *me.*"

"You be careful, okay?" she says, dismissing this, coffee cup held between both of her hands. "Especially out there in Holly-wood. She's gonna be in over her head, and you're gonna need to be there for her."

It *should* be hard to picture Caroline there with me, but it's just . . . not. The more I've thought about it, the more confident I feel about this all working.

I know she wanted to go to Columbia, but there are also plenty of good journalism schools out in LA. I mean, heck, she might not even have to go to school anymore. I've got a ton of connections, people who could hook her up with a job at any magazine or newspaper she wants to write for.

"I'll take care of her," I say. She looks like she wants to say something else, but her eyes flick behind me to the clock hanging on the wall just above her.

"You better get going," she says, and I nod, taking one more swig of coffee before we pull on our jackets and head out the door.

"Well," she says, squinting into the distance as we stand on the welcome mat. "I'm going to miss . . ."

I tear up.

"That car."

I follow her gaze to the Corvette in the driveway. I shake my head, pretending to be disappointed.

"You know, I *thought* you were going to say—"

The words aren't even out of my mouth before she wraps me in a hug. "I miss you all the time, Arden," she says, and I clench my jaw to stop the tears from flowing. "Every day."

When she releases me, she digs in her jacket pocket and pulls out a small present, wrapped in red-and-white paper, tied with a string. "Merry Christmas," she says, handing it to me.

"Thanks, Grams," I say, smiling at her in the glow of the porch light, trying to remember every wrinkle around her dark eyes, every strand of her salt-and-pepper hair, the way I feel standing here right now.

She wipes quickly at her face with the back of her hand before pushing me forward. "Open it later. Now get out of here. You're going to miss your plane."

I nod and pocket the gift as I turn toward the driveway and pause.

"Oh, I almost forgot . . ." I spin back around to face her, digging in my pocket until I pull out the keys to the Corvette. "Merry Christmas." I place them into her palm and close her fingers around them.

She opens her mouth to protest just like I knew she would, but I hold my hand up to silence her.

"It's done and paid for. And it's exactly what you deserve," I tell her, and her face softens. "Plus, I just don't think anyone else would look half as good driving that car."

"Well, I can't argue with ya there," she replies, squeezing my hands. "Thank you."

I nod before walking slowly to the other rental car I'd had dropped off this morning, my suitcase wheels ricocheting off every crack in the pavement. I squeeze it into the trunk with my other bag before pulling open the driver's-side door.

Taking a deep breath, I glance up to see Grams still standing there in the glow of the Christmas lights I put up, one hand raised in goodbye.

Before I know it, I'm closing the door and jogging back up the drive, wrapping her in one more hug.

"Come visit me, okay? Call me anytime and I'll book you a ticket," I tell her.

"I only fly first class," she jokes, making me laugh.

"Damn right you do. I'll miss you, Grams," I say, and she nods, as both of us give in to crying now.

"I know, sweetie. I know." She squeezes me tighter and I wish I wasn't leaving her. I wish I wasn't leaving Barnwich.

But soon I'm driving along Main Street to Caroline's house. Soon I'm parking outside. Soon I'm texting her I'm here so I don't wake up all the Becketts. I already said goodbye to them all last night. Riley only let me leave if I promised to come to see her play at states if they make it, and this time I felt confident about saying yes. Besides, I'm actually afraid of what she'll do if I don't.

As I wait, I pull the gift Grams gave me out of my pocket and carefully unwrap it to reveal a framed picture. It's the two of us standing on the bar of Edie's Eatery, big smiles on our faces. I flip it over to see her meat loaf recipe taped to the back.

I picture it hanging on my stainless steel fridge at my house in Malibu or in the hands of a hired home chef. I wonder if they'd change it, garnish it, make it into something it's not, something other than the perfect brick of meat it already is.

I jump when the car door opens and Caroline chucks a duffel bag into the backseat. When she slides into the front seat, she studies my face, frowning.

"You okay?"

"Yeah. Everything's fine." I nod, stowing the picture frame in my purse and shifting the car into drive.

Still, she squeezes my hand as I pull away, telling me she knows it's not.

• • •

I stifle a laugh as Caroline plays with all the buttons in her first-class pod on the plane, gasping every few seconds as she discovers a new feature.

"Arden," she hisses. *"Arden."*

"Yeah?"

"Look how far this seat goes back," she says, and I watch for about thirty seconds as her chair slowly squeaks into a full recline. She pops her head up. "This is ridiculous!"

She practically passes out when the flight attendant takes our orders and the food and drinks come out.

"A whole-ass sandwich, all these snacks, and you just got a coffee?" She leans across the aisle. *"What* is wrong with you?"

"I'm just . . . not hungry," I say, glancing out the window at the sea of white clouds, the ground below us not even visible.

"That means you're nervous," Caroline says through a mouthful of food. I snort and look back over at her.

"Me? Nervous?"

"Yes, *Arden James.* I know you."

She's right, obviously.

"What are you nervous about?" she asks.

I shrug. "I don't know. The party. Being back in LA. Bianchi finding out the truth. Generally everything."

"You know I'm a good journalist. Bianchi doesn't have to know that we were ever fake dating," Caroline says, then takes another bite.

Were. As in we *were* fake dating, but now we're regular dating?

We stare at each other for a long moment, until I push my sunglasses back on and take another sip of my coffee. "You're right."

We still haven't talked about . . . *us*. I keep waiting for her to say something, or wanting to say something myself, but even though I'm all in (I mean two hours ago I was already planning our future), I want to give Caroline a chance to see what she's getting into before I put that kind of pressure on her. I want her to know what she's signing up for, give her the opportunity to change her mind.

But I hope she won't. Pretty much everyone in Barnwich told me to watch out for her in LA, and that's what I intend to do.

Anyway, even if I wanted to, it's not like I could lean across the airplane aisle right now to have a little chat about it. I look up and down the plane to see if anyone is watching, listening, already feeling the weight of what my life is going to turn back into once we touch down in LA.

"Well, I should get some more work done. Gotta have this to *Cosmo* by eight in the morning," Caroline says as she pulls out her laptop.

"So you'll finish it after the party tonight?" I ask, and she nods. "Let me read what you have so far." I reach across to grab her laptop, but she moves it away just in time.

"No way! Not until it's finished," she says, surprising me.

"Come on. Are you serious?" I ask, but she just ignores me.

I watch her type away, wondering what she's writing, how she'll make me look, how much personal information she's putting in there. I've never been interviewed by someone who really sees me before, and I'm both terrified and dying to know what she's saying.

"Don't you want some outside input?" I ask, leaning across the aisle to try to get a peek, but she angles the computer away again.

"Why don't you order a backup sandwich? Maybe you'll want it later in the car on the way to your house."

"You want me to just . . . get a sandwich and put it in my pocket for later?" I ask, ignoring the fact that she's dodging me.

"I mean, in your bag or something, but . . . yeah. You never know."

"You're ridiculous." I shake my head and put my earbuds in, resisting the urge to kiss her for the thousandth time today. It weirdly makes me feel a little more reassured. Nothing's going to change Caroline, not even Hollywood. We're going to be able to make this work.

So the next time the flight attendant passes by, I get the backup sandwich.

You never know.

CHAPTER 27

CAROLINE

DAY 12

The second we land in LA, I can feel a shift in Arden.

I try to make eye contact as we ride in the backseat of a tinted black Escalade, but her hood is still pulled up over a baseball cap from our power walk through the airport, and now she's just . . . staring out the window, thumb flicking open one of the arms of her sunglasses and then closing it, over and over.

I swallow the slightly sick feeling growing in my chest. The one that reminds me of those last few days in Barnwich before we kissed, like I was already losing her just when she was finally, *finally* in reach.

I turn to look out at the road as I try to shake it off. I take in the palm trees, the traffic, and not a single flake of snow in sight even though it's Christmas Eve. Everything is so different from Barnwich here. I knew it would be, but actually seeing it is something else.

My phone buzzes, and I look down to see a video from Riley of her and Miles and Levi at Restaurant Depot. They're loading up on potatoes and eggs and candles for the Hanukkah candle lighting party tomorrow night at the bar, following the carefully curated list of instructions I left them. Levi's pushing the cart at breakneck speed, while Riley surfs on top of the potato bags, and Miles chases after them both, trying to get them to stop.

I smile to myself and turn my phone to show Arden, but she's still looking out the window, a million miles away.

Eventually we cross through a big set of gates and pull into her development. The houses are eighteen times bigger than anything back home, sprawling mansions that loom large enough to block the ocean on the other side. We turn right into the driveway of a black, angular modern house, all windows and steel. It's so far from what I would picture for Arden that I'm surprised when she unbuckles her seat belt.

The car stops and Arden murmurs a thank-you to the driver before we climb out to find a woman with curly hair waiting for us outside the enormous glass door. The salty ocean smell wraps around us as she bustles over, glancing at a watch on her wrist.

"Cutting it close, James!" she says, but then her eyes flick back up to give me a fast scan, and a big smile creeps onto her face. "Well, aren't you just the cutest."

I glance down at myself in an attempt to see what exactly she's looking at, but her perfectly manicured hand shoots into my field of view. "I'm Lillian, Arden's agent."

I stiffen after what Arden's told me, but shake it. "Caroline."

I barely let go before she's guiding us inside. My neck tilts back as I take in the high ceilings, the artsy chandelier, the glass staircase, the white straight-backed couch.

It's nice.

Big.

But . . . sterile.

There are no pictures on the walls, no stuff lying about, and that couch looks so uncomfortable it would probably suck to have a movie marathon on it. There's nothing that makes this place feel like a home. Nothing that feels like *Arden*.

"All right, hair and makeup will be here in half an hour. Jenna . . ." Lillian pauses, then adds, "Arden's stylist will be here an hour after that. There are cold-pressed juices in the fridge if you're peaky. Coffee on the counter. You two both must need to shower, right? Airplanes are always so . . ." She grimaces, her whole face scrunching up. She glances down at her buzzing cell phone, and without even taking a breath, she beelines out of the room. "I gotta take this."

We both watch her go.

"Is she always so . . . ?"

"Yeah," Arden says with a laugh, but it's forced. "That's why she's the best in the business." I think about what she told me about the carefully curated *Arden James* image that Lillian spearheaded, everything she said two days ago at her old house about losing herself to the lie.

And how *the best in the business* didn't necessarily sound like a good thing.

She nods upstairs. "We should probably get going. I'll show you where you can shower."

I grab my duffel bag, already carefully placed by the driver in the entryway.

"Should I try one of those 'cold-pressed juices'?" I tease as we walk up the steps, and finally Arden grins.

"You're in LA now. They'll probably put you right back on

the plane if you don't," she says as I follow her down the hallway. She slows to a stop, then pushes open a black door to reveal an enormous guest room. The perfectly made bed is half a football field away, and an open door next to it shows a white tile bathroom attached.

"This is *huge*," I say, gaping as I take it in, my duffel bag sliding off my shoulder.

Arden nods farther down the hallway. "My room is even bigger."

"Oh my God, can I see?" I ask. Arden shrugs and grabs my hand, pulling me to the very last door. Her smell wafts out of it the second she opens it, the first time this place has really felt like hers.

"Holy shit."

A king-size bed. A wall of windows overlooking the ocean. A cool modern art painting above the dark wood headboard. A *fireplace*.

She motions me through another door, and my eyes practically pop out of their sockets when I see her closet. Floor-to-ceiling shelves. Jackets, and shoes, and shirts, and dresses, and purses on every available space. I see items she's worn in shows and movies, taken from set, and red-carpet dresses I recognize from pictures Riley shoved under my nose after every premiere or awards show.

My hand reaches out to drag along sequins and velvet and chiffon as I try to make sense of *this* Arden, to see where *my* Arden fits into it all.

This giant, empty house. The tinted Escalade. The sunglasses and baseball cap.

I want to get to know, to learn to love, the other half of her, because I know how much acting means to Arden. The career that she's built, this role with Bianchi.

But ever since we got off the plane, maybe since after we first kissed, there's been a little voice in my head asking how I can fit into all of this. If she'll even want me to. A voice I've been trying desperately to silence.

"Everything is so *neat*," I say. "This whole house. Don't you have any, I don't know . . . *mess?* Some mail? A diary? Dirty under-wear?"

She laughs and runs her fingers through her hair. "Yeah, I mean . . ." She sits me down on the edge of her bed and pulls open the drawer in her bedside table.

It is just *filled*. Books, torn-out pages from screenplays through the years, highlighted over and over again, letters in Edie's handwriting, Polaroids from film sets and award shows. This twelve-by-twelve drawer is the most Arden thing in this five-thousand-square-foot house. And *wait* . . . in the mess, right on top, I see it. The friendship bracelet I made her the winter before she left and tied onto her wrist at that year's tree lighting.

I reach out and pick it up, thumb gliding along the braided knots. "You kept it?" I say.

"Of course I did."

She says it so quickly, with so much certainty, it makes me look up and meet her dark eyes. My fingertips tighten around it, and I feel the thread I can hold on to. Because if Arden can hold on to this, maybe she's capable of holding on to me too.

"Caroline—" she starts, but Lillian's voice shouts up at us from downstairs.

"Fifteen minutes, ladies! You better be ready for makeup when that clock strikes three!"

Arden takes the bracelet from my hand and puts it back in the drawer, before closing it with a soft thud. I nod toward the hallway. "I should probably . . ."

"Right. Yeah." Both of us hurriedly stand, and Arden shoves her hands into her hoodie pocket. "See you in a little bit."

I head to the door, wondering what she never got a chance to say.

"And, Caroline?"

I skid to a stop and turn around, my heart rate kicking up as I look back at her. "Yes?"

"I'm, uh . . ." She hesitates for a moment before shaking her head. "I'm really glad you'll be there with me tonight. Thanks for coming."

"Me too, Arden," I say, although I'm not sure it's the whole truth.

She tosses me a lump of brown paper and I manage to catch it, unwrapping a corner to see the saved sandwich from the plane. "Might pair well with the pressed juice," she says with a grin.

I take a big bite and leave laughing, feeling a little bit better.

A couple of hours later, my scalp hurts, my fake eyelashes are bothering my eyes, and this dress might break one of my ribs, but I look . . . well, *hot*.

Almost unrecognizable, but still. I don't think I've ever looked this good.

I turn side to side in the mirror, taking in the flowing emerald-green dress and my hair, half-up, the rest curled to perfection, a matching bow standing out against the strawberry blond.

These Hollywood people sure know what they're doing.

I send a picture to Austin and Maya in our group chat, and an explosion of heart-eyes and exclamation points comes back almost immediately. I smile to myself, slipping my phone into the clutch Jenna gave me to pair with the outfit before heading out of the room and down the hallway.

I'm about to start down the steps when a hand grabs ahold of my wrist, spinning me around.

"Arden," I hiss, as we come face-to-face, but my breath hitches when I see how stunning she looks. All those Instagram pictures Riley showed me over the years pale in comparison to seeing her glammed up in front of me.

She's wearing an off-the-shoulder red dress, her full lips a matching color. Her hair is pulled back, showing off her sparkling earrings, and her eyes are almost too beautiful to look at.

Her hand slides up my arm until it's gently touching my face. "I want to kiss you," she whispers. "But I don't want to mess up your makeup."

"Maybe Bianchi will find it more believable if you do," I say, and she smiles, white teeth flashing.

But then her face grows serious. "Caroline, things at the party might . . . I don't know. It's going to be a lot. And Bianchi is going to be trying to suss out the truth, so we're *really* going to be under a microscope. But I'll be there for you, okay?"

I nod. "I know you will be."

"Ladies, this house is an echo chamber, and if either of you mess up as much as a single eyelash, I will personally brawl with you in the driveway," Lillian calls up to us from the living room.

Arden rolls her eyes but still only lets her lips brush ever so lightly against mine. Even so, I forget how to breathe.

Before I can remember, we're heading downstairs and out the door to the waiting Escalade.

We've barely sat down in the car before Lillian's curly hair pops in through the open window. "Good luck tonight," she says. Arden nods, but her face gets far more serious when Lillian adds, "Don't fuck this up, okay?"

Lillian doesn't say anything else, and with a wave of her wrist, we're off to Bianchi's house while I bristle in the backseat over the implication that Arden hasn't worked hard, that *we* haven't worked hard, to make this happen. I clasp my hands in my lap as I try to steel my nerves for what's ahead, but despite my best efforts, I can't stop my leg from bouncing. Soon, we're pulling into another gated development and up a long cobblestone drive-way to an Italian-style villa that is so picturesque it makes me feel like *I'm* in some kind of movie.

"Hey," Arden says, hand reaching out to still my bouncing leg as the car comes to a stop. "We've been pulling this off for *twelve* whole days now, around people who know us *way* better. A few more hours is going to be easy, okay? Just one more take."

Are we still pretending?

Confused, I think about asking her that, but I stop myself. Instead, I open my mouth to tell her I am clearly *not* an actress, but the door behind her opens. Arden slides out of the car easily and comes around to help me out, taking my arm in hers in one smooth motion.

I feel like I'm going to black out as we walk up the stone steps and through the wooden doors, so I force myself to focus on the details instead of the people. Marble floors and high ceilings. Christmas garlands and lights strung around banisters, candlesticks romantically placed. It's breathtaking, but it doesn't feel warm or cozy like real holiday decorations. Not like Barnwich. It feels almost staged, like a movie set, which I guess makes sense.

"Champagne?" a man in a white tux asks, holding out a tray, and Arden scoops two off the silver serving platter.

"Don't tell your mom," she whispers, and I laugh. I take a surprisingly bubbly sip and try to play it cool as we mill about the room, passing celebrity after famous celebrity.

"Love the dress," Arden says about a poofy gown I know she despises.

"Such a huge fan of your latest," she says about a movie that *nobody*, not even my grandma, thought was good.

It's so surreal to watch her casually greet and schmooze these people like they're regulars at Edie's Eatery and not Academy Award winners.

Which . . . I guess they are for her.

But this is the most up-close look I've had at *Arden James*. And I can't help but notice how fake it feels. How messed up it is that Arden is so great and these people just want the bullshit version of her.

And I definitely can't ignore the sting when Melanie Jacobs, someone I've definitely seen in a tabloid with her hand around Arden's waist, comes up to us. Of course she's gorgeous and she plants a slow kiss on Arden's cheek, leaving a red lipstick stain behind.

Without thinking, I reach up to wipe it off, but Arden grabs my hand before I can, stopping me.

"It's not a big deal," she murmurs, and takes a quick swig from her glass.

It's a big deal to me.

"You must be Arden's girlfriend," Melanie says with an appraising look, followed by an amused smile that makes me feel about two inches tall. She leans into Arden and whispers something in her ear before laughing.

For just a moment I see a glimmer of something recognizable flash across Arden's face, but then she laughs and it's gone. She even drops my hand while I finish the rest of my glass.

I don't know why I thought she'd be there for me when she can't even be there for herself.

"Well, well, well," a voice says as we enter a dining room just off the entryway, Arden wiping her cheek quickly now that Melanie is gone. Bianchi himself saunters toward us in a black tuxedo, glass in hand, his hair as unruly as ever. "What do we have here?"

I see Arden shift slightly, her body almost a buffer between me and Bianchi. But he reaches his free hand past her and holds it out to me.

"Caroline, right?" He grins as I take it and nod an affirmation. His eyes flick from my face to Arden's, gaze intense, like he's searching for something. Trying to sniff out the lie. "You two have caused *quite* a stir."

"Like I told you," Arden says, a smirk I don't recognize pulling at her lips. "I'm good at staying trending."

He laughs and slides his hand into her palm. Then he leans forward and whispers, "Let's find a moment to talk this evening. Alone. About the movie." Leaning back, he studies both of us again, eyes moving this time to where my arm is laced through Arden's, hand gripping at her forearm. "Looking forward to reading the article tomorrow, Caroline." But he moves on before I can say anything at all.

As the evening wears on, we eat fancy appetizers from sparkling trays, and Arden continues to transform into someone else entirely, all fake smiles and forced laughter and letting people talk down to me, while I stumble through conversation after conversation with people whose eyes glaze over with disinterest immediately.

"How quaint," Steven Bronkowski, two-time Academy Award winner, says after I tell him about the article I wrote on the five-generations-old Christmas cookie recipe, murder and all.

"Oh! How, uh, *fun*," Alana Patrick, Oscar-nominated director, says when I make a joke about me and Arden stealing a tree from Swanson's, before she floats away without another word.

"That's . . . fascinating," Julia McDower, former child star, says after I talk about how old a tradition our tree lighting is.

"Like that speech Garry Ryan gave this year at the Emmys," Arden says, sending the two of them dissolving into laughter. Julia nods in agreement while I turn about six different shades of red. "*Speaking of which*, you are due to win. Your new show sounds incredible!"

Once again Arden has deftly steered the conversation in another direction, and what she told me in her driveway about her persona makes more and more sense. The hiding who she is makes more and more sense.

Because people here just don't care about who we are and where we call home.

And it makes me miss Barnwich even more. Miss the Christmas Eve we could be having, cookies and laughter and snow. Meeting up with Austin and Maya to exchange gifts. Wearing ugly sweaters with my whole family per Beckett tradition.

With every minute that passes, that thread of my Arden I found back at the house gets harder and harder to hold on to. And my fears become more and more real.

That I don't have a place here at all. That I could never quite fit into whatever life she's made out here for herself.

That my Arden isn't the whole, but a piece of her she doesn't want anyone else to see, no matter what the past twelve days in Barnwich were like.

"Caroline?"

My eyes snap to her face, and I realize she was talking to me. "Yeah?"

"I asked if you wanted to take a picture." She points to a guy walking around with a camera, only a few feet from us, snapping photos of some of the guests.

I nod as Arden calls him over, and without a trace of awkwardness or hesitation, she takes my hand. My eyes move quickly to her face as he holds his camera up, to take it in for just a moment, before the flash hits us. And I can't help but feel my heart sink when it looks like a stranger is standing beside me.

We pose and smile, and when the photographer walks away, I see Bianchi wave at her, motioning for her to come join him finally in a study just off the entryway.

"Wish me luck," she whispers, hand sliding so quickly out of mine I couldn't hold on even if I wanted to.

And as I watch her go, a blur of red, I know she doesn't need it. She belongs here.

She's the best actress I've ever seen, because she almost convinced me that what we had could be real.

CHAPTER 28

ARDEN

DAY 12

Fifteen minutes after leaving her, I bust out of the study, my eyes scanning the crowd for Caroline.

I finally spot her in the corner, clutching her champagne glass tightly. I slide around the room full of people toward her, nodding hello to a past co-star who I absolutely hated. But I won't let even his slimy face ruin my excitement.

"Come here," I say, putting her drink down and pulling her into the next room, which is just as gaudy as the last one, full of people slow dancing to the live band playing instrumental Christmas music.

I pull her close, her sweet-smelling hair brushing against my chin. "I got the role," I whisper. She pulls her head back to look into my eyes. "We did it."

"No way, Arden." She smiles, hand tightening on my shoulder. "I'm so happy for you."

I study her face. She's smiling, but something's off in the corners of her mouth, around the edges of her eyes. She must be upset about the article. The fact that I got the role before it even went live, so it's kind of moot. "Look, the article will still go live, and I can't *wait* to read it. To see how you see me." I run my hand down her face, gently as a feather, waiting to see a change in her expression.

"Just . . . finish this dance with me," she says, pulling me closer.

"Caroline—"

"Arden."

My blood runs cold, even as her cheek brushes up against mine. I squeeze my eyes shut, wanting to stop time, afraid of what's to come when the song ends. What could have happened in the last fifteen minutes? How could I have messed things up so fast?

I mean, yeah, it wasn't a perfect night. It was a little awkward at times trying to navigate conversations with all these people, but I didn't think it was *that* bad.

I try to calm my panicked thoughts and soak her in as much as I can. Her smell, the way she feels in my arms, the way *I* feel when she's this close to me. When she's even *near* me.

I think of the look on her face the first day I showed up at the diner, and the way she chopped down that Douglas fir like a damn lumberjack, and her fingers sliding down my arm to intertwine with my own on her bed. I think of her mouth tasting like hot chocolate and peppermint when she kissed me, her friendship bracelet that collects dust in my bedside table, her box of articles. Her *I see you*.

I'm not ready for any of it to end.

When the final note plays, we stay where we are. I'm afraid to move. To even breathe.

Finally, she pulls away, leading me out a door onto a dimly lit stone balcony that stretches the entire length of the house.

"Arden," she says, her voice cracking, brown eyes squeezing tightly shut. "I . . . think we need to be realistic here."

"What do you—"

"I never thought I was going to see you again," she says, eyes opening and locking on mine. "When you didn't come home that very first Christmas, and one Christmas turned into two and then three without a call or a visit. I told myself that was it. I never thought I'd fall off a ladder at Edie's and see you looking down at me."

She pauses, a tear rolling down her cheek. I reach out to brush it away, but she catches my hand and pulls it down between us.

"I think . . ." She takes a deep breath, looking back up at me. "I think we need to be honest with ourselves. You have a *life* here, Arden. A life that I don't fit into. A life that doesn't, and has never, included me. And you just got the role of a lifetime, which is only going to make that more true."

"Caroline, it doesn't have to be like that. You can fit. You *can*." I take a second to strip the desperation out of my voice. "Listen, I know I was scared at first, but I've spent a lot of time thinking, and there are *plenty* of good journalism schools out here. I mean, you could move out here in the fall and I could probably get you a writing job anywhere you want. Like you've been dreaming."

She shakes her head. "But that isn't my dream. It's yours, Arden. This can never work, but I think you already knew that." She squeezes my hand, but I can feel her fingers wrenched around my heart instead. "It's why you stayed away all those years. Why you tried to warn me before we kissed. Why you never got in touch. It wasn't just because you thought you'd never be able to leave. It's because you knew, deep down, that you'd never be able to take me with you either."

I don't say anything.

I can't say anything, because on some level . . . she's right.

And I fucking hate that.

"We might have had these past twelve days together, and *God*," she laughs, eyes filled with tears. "I'm so glad we did." Her hand slides up my arm until it rests against my cheek. I turn into it, trying to memorize the pressure of her fingertips, the way her palm feels against my skin. "But that's all we'll ever have."

She stretches up and her lips brush against my cheek. Then I close my eyes, bending my head down until our foreheads touch. "I'm going to be the one to leave this time," she whispers, and then I feel her slide away from me, light as a feather.

When I open my eyes, she's gone, leaving empty air where she was just standing.

I clutch at the ornate gold banister, trying to catch my breath, but my head is spinning.

Caroline. She just . . .

"Fuck," I gasp out. "*Fuck!*"

"Need a cigarette?" a voice asks from the darkness.

I whirl around to see Bianchi strolling toward me. He leans against the banister next to me, a cigarette dangling from his fingertips.

"No, I . . ." I wipe at my face with the back of my hand and try to compose myself. "What are you even doing out here?"

"Hiding from it all." He chuckles. "Never was a huge fan of parties."

I rip my hand away from the cool metal and start to pace. Bianchi tracks me with a curious expression on his face.

"I . . ." Tears sting at my eyes and I fight to swallow them back. But then I skid to a stop in front of him. "You know the real reason I wanted this role? I wanted something that felt real and honest. Something that felt true to *me*, because nothing in my life or even my career has in so long."

He nods, studying my face as he takes a drag.

"But the irony is, you only gave it to me because I lied," I say, laughing humorlessly. "I *lied*. I never dated Caroline until last week. Sure, I *was* the small-town girl with a crush on my best friend and dreams of getting out of good ol' Barnwich, but I left one day, said I was going to come back, and I never did. Not once!"

"Until now," he says.

"Like it matters." I shake my head and then let it fall back until I can see the stars.

I wait for him to tear into me for everything I've done. I wait for him to rip the role right out of my grasp. But instead, when I turn my head to look, he just smiles to himself and takes another puff of his cigarette.

"You know," he says, "I like you a hell of a lot more when you *are* being honest. Your audition was damn good, but this . . . this was better." He puts the cigarette out and stands face-to-face with me.

"What?" I ask.

"Arden, come on. Do you really think I bought that whole routine between you and your agent?" He laughs, shaking his head. "You do much better with a script."

"You knew this whole time? And you just let it drag on?" I ask, and he nods. "But why?"

"I wanted to see how far you were willing to go for this. I wanted to see that you are as committed as I am," he replies.

"Great," I reply, pissed off. I drag my hands down my face, until I remember I'm wearing a full face of makeup.

"You know, you and I aren't so different, Arden James. I grew up in a small town in Ohio, which to these people"—he motions to everyone on the other side of the windows—"basically means we're from the same place."

I can't help but laugh at that. I never knew that about him. Like no one knew about Barnwich until this week.

"I gave up a lot to be where I am today. Things I never wanted to lose. But jobs like yours and mine can be . . . all-consuming at times. Now, looking back, I'm not so sure I had to give up everything. This business can be so all-or-nothing, but life doesn't have to be. You know, Arden, there's nothing wrong with having someone who helps you find your way when you can't see the forest for the trees. If I had, maybe things wouldn't have played out like they did."

"What are you saying?" I ask.

"You know as well as I do that you can believe *some* things you read on the internet," he says, flipping my own words around from the audition.

The alcoholism.

It *wasn't* just gossip.

"I lost family, friends, and more of myself than I care to admit, even to my therapist. I see a lot of myself in you. The only difference is . . . I'm forty-six and you still have your whole life ahead of you. I see what this industry does to teenagers. I've watched what it's done to you the past few years. Just . . . don't let it cost you anyone else," he says, pushing off the banister to head toward the door. "Don't let it consume you further. You've got too much talent for that," he adds, before disappearing back into the crowd.

I stand there, looking through the wide glass window at the people milling about inside, feeling so . . . *separate* from them even though I *am* them. All night I've been just as fake. Just as disingenuous. Hell, we're all here on Christmas Eve instead of with the people we actually want to be with. All because it's expected.

But . . . I never wanted to be on every magazine cover, at every A-list party, at the bottom of every bottle.

All I ever wanted was to act.

The rest of this life was chosen for me by people who wanted to profit off me. Who told me it was necessary when I can see now it wasn't. People like . . .

Lillian.

CHAPTER 29

CAROLINE

DAY 12

"It's for the best," Lillian says, watching me shove everything into my duffel bag as quickly as possible, my makeup smeared everywhere, I'm sure.

When I got back from the party, she had my ticket back to Barnwich booked before I could even take my shoes off.

She shrugs and looks down at her phone, thumbs tapping away. "I mean, this homegrown image is working for this project, but who knows what'll happen after this movie. Who *Arden James* will need to be next."

I focus on squeezing my toiletry bag into a side pocket, trying to fight the words that threaten to spill out.

But I can't. Maybe it's the champagne, or maybe it's the fact that Arden has never had anyone to stand up for her these last four years. Either way, even though I'm heartbroken, I won't just sit here in silence and let this woman act like she cares about Arden.

"She's a person, not an image, Lillian. She's . . . *Arden*," I say, and her gaze meets mine again. "Can't she just *be* Arden?"

Lillian smiles, but it's condescending. "Oh, Caroline. Don't take it personally. It's just business." She flicks her head at Arden's face on the cover of a spread of magazines on the dresser. "*Good* business, at that."

An Uber notification pings into my phone. I return her shit-eating smile as I reach down to scoop up my packed bag. "Is it? Because Arden's already famous. She did it. So what's going to happen when she realizes she doesn't need someone manipulating her to continue having a huge career? Because it seems to me like one day, even if it's *years* from now, she'll figure out she wants to be herself a whole hell of a lot more than whatever the fuck you want her to be. The cracks are already forming." I think about Arden kissing me outside her old house. Her smile at Cemetery Hill, sledding with my friends. Running down the hallway after the basketball game. "And you better be careful. Because then? There'll be no business for you at all."

Lillian's eyes are wide as I step past her into the hall and slam the bedroom door behind me. She doesn't say a word as I go down the stairs and out to the car that will take me to the airport, toward home.

Still, no matter how strong I pretended to be in that moment, I cry the entire ride and then the flight back to Barnwich. I keep my hoodie pulled up as I stare at my laptop screen through tears, bits and pieces of an article I need to finish writing staring back at me, all of which feel different now. Painful.

Just a few hours until my deadline. What am I going to do?

CHAPTER 30

ARDEN

DAY 12

Before I know it, I'm pushing through the front doors and running down the cobblestone drive, hopping into my waiting car. "Home, please! Quickly."

We speed through the night, my fingers tapping anxiously on the handle of the door. Eventually I reach up and pull the pins out of my bun, letting my hair cascade down over my shoulders. The whole time all I can think is all these years, all this time, pretending to be someone else, there was still someone who always saw *me*, the real me, even when I couldn't.

And even after the last twelve days, I just chose all *this* over *her*. Again.

The winding drive to my house feels never-ending. It feels like hours later that I finally see the glow of the front porch light.

I hop out of the car, heart pounding, and push inside, calling out her name into the foyer. "Caroline?"

I kick my heels off and run upstairs, then down the hallway, before finally bursting into the guest room.

The *empty* guest room.

I flick on the light to see the bed carefully made. The only signs she was here at all are the dress she was wearing lying neatly across it and a Barnwich postcard she bought in town the day we kissed centered on top of it.

"She's gone," a voice says from behind me, and I turn around to find Lillian leaning in the doorway.

"What? How? I was just with her an hour ago," I reply.

"She doesn't belong here. And you don't belong there. Arden, I did you a favor, sweetie."

A favor?

I walk toward her, my hand curling into a fist at my side.

"What did you do?" I ask.

"I got her on a flight ASAP before she could change her mind." She shrugs, a smug smile spreading across her face. "Don't worry, we'll let the article go live so your little friend can get something out of all this."

Little friend?

Lillian places a hand on each of my shoulders.

"Now you can focus on what's really important. This movie. Then awards. Ads. Who knows what else?" Her eyes light up at the thought of it all. "Now, come on. I'll call Jenna to come fix your makeup so we can get you back to that party. Maybe you'll even find a girl to make you forget about all this." She waves her fingers around vaguely, but the thought of that makes me feel nauseous.

I shake my head, finally able to fully see the truth.

"When I was sixteen and got emancipated, I put all my trust in you, Lillian. I actually thought you were taking care of me this whole time, looking out for me like my parents never did, but now I can see it clearly. You've never been any better than them. I've spent these last twelve days being reminded of what it's like to have people actually care about me. And I'm not going to give them up. Not for fame or money . . ." I take another step until we're face-to-face. "And *especially* not for you."

"Okay. You can kill the dramatics, sweetie."

"You're fired." I take another step toward her, making her step back into the hallway. "Get out of my house."

She stands there with her jaw practically on the floor. For once, there isn't a single word coming out of her mouth. She stalks angrily toward the hallway.

"Oh, and, Lil?" I say. She turns to look back at me with a smugness like she knew I wouldn't really fire her. "Feel free to grab a cold-pressed juice on your way out. Sweetie," I add, before shutting the bedroom door in her face.

I step backward until my calves knock into the bed frame, then fall back on top of Caroline's dress. I reach behind my back and grab the postcard. A map of Barnwich. The familiar roads. Edie's Eatery. Home.

Tears fill my eyes as I hold it to my heart, alone in this big, empty house once again, wondering how I convinced myself that loving her could've ever been fake.

CHAPTER 31

CAROLINE

Once the plane lands, I practically run through the airport and into the arms of Austin and Maya, who've come to pick me up. I called them at the gate at LAX to tell them what happened. They hold me close, and I burrow my face into Austin's chest.

"Thanks for coming on Christmas," I gurgle out.

"Anything for you, Beckett," Maya says.

"My great-aunt Bett's snoring in our guest room has kept my entire family up all night anyway," Austin adds, making me laugh as he squeezes me tighter, then takes me out to the waiting car.

Maya sits with me in the backseat and lets me rest my head on her shoulder, while Austin drives us the two hours home. As we head down a deserted Main Street, I stare out the window at the glittering Christmas tree in the center of the square, remembering the glow of it on Arden's face, the feeling of her cold lips pressed up against mine.

Only now the memory hurts.

"I have no clue how I am going to get this article done by eight a.m." I laugh through my tears, shaking my head.

"You're Caroline Beckett," Austin says. "You'll find a way."

"Team Caroline," Maya agrees, squeezing me tighter. "And if you don't, your Columbia portfolio is so good it never needed this to begin with. Take care of *yourself*."

"Let us know if you need anything, okay?" Austin says as he slows to a stop outside my house. "I've got a new white chocolate mocha I think you'll like."

"We're just a text away," Maya adds. "Merry Christmas, Caroline."

The two of them hug me before I grab my bag from the trunk and head inside. The house is dark and quiet except for our tree glowing in the living room, our well-worn stockings waiting for us just underneath. My parents were probably fast asleep by the time I texted I was leaving LA, not expecting me until the afternoon.

I tiptoe up to my room and turn on the light.

"Jesus Christ."

"Howdy," Riley says, taking a casual bite of a carefully decorated sugar cookie in the ugly sweater I got her, like she didn't just give me a heart attack.

"What are you doing in here? And are those Dad's Christmas cookies? It's like six a.m.!"

She crunches noisily on it, unfazed. "Austin and Maya told me you were coming home."

I groan and collapse on the bed next to her. She holds out the other half of the cookie, and I take it.

"You good?" she asks, lying back next to me.

I let out a long sigh. "I don't know."

"That's okay."

We lie there in silence for a long moment. "I don't know how to finish this article."

"What do you mean?"

"When I first agreed to it, I thought it could be just like all my other articles. Asking questions, capturing the story, the person, in a new and honest light. Writing it without being too deeply in it, even though I technically was."

Riley nods, turning her head to look at me.

"But it feels like I can't do that anymore. Because I *am* so deeply in it. I can't be objective because . . ." I let out a frustrated sigh. "Because of what I feel for her. To write the article they're expecting I have to pretend to feel things I actually feel but can't let myself anymore. It's like I don't know the truth at all, Riley. And I'm stuck because I don't want to mess this up for her with Bianchi and—"

"Just . . ." She exhales. "Write the article that will show people Arden exactly how you see her. Because, Caroline? That's the real Arden. That's the Arden the world deserves to know. The Arden that *Arden* deserves to know again."

I chew my lip and turn to look at her, stunned. "That was actually pretty decent advice."

She grins at me and steals the last bite from my hand. "Yeah, well, in addition to being the best-looking, I'm clearly the smartest in the family, so . . ."

I shove her shoulder, and we both laugh.

"You need anything else?" she asks, and I shake my head. Riley sits up, cookie crumbs falling off her shirt as she heads for the door. "I'm hitting the hay for a few hours before Dad wakes us up for stocking stuffers." She stifles a yawn. "Merry Christmas, Caroline."

"Happy Hanukkah, Riley," I say, before she slips out the door and back to her own room.

Then I sit up, get my laptop from my bag, and open it to see I only have two hours to get this article in. But that's okay. I pull up my Word document, finally knowing exactly what I need to say.

CHAPTER 32

ARDEN

I wake up to my phone buzzing noisily against my pillowcase.

Groaning, I rub my eyes and grab it, sitting up to see a sea of notifications as far as the thumb can scroll.

On Christmas?

I throw my legs over the edge of the bed, the marble floor cool underneath my feet as I tap on the link that's being shared a million times.

Caroline's article.

My heart clenches as it opens. When the page loads and I see the title, my eyebrows shoot up to my hairline.

"My Twelve Days of Arden James."

I steady myself before I keep reading.

I've always thought of her as two separate people.

There's Arden James. The girl you all see. The one on the covers of magazines and in the movies. The one who lives in the modern and somewhat cold mansion on the Pacific and who seems to go out more than she stays in. The enigma.

Then there's Arden. Just Arden. The girl from Barnwich, Pennsylvania, who cares more deeply about the people she loves than she likes to let on and who wears her heart right on her sleeve.

I would know, because that Arden has been just about everything a person can be to me.

My best friend.

My confidante.

My first crush.

At times she's been the very last person I've wanted to see . . . but most times she's been the first.

There's one thing that I've known to be true through it all, though:

I have always, always, loved her.

I loved her when she gave me her jacket to tie around my waist when I peed my pants in third grade. I loved her when she put hot sauce in Matt Fincher's chocolate milk after he made fun of my braids. I loved her when she used to dream about a life grander than the one she had.

And I loved her when she moved to California and left me behind, standing on the sidewalk with tears staining my cheeks. I think that's when I loved her the most. It kind of sucks that sometimes you don't really know how you feel about a person until they're gone.

So when she finally, finally came home for Christmas, it felt like a second chance at rediscovering my Arden (well, after I got over wanting to punch her). And these last twelve holidates spent with her in Barnwich were more than I could have possibly hoped for.

Tears fill my eyes as I read about all our adventures around Barnwich, seeing it all through Caroline's eyes. She brings the town to life, but even more than that, she brings *me* to life. A me I actually recognize, even if I'm still piecing her together.

I don't know what will happen to me and Arden, but what I do know now is there's really only ever been one Arden. She's just still figuring out exactly which parts belong to her, which parts belong to all of you, and which parts never belonged at all but were simply part of a Hollywood narrative that was written for her when she was far too young to know that she never needed it in the first place.

Because that's the other truth. She never needed it. For me, she never needed to be anyone else but her. I hope in reading this, you'll feel the same way.

I'm so grateful for all the different ways I've been able to fall in love with Arden.

I never got to ask her a twelfth question on our last day together, but the one I have now is the one I wish I'd asked most.

Arden, do you think you'll ever come back to Barnwich? Maybe one day you will. Maybe you never will again. Either way, I know a part of me will always be waiting.

I drop my phone onto my bed and lie back into my pillow, my heart pounding heavily in my chest as I let her words sink in.

Caroline sees me.

Caroline loves me.

Caroline's waiting.

Do you think you'll ever come back to Barnwich?

And that's when it hits me.

I don't have to do this again.

I'm the one making the decisions now. About what I do. About where I live. About *how* I live. I don't have to give up my life, my home, and the people I love to have a career. Yeah, I might miss out on things sometimes on one side or the other, but not everything. Not the things that matter. My roots can dig deep into the ground and still stretch a long way, like Grams said. I can't have everything, but I can have a hell of a lot more than I did.

I can have . . .

I sit bolt upright, my eyes darting to my still-packed suitcase sitting in the corner of my room.

. . . *Caroline.*

CHAPTER 33

CAROLINE

"Incoming!" I call out as I deliver a steaming tray of latkes to a table already piled with food. People descend on them the second I let go. Mr. Green, finally out of his Santa suit, literally elbows me out of the way.

"This is a great idea, Caroline," he says through a mouthful of food. "Always wondered when Barnwich would start including us Jewish people in the holiday festivities."

I nearly collapse in the middle of the bar. *"You're Jewish?"*

He points a latke at me. "Don't let the Santa suit fool you."

I smile and lean against the counter of the bar as he walks away to go sit with a group of tourists in the corner booth. Riley swivels around on her stool, while Miles and Levi rest their elbows on the opposite side.

"A Hanukkah event in Barnwich on Christmas," Levi says with a whistle, as all of us look out at the packed room.

Barnwich *showed up*. I scan the crowd of familiar faces, my parents, our caroling buddies Josephine and Ruth and Shirley and Clara, a few small business owners, even some people I know from school, laughing with Austin and Maya by the door.

Riley nods. "Who'd have thought?"

"Looks like the Becketts made their very own Barnwich tradition," Miles says, whacking me lightly with his bar towel. I look over at him and he smiles. "Now you'll *have* to come home from the big city next year."

"Holidays in Barnwich?" I say, returning the smile. "Wouldn't miss it for the world."

It's true. It feels amazing knowing we'll always get to celebrate all the parts of us with the people we love most from now on. So I hate the fact that in a room as full as this one, it still feels like someone is missing.

As Riley tries to convince Levi and Miles to give her a *whiskey on the rocks*, I turn to head back into the kitchen to see if Edie needs help. She's taken over for the day, with Finn's and Tom's help, the two of them inexplicably wearing their matching bandanas again.

"How's it coming, Edie?" I ask as I push inside, and she immediately slings an arm around my waist while she stares at the brisket in the oven, prepared with my grandma's stolen recipe: Levi sweet-talked it out of her and she gave in when she heard what we were doing. Or maybe it was the piña coladas on their cruise.

"It's coming." She gives me a squeeze, then turns her head to look at me and says, her voice soft, "That was some article, kid."

"Thanks, Edie," I whisper. "I just . . . had to write the truth. Show Arden how I've always seen her."

"Well, you certainly did that."

"Have you heard from her?" I ask before I can stop myself.

She shakes her head and I nod, trying to blink away the tears that sting at my eyes.

Of course not.

"I'm gonna get some air," I say, and she pats my side before letting me go.

I don't even bother putting on a jacket before I push through the back door. Barnwich is so quiet and snowy and perfect on the other side, I don't even mind the cold as I walk slowly around to the front.

I let out a long exhale and tilt my head back, squeezing my eyes shut.

I expect the tears to fall, but in this moment, despite everything, I can't help but feel like . . . well . . .

Enough.

Not just Jewish enough or Christian enough, but like *I'm* enough. Me. Caroline Beckett. Even if I don't get into Columbia with the application I submitted this afternoon. Even if I don't fall in love with someone else for another decade. Even if I never see or hear from Arden James aga—

"Yes," a voice cuts through the silence.

I open my eyes, head swinging down to see a figure standing underneath the orange glow of the streetlight.

"Arden? What are you doing here?" I want to move toward her, but my feet feel frozen to the concrete.

"Yes," she says again, and I frown.

"What?"

"Your question. In the article," she says, doing what I can't and taking a step closer. "Yes. I'll come back to Barnwich."

I tilt my head to the side, scared to let myself believe this means something more.

"But for how long?" I ask, my voice cracking.

"Well, at least until the summer. Maybe longer if I can convince Bianchi to shoot the movie here."

I start. "Wait. *What?* Here like . . . in *Barnwich* here?"

"Yes, Caroline." She laughs, and the sound fills up all the empty parts of me.

"You still got the part?"

She nods. "Pays to be honest." We stare at each other for a long moment. "You would know that," she says, quieter now.

"Arden, I—"

"You wrote one hell of an article, Caroline," she says, cutting me off. "Everything you said, it . . . *God*, it hit home." She looks down at her feet. "I love acting, but the choices I made at fourteen have just slowly been killing me, in more ways than one. I think after this Bianchi role, I . . . I need some time off. To figure out what exactly I want to do. What I want this acting thing to look like."

"I'm sure Lillian is thrilled about that."

She smiles at that and shakes her head. "I fired her last night."

"You *what?*"

"She never saw me. She was just as bad as my parents. Caroline, being back here, being home these last two weeks, has left me feeling more whole than I've felt . . . ever. It's made me realize what I want. Who I want to be. To Grams. To the whole world. To myself, and . . . to *you*. Even if it takes me a little while to figure out how." She takes a deep breath and takes another step closer until she's just a foot away. "Watching you walk away yesterday was . . ."

She doesn't finish her sentence. She doesn't need to. Because

I know. It was just as hard for me to be the one doing the leaving as it was to be left behind.

"I shouldn't have rushed out like that," I admit, and this time she lets me talk. "I was . . . scared, to be honest. I felt so out of place. Like I didn't belong there with you."

"I get it."

"I know. And that's what I realized when I left. That maybe I should have more faith in you."

"You should," she says, swallowing. "Because I—I love you, Caroline. I've loved you for so long it's . . . ridi—" She laughs, shaking her head. *"Ridiculous."* But then she gets a serious look on her face. "I know I have fucked up a lot in my life, run away from a lot. But I want to show up for you. I want to come home. And I don't know if this will work out. You could hate my guts in a week, be sick of me by Valentine's Day. Hell, you might even end up wanting to take Taylor Hill to prom. All of that scares me, but, Caroline, I want to try. Because if I don't, I'll spend my entire life wondering—"

The words aren't even out of her mouth before I throw myself into her, my lips clumsily finding hers. She wraps her arms around my waist and then walks me backward until I'm pinned against the brick wall of the bar.

Arden James, Arden James, Arden James.

Her name dances around my head, filling my chest until it feels like the only thought I've ever had.

We kiss on the snowy streets of Barnwich, where we first fell in love. Where she left me and where she came back to me.

"Unbelievable," Riley says from the doorway, startling the two of us apart. "I came to see if you wanted to do the honor of lighting the candles, and I find you *making out*? Some party host."

We both laugh, and Arden shoots her a sheepish grin.

"Happy Hanukkah?" she says. Riley rolls her eyes and then runs inside ahead of us.

Arden reaches out to grab my hand, and the contact sends sparks through me just like all those years ago. Her mouth pulls up into that lopsided grin of hers, and for the first time since she came back, I don't want time to slow down. Now I can't wait . . .

To discover all the pieces of her that are new, all the pieces of her that have stayed the same, all the pieces of *us* that don't even exist yet.

And as she pauses in the doorframe to pull me into a kiss underneath the mistletoe, I can't help but wonder if my twelve days with Arden James can turn into a lifetime.

ACKNOWLEDGMENTS

Alyson

I'd like to thank my editor, Alexa Pastor, for giving the most constructive notes a gal could ask for, while also cheering me on the whole way. Three books in and I still don't know how you manage to look at a first draft and pull out the best parts of every story. And thank you to the rest of the crew at Simon & Schuster.

Thank you to my agent and friend, Emily Van Beek, for always making yourself available for whatever we might need. And for helping us find the right stories to tell.

To Mom, Dad, Luke, and Aimee, thank you for always supporting me. And thanks especially to my brother, Mike, who drove to our house to watch Poppy more days than I can count so that Rachael and I could hit our deadlines.

To my wife, thank you for taking charge of drafting this book when I was struggling. And for always knowing exactly how to quiet my anxiety when it gets too loud. You're my light in the dark and I love you so much.

To Poppy. You are the reason I will always continue to write! Everything I do from now on will always be for you. You are the bravest, toughest, most beautiful little person I have ever met. I hope one day you can read all these books your mama and I are writing and find pieces of yourself. I hope they help you in some small way. I love you, Linguine.

Rachael

I feel tremendously grateful every single day to the people below who make it possible for me to write stories and share them with the world. Not a single one of my books would exist without them.

First, as always, a big thank you to Alexa Pastor, who has been by my side for every single one of my six books. What a journey we have been on, and to have someone as talented as you, who always brings out the best in my ideas, is something I never take for granted.

To Justin Chanda and the rest of the incredible team at Simon & Schuster, all of whom have gone above and beyond to show me so much support and care through the years.

To Emily van Beek, the best of the best. To have you in my corner is the greatest of gifts. I don't think anyone has made me feel more excited and inspired about the possibility of my career and the books to come.

To Sydney Meve and the rest of the team at Folio Jr.

To my friends and family, Mom, Ed, Judy, Mike, Luke, and Aimee. Even if Luke wins every game of Moonrakers for the rest of eternity, game nights will always be my favorite nights.

Thank you, thank you, *thank you* to my readers. Your messages, your posts, your words, your comments. You are why I put stories into this world.

As always, to Alyson. Alyson, our love story is better than any book I could ever write. You have given me the greatest gift.

And, to Poppy. You are the best of me. But, please, stop jumping off the couch. I love you, Scoob.

ABOUT THE AUTHORS

Rachael Lippincott is the co-author of #1 *New York Times* bestseller *Five Feet Apart* and *All This Time* and the author of *The Lucky List* and *Pride and Prejudice and the City*. She holds a BA in English writing from the University of Pittsburgh. Rachael is originally from Bucks County, Pennsylvania.

Alyson Derrick was born and raised in Greenville, Pennsylvania, a town where burn barrels take the place of recycling bins. After making her great escape to Pittsburgh, where she earned her BA in English writing, Alyson started her own food truck but soon realized she much prefers telling stories over slinging cheesesteaks. She is the author of *Forget Me Not*.

Rachael and Alyson currently reside in Pittsburgh with their dog, Hank.